ONLY A VISCOUNT WILL DO

TO MARRY A ROGUE, BOOK 3

TAMARA
Gill

COPYRIGHT

Only a Viscount Will Do
To Marry a Rogue, Book 3
Copyright © 2017, 2020 by Tamara Gill
Cover Art by Wicked Smart Designs
All rights reserved.

ISBN: 978-0-6489050-7-3

ONLY A VISCOUNT WILL DO

TO MARRY A ROGUE, BOOK 3

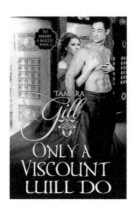

Lady Alice Worthingham never conforms to Society's norms. Ever. She loves adventure, new experiences, and approaches life with a sassy attitude Society can take or leave. But even for her, robbery by a highwayman is a bit much.

Lord Arndel, Lady Alice's neighbor, is playing a dangerous game-- acting the proper viscount by day and the Surrey Bandit by night. And to brazenly steal from the woman who's captured his attention is no mean feat, or the wisest of moves.

When Lady Alice learns the truth, the viscount finds that when a well-bred woman seeks revenge, she'll make a gentleman thief pay for his crimes with everything...including his heart.

PROLOGUE

*C*allum squinted, the light in the room blinding as the blindfold was ripped from his face. He blinked, growing accustomed to the brightness in the room.

He didn't recognize any of the men staring at him, but he could understand the menace that glistened in their eyes. Callum rolled his shoulders, the bands about his wrists leaving his hands almost numb.

"Who the hell are you?"

The man behind the desk, a rotund, balding gentleman, stared at him nonplussed. "I'm a moneylender. One who's come to collect."

Two more burly men came into the room and stood behind the man at the desk. They crossed their arms over their chest and Callum understood the unspoken threat. "I don't owe you any funds."

The man laughed. "*Tsk tsk*, a minor detail that you'll soon be remedied of. *You*, Lord Arndel may not owe the money, but you have inherited the debt of your late cousin, along with his title." He shrugged. "I'm sorry to be the bearer of bad news, but the debt your cousin owed me is perhaps more than you can pay, and, therefore, just as your cousin was asked to do, you, too, shall have expectations toward us that will be met."

"I'll do nothing you ask of me. I have no idea of this debt that you speak, and I fail to see why I should inherit it."

"All true," the man said, his eyes narrowing slightly. "And yet you do inherit the debt and you shall do as we say or your sweet, loving family shall be, how do I say this," he said, tapping his chin, "hurt."

Callum swallowed, the need to hurt the bastard increasing tenfold. If only he wasn't tied up, he'd pummel the man within an inch of his life. How dare he threaten his child? "You touch my daughter, even one hair on her head, and you will rue the day."

"You will rue the day if you think I am joking, my lord." The moneylender took a sip of his amber liquid, placing the glass down as if he had not a care in the world, and hadn't, in fact, just threatened a man and his family with who knows what horrendous consequences. "Before your cousin died, we had a contract written up, in case his demise was earlier than foreseen. Now that you've inherited the estate and title, we have forwarded the contract to your solicitor, and I'm sure in the coming days he will ask for an audience with you."

"How much is the debt?" With any luck it wouldn't be as much as he feared, though his cousin Robert had lived a misbegotten lifestyle full of vice and debauchery, which apparently involved large wads of blunt.

"The debt is in the vicinity of eighteen thousand pounds. More than I know you have."

Callum tried to take a calming breath and failed. The room shrank, and for the first time in his life he thought he might pass out. "Eighteen thousand pounds...no doubt you thought nothing of lending such sums to a man who you knew would never be able to afford such debt. How dare you act so criminally."

The moneylender laughed, his gut shaking in mirth. "Alas, my lord, if it hasn't escaped your notice, I *am* a criminal and I will get my money back, and with your help." He reached into his desk drawer and pulled out a file with a multitude of papers within it. "Would you like to know the details of the services that will render me happy?"

"Do I have a choice?" Callum asked, his words cutting, severing any hope he may have had of his and his family's future.

"In this folder is a listing and drawings of jewels that I want you to procure for me. Each piece is of high value, made of the finest quality jewels and will make me so rich that you may even see me gracing the ballrooms of the *ton* in the years to come."

Callum doubted that very much, nor did he want to think about what the moneylender's words meant. He wracked his brain for a way to remove himself from the situation, to walk away without debt nor any links to the man before him, but his mind came up blank. There was no way out for him. He had no money of his own; he had the estate only and most of that was entailed and untouchable.

"You, Lord Arndel, shall steal these jewels from these rich toffs, and deliver them each month until the debt is paid. And just to sweeten the deal, some of these jewels are worth up to a thousand pounds, so do not despair that I'll be requiring your services forever."

"You want me to become a thief, stealing into these people's homes, people who I shall see most nights at Town events and such? Damn you. I shall not do it."

The moneylender gestured to one of his guards, who then went and opened a door, mumbling to someone inside the dark space. Rage unlike any he'd known consumed him when they carried out his daughter, her body limp in the man's arms.

"What have you done to her?" he roared, standing and throwing the chair his hands were tied to against the wall. A satisfying crack sounded and he did it again, the chair giving way, enough so he could pull his hands free.

As he went to his daughter, the second burly man tackled him to the ground, his weight and solid punch to his lower back winding him. "Tell me what you've done?" he wheezed, his gaze blurring with the horrible realization that they may have killed his little girl.

"She's alive, for now. Too much liquor in her tea, unfortunately. Knocked her out cold." The man laughed and Callum promised he'd kill the bastard. Maybe not today with his daughter's life still in the fiend and his cronies' hands, but one day. One day, the man laughing down on him would pay for daring to take her from his home.

"In one month's time the first jewel is due. There will be no sneaking into their homes. You must wait for them to be attending a ball, or traveling to or from their estates after a jaunt. It is at these times you must strike, steal their valuables, and bring them to me."

"So I'm to be a highwayman?" The absurdness of the situation was too much for his brain to register. Just when his life had taken a positive turn, and now this. He fought to move, to get up. The moneylender gave one curt nod and the man took his knee off the middle of his back. Callum ran to Amelia and wrenched her from the second guard's hands, hating the fact these bastards had been anywhere near her, had stolen her from right under his nose with nary a problem.

"Fine," Callum said, holding his daughter tight. "I shall do as you ask, but if you ever come near my child again I will kill you. Even if I hang before all the *ton*, do not doubt that I will allow you to live, should you hurt one hair on her head."

The moneylender threw him an unamused glance. "I will have no reason to hurt anyone should you do as I ask, within a timely manner."

"Give me the list." The man held it up and Callum ripped it from his grasp, striding to the door. He stopped when one of the guards stood before it, his arms crossed over his chest.

"Let Lord Arndel pass. Our business today is complete."

Callum strode from the room, his steps faltering when a bevy of half-naked women stood along the walls, watching him, some of their eyes beckoning him to join them in the rooms behind them. How dare the bastard take his daughter into such an establishment. Amelia mumbled in her sleep and Callum frowned. What liquor had they given to her? What if they'd killed her by accident? If his cousin Robert wasn't already dead, he'd kill the man himself for placing his daughter into such a predicament.

Stepping free of the building, Callum made his way out of the circular square that had buildings in dire need of repair and headed toward where a busier road lay beyond. He would get Amelia home and then he would decide what was to be done and how he would face the next few months under the order of such a man as he'd just left.

It wasn't to be borne, and yet somehow it must. Callum couldn't see a way out of the situation. He was beholden to him until he paid off a debt that wasn't his.

Damnation.

CHAPTER 1

Surrey, two years later

*A*lice met her mother's startled eyes and then turned to look out the carriage window. No one graced the road between home and Ashford, the small village they'd traveled from. Tony, their driver, yelled and the carriage jerked forward at increasing speed. Alice reached for the leather strap and held on as best she could.

"I cannot see anyone, Mama." She sat back and clasped the squabs with her free hand. "And yet I can hear what sounds like a rider coming up hard behind us."

Her mother removed her handkerchief from her lips long enough to answer. "Who do you think—"

"Halt the carriage!" a deep, muffled voice commanded, followed by a loud crack of a gun that sent shivers down Alice's spine. *Is Tony being shot at—their horses? Dear God, what is going on?*

Again, Alice looked out the carriage window then jumped over to the other seat and opened the portal to speak to

Tony. "Are you all right to continue? We're so close to home, I don't want to stop."

Tony kept his eyes on the road but crouched lower on the box. "Right ye are, miss. I'll not let him catch us."

Another shot rang out just as the words flew from Tony's lips. Alice gasped and grabbed her mother's hand, not liking her pale gray color.

"Get down, dearest," her mother tried to shout over the crunch of wheels on the gravel road.

The carriage continued to barrel up the thoroughfare at a blistering speed. Alice sat on the floor and pulled her mama down with her, before turning to look under the seat for the pistol their father used to keep there. She sat back on her haunches as her search turned up nothing more than empty space and a cobweb.

Tony cursed before yelling out that he couldn't continue without putting their lives at risk. Sickening dread pooled in her stomach. Her mother threw her a frightened glance, her lips in a thin line of fear.

"Even under such circumstances I don't believe Tony should say such words, cursing is never acceptable."

Alice beat back the urge to roll her eyes. They had bigger things to worry about than a swear word. Had she been on the box and some idiot was shooting bullets at her, Alice was sure more than a few curse words would fly out of her mouth. "Tony is slowing down, Mama. If anything, that is what you should be worried about."

"Alice, come sit closer to me and don't let go of my hand, under any circumstances."

Alice did as she was told and held on tight to her mother's shaking fingers. "It'll be all right, Mama. I'm sure he only means to rob us, and then he'll be on his way." At least that is what Alice hoped, but who knew with this highwayman. Anything was possible.

Her mother nodded but clasped her hand in a punishing grip as the carriage rolled to a stop. Alice listened to the sounds outside and the carriage when Tony jumped down. He came to stand at their door, his head looking in either direction, no doubt trying to garner the fiend's whereabouts.

They waited like sitting ducks for the elusive fox to attack, but silence reigned.

"Who do you think he is?" her mother asked.

Alice frowned, wondering the same. "Perhaps he is the highwayman who has been terrorizing Surrey for the last year or so." His escapades had London all a titter over the jewels he'd stolen, the wealth he'd amassed from the rich. Now it looked like they, too, would fill his coffers. She took a fortifying breath, not wanting to believe her own words. She had thought it such a lark that the gentleman stole from the rich and left the poor alone. But now, as one of the unfortunates to come under his ire, she didn't think too highly of it, after all.

"What do you want?" Tony shouted toward the trees.

A shiver of unease crawled across her skin as the question was met with a deep masculine chuckle. A laugh that was both cocky and condescending at the same time.

"Get the ladies out. Now!"

Alice shushed her mother's whimpering and nodded to Tony to open the door when he looked back for approval. He helped them down, then stood before them like a knight in shining armor. Alice inwardly smiled at the devotion her mother's coachman had for the family, especially since he was older than England itself.

She looked down the road, bordered by thick dense trees that cast moving shadows everywhere. Her mother's eyes were huge and full of fear as a ghostly apparition of a dark horse and rider stepped from the dark canopy. The horse's ragged and uneven breathing made it seem dangerous, and not of this world.

Alice was sure at that very moment, they were going to die. Nothing that looked so evil could possibly do any good in this world.

"Well, well, well. Look who we have." The rider jerked his mount to a stop, the horse's eyes flaring at the sharp pull of the bit.

"That is none of your concern. Take what you want and be gone with ya," Tony said, throwing them a concerned look over his shoulder.

Alice's eyes narrowed at the *tsk, tsk, tsk* that sounded from the highwayman. She looked at the horse and wondered how a robber could own such a beast. Or perhaps, stolen would be a better summation. She studied the man, his breeches tight to his well-formed legs. His jacket and shirt, though not the best in quality, were clean and pressed. As for his face, she could not make it out at all, due to the black bandanna covering his nose and mouth. But his eyes, dark as night, were intelligent, calculating, and right at this moment, making a study of them. Thoroughly.

The highwayman bowed low on his horse. "I do believe the Duchess of Penworth is to be my quarry this day. And that lovely brooch you have upon your person will do nicely as my payment. Hand it over and no harm will come to you."

Alice comforted her mother as she gasped, in vain trying to hide the brooch that made the robber's eyes gleam with sickening greed.

"Who gives you the right to take what doesn't belong to you, sir?" Alice raised her chin in defiance. The thought of her mama losing such a treasured family jewel made the blood boil in her veins.

She stilled as the man's attention swung her way, the lift of his eyebrows declaring he had not noticed her, or had been ignoring her. Alice pushed down the sickening nerves that racked her innards when he proceeded to dismount, then walk toward them with a swagger that oozed confidence.

Alice lifted her chin further and refused to look away, even though her mind froze in fear. He was tall, strong, and could break them both in half, if he wished, if the size of his arms were any indication. *Oh, dear, please don't hurt us. I'm sorry I spoke.* She swallowed as he came to stand before her, much too close for her comfort.

"You are a beauty, my little blond goddess. Perhaps I should steal you, instead of the man-made ornaments." He reached out and flicked her mother's brooch, dismissing it as nothing of value.

Alice gaped and then snapped her mouth shut at the man's impudent gesture. Surely, he had not said what he had? But at the gleam in his eyes, Alice realized he was deadly serious.

"You sir, will leave my daughter alone." Her mother moved in front of her, which pulled Alice from the trance she seemed to have fallen into while looking at him.

He smiled then walked over to Tony, and as quick as a flash, pushed the man to the ground, tying his hands with a well-versed ability that under different circumstances would've been impressive. Dismayed, Alice watched their only means of protection wiggle on the ground, no longer any help. The rogue turned back to them, his eyes darting back and forth.

"This is not the time to throw orders around, Your Grace." He came over to them and unclasped the emerald brooch. Alice clasped her mother's hand as her parent's eyes filled with tears. She looked back at the robber, his eyes not sparing the jewel a second glance as he slipped it into his pocket.

"Your Grace, if you will return to the carriage, I'd be most appreciative. I have something to say to your daughter…in private."

"You have nothing to say to me, sir. You've got your payment, now it's time for you to leave us alone." Alice held on to her mother, not wanting to hear anything this brute had to say. Fear crept up her spine that he would molest her in some way. Perhaps he wasn't the highwayman Surrey was being harassed by, for she'd never heard of him attacking women while he robbed them of their worldly possessions.

He laughed and held the carriage door open. Then with a yank, pulled them apart and escorted her mama to the door. The pistol appeared again and when her mama hesitated at the door he jabbed it into her spine. Her mother refused to move and Alice read the defiance in her stance, but the last thing she wished was for her mother to be hurt. She had lost one parent, she wasn't ready to lose another.

"Wait in the carriage, Mama. I'll be quite all right. I promise."

Her mother finally conceded, and Alice flinched as the carriage door slammed shut. The fiend walked back to her, though perhaps stalked would be a better word, before pulling her behind the carriage and out of her mother's sight even as she leaned out the window, determined to keep her daughter in view.

He watched Alice for a moment. His eyes, which she'd thought to be black, were in fact, blue with tinges of gray through them. Any other time, Alice would've termed them attractive, but today, they were a window into hell.

She started when he leaned toward her. "You are a beauty, Lady Alice." The whispered words against her ear spread a peculiar warmth through her bones. Alice put it down to her fear and the knowledge that she didn't know who this man was, nor what he was capable of. She stood still and waited, refusing to say or react in any way, lest it stimulate him to do worse.

"A shame that a woman like you will enter a marriage of convenience. Such delectable flesh should be loved a great deal and pleasurably so." His hand clasped her shoulder and pushed her against the multitude of parcels tied to the back of the carriage. He leaned in closer than she'd ever allowed a man to do. "It's been a long time since I've had a woman like you under me. Oh how I'd love to partake in mutual pleasure that would ruin you for anyone else."

Alice swallowed, hating the fact that deep down, her body was reacting to his absurd, scandalous words. She shouldn't allow him to say such things. She should knock him in the head, but at this moment she didn't have anything to do the job with, so it was a moot point.

"How do you know me, sir?" she managed to ask, her breath stuck in her lungs, her nerves frayed by the thought of this man atop her, pleasuring her as his words promised. There was something seriously wrong, if such thoughts, instead of being vile, left her wondering what it *would* feel like. Other than his occupation as a felon, he seemed healthy, the whites of his eyes were clear, not bloodshot or yellow in color. But probably the oddest thing of all was that, although he was robbing them, had already stolen a brooch, and shot at their equipage, he didn't frighten her.

Not one little bit.

He chuckled, his eyes stealing over her flesh. "I always learn about the people I plan to relieve of their possessions. You are not too angry at me, I hope," he asked.

Alice raised her brow, knowing by the gleam in his eyes that he was smiling, laughing even.

"Perhaps you will grant me a boon if I do not steal those lovely earbobs you have on."

"If I give you the earbobs, will you return the brooch?"

"What about," he said, stepping closer, "you give me a kiss and I'll think about the trade?"

Alice swallowed as the highwayman's hand clasped her hip, his fingers flexing against her body. Their eyes met and she was surprised to see his darken with some emotion she didn't want to delve too deeply in. *Who is he?* And how did she know, no matter his words, that he would not force her into anything she did not wish to partake in? It was very perplexing.

"Will you not kiss me, my lady?" he mocked, challenging her.

Alice ran her hands over his shoulders and into the dark locks at the nape of his neck. His hair was soft and the scent of lemons wafted in the air. How bizarre for such a man to be clean and fresh smelling. She played into his mocking and gave him the best saucy look she could muster.

"Sir, you don't know how long I have waited to meet the famous Surrey Bandit, if that is who you are. And if your lips are as tempting as your voice, I would be honored to grant you my favor, but you'll have to remove the bandanna to do so."

Alice stepped into him with all the supposed desire she could muster. She suppressed the fear that rose within her that she was playing with the wrong kind of man. For all his desirable eyes and clean body and clothes, he *was* a highwayman. Ruthless and possibly more dangerous than one supposed. She prayed she'd not mistaken her insight and was not heading down a road of no return.

His lean muscled body touched all the way down the front of hers, and Alice blamed the lack of air entering her lungs on trepidation over what she was about to do, not what he made her feel after only knowing him a few minutes. A thief, no less. Her hands ran down his neck and settled on his shoulders. She leaned forward, so much so, that the man's breath through the bandanna warmed her lips.

Her attention snapped to his lips when he lifted the cloth away to give him the ability to kiss her. She swallowed, her mouth going dry at the sight of a mouth made for sin. His lips were too perfectly formed to be fair for the opposite sex. How she'd always wanted lips as full as his, if not a little more red in color to tempt the opposite sex to kiss her, which unfortunately had never happened. And now, it looked as if her first kiss would be with a man who was robbing her.

Alice licked her lips and realized her mistake the moment his blue orbs darkened with hunger. Her breath increased and she tried to calm her beating heart, which threatened to jump out of her chest. She wasn't supposed to want his kiss, but some scandalous part of her wanted it more than anything in her life.

"Kiss me, beautiful."

Had she been able to, she would melt on the spot, like snow under a summer sun. Oh, that deep, masculine voice was temptation incarnate; it beckoned something wild within her to kiss him and be damned her manners and the expectations foisted on her, due to her heritage. Alice would never know how she tore her attention from his lips.

Instead of leaning forward and taking what they both desperately wanted, she mentally shook herself. She did not want to kiss him. It was the blood rushing through her veins that was making her feel giddy and...whatever else it was that flowed throughout her body. Not the man or the pleasure he tempted her with. Alice steeled herself to do what she must and so, just before their lips met, and with all the might she could yield, Alice lifted her leg and kneed him firmly in the groin.

He fell to the ground, his howls of pain loud in the quiet

forest. Alice watched him for all of a second before she turned and ran to the front of the carriage, welcoming the sight of Tony staggering to his feet.

"Tony, get in the coach. I'll drive."

"But, my lady—" he stammered.

"No buts. Do as you're told and now." Alice climbed quickly up to the box and grabbed the reins. The highwayman was still on the ground clutching himself, and Tony still stared at her with widened eyes. "We haven't much time. Move! Now, man," she yelled.

He did as she bid, and she whipped horses to an immediate canter just as the carriage door slammed shut. With a cloud of dust, she left the fiend where he belonged, on the ground and alone. She cracked the whip over the horse's ears and frowned as the realization of what she'd done hit her with as much force as she'd hit him. The knee to his groin had been quite hard, perhaps harder than she ought to have done, and a small part of her hoped she hadn't hurt him too much, for all her anger at his robbing them.

Robber he may be, but he had smelled very nice, like summertime fruits or something. And his breath, when he'd spoken, had not reeked of stale beer or yesterday's meals, but of mint, fresh and tempting. Had he been a gentleman at a masquerade ball, he would have received the kiss he so willingly wanted to bestow. And no doubt it would have been an enjoyable, delectable few minutes. Her sister Beth had told her of a man's kiss and Alice had longed to have one, but she drew the line at kissing a highwayman. She would not do it, no matter how much she may have wanted to rile against expectations and live for the moment. Rakes and libertines, such as the fiend on the road behind her, were always good at seduction, but were not to be trusted or enjoyed. Ever.

She inwardly sighed. Her life of late seemed one drama

after another. Perhaps, she should do as her mother wanted and find a husband of her own.

She checked the horses' speed as her body rebelled at the notion of being married. If she were married, she would be expected to cater to her husband's every whim, give him babies and make him happy. Not that she objected to being happy, but only the deepest love would entice her into the marriage state, and all the men she'd met so far, since her first Season, had been less than inspiring.

Of course, they'd been rich, titled even, and with estates that would please even royalty, but as boring as watching water droplets dry on grass. And certainly none of them had inspired intrigue or attraction. The first time she had experienced that was today—with a thief.

Although that wasn't *quite* true, since she *had* reacted to a man before, none other than their neighbor Callum Edwards, Viscount Arndel.

Alice stared at the road, not really seeing anything other than the horses cantering along. Maybe her mother was right and she needed to stop being so picky and viewing the wealthy as overprivileged idiots, because if she was reacting to bandits there was something wrong with her.

The piercing blue eyes of the man she'd left writhing on the road flashed before her and she grinned, hoping she hadn't hurt him too much. Why, she couldn't fathom. He had pulled a gun on them. He'd deserved everything he received. However, never in her life had she been so exhilarated and fearful at the same time.

It was an absurd reaction. The man was a scoundrel, not at all worthy of her attention. He deserved to be in Newgate for his crimes, and yet he had raised in her a devilish spirit, that was forever trying to break free. A spirit that yearned for a love match and a man who would spark her desire—every day of her life. Not someone who'd marry her for her wealth and the pretty face her mother was forever stating she had. Alice didn't want to be anyone's ornament. Someone who was hung in a grand home, admired and tittered over, but otherwise ignored. She slowed the horses as she turned them through the gates of Dunsleigh and sighed.

No doubt the fiend lived a wild existence that was neither hindered by Society nor family obligations. How she wished she could be as free as he was. Well, until he was captured and hanged for his misdeeds. That wasn't the sort of ending she cared for at all.

But then what was life if one could not dream of possibilities? No doubt, no matter what she wanted, and yearned for, eventually she would settle down and live the life that was expected from the daughter of the Duke of Penworth. Although, no matter how much pedigree she held, it could not stop her from dreaming otherwise.

---

*C*allum Edwards, Viscount Arndel, sat up on the dirt road and leaned on his knees as he watched the coach barrel down the road and leave him in a pool of dust. He shook his head and frowned, wondering what the hell had gotten into him to act so reckless. He cringed and hoisted himself up to stand, dusted down his buckskin breeches, and whistled for his horse. As his trusty stallion Bandit trotted over, Callum pulled out the prized jewel from his pocket and grinned at the green gem. The trinket was the last gem required to resolve the debt to the moneylender—just as soon as he traveled to London to rid himself of it.

The rich, dark green emerald in a gold brooch twinkled up at him, the diamonds around the rectangular-shaped stone set off the jewel to perfection and anyone could tell it was worth a fortune.

He pocketed it and clasped the reins of his horse, lifting his leg into the stirrup without success as pain shot through his groin. He swore, rubbed his cock, and adjusted himself a little before trying again. After some time, he succeeded and cursed the little hellion to Hades. Lady Alice Worthingham had surprising strength in that delicate leg of hers, far more than he'd imagined.

Callum moved about on his seat, the blasted saddle causing throbbing in his own jewels and shooting pain up into his gut. He guided his horse toward home, needing a cold compress and a well-aged brandy, if not bed, after Lady Alice's well-aimed knee.

Checking to see no one was about, he made his way across the fields toward his home, Kester House, and shook his head over his words to a woman well above him in social stature, but too young or too innocent to understand what his intent had meant.

What had he been thinking? Well, he knew what he'd been thinking, and damn him for the rogue he portrayed himself to be. It couldn't be further from the truth. He'd never acted such a cad before. He'd taken what he wanted and run from all his other holdups. He had not played with his victims like a boy playing with wooden soldiers.

And he hated the fact that it seemed as if Lady Alice had not been fooled by his bravado or threat. If anything, he had the impression that she'd been laughing at him, daring him to try and seduce her.

Scamp came to mind when he thought of Alice and he laughed, absurd as it was. He'd not thought she had a rougher side, but for all her toff upbringing someone had obviously taught the girl to stick up for herself, both with her body and her mouth.

A mouth that he was sure would haunt his dreams for many a night to come. Delectable and succulent came to mind when thinking of her lips. She probably tasted as sweet as she looked.

Callum cantered across the meadow and welcomed another wooded grove that marked the border of his lands. The dense forest was as old as the estate and had been there ever since the family had bought the land in the 1600s. The old trees cloaked him in shadow and he paused a moment, taking the time to pull off his bandanna and wipe his face of any grime.

His horse ambled its way back to Kester House, as if it knew the direction on its own, and so it should, since the stallion had come with the estate when he'd inherited it. Soon, his future would be his to command again. With the emerald brooch in the moneylender's hands, the estate's debts to the fiend would be at an end, and if he could secure the sale of some lands that adjoined the Duke of Penworth's estate, it would give him enough money to make the estate profitable again. Amelia and he could start afresh.

He'd longed for two years for this moment. He had a lot of missed time to make up for putting his family through the ordeal of never knowing if he'd return.

Callum frowned at the obscene amount of debt his idiotic cousin Robert, the former viscount, had left him floundering in. Such a waste of funds had been spent on gambling and the never-ending pursuit of women who had graced the stage. It had required a small fortune to keep those women honest. Not that they ever had, no matter how much Robert had paid them.

And Robert's mother, who had allowed her son to run their only estate into the ground, was also to blame. Not that the old battle-ax would ever think her dearest, and now departed boy, could ever do any wrong.

He avoided the open fields at the front of the estate and, instead, made his way through the dense undergrowth of the trees, not wanting anyone other than his stable staff to see him dressed in the common man's attire. The talk of the Surrey Bandit was all anyone was speaking about, and the detailed sketches of the fiend posted in the towns and roads were well done, too well done for his liking.

Should anyone take a good look at the wanted poster, they'd notice the little mole that sat on his right temple. Not to mention, his arrival home at all hours of the night, without the dress of a lord, would raise any staff's curiosity, and that was the last thing he needed. His life of crime was so close to being over he could taste it, and nothing and no one would get in his way of a future brighter than his past had been.

Stuffing the bandanna into his saddle bag and slipping the brooch into his chest pocket, he made his way out of the trees and kicked his mount into a canter toward home. Tomorrow he would call on the duke and then make arrangements to travel to London for the sale of the gem. He couldn't hie off to Town so soon after the theft. It would look suspicious, if he did. Time was his ally, and he would allow the local scandal to settle down, and once it did, then he would finally be free of the trouble he was in.

Then and only then, would he be able to breathe easy, to be free to take responsibility for the estate he had inadvertently inherited—without the ever-tightening noose that threatened to choke the life out of his future.

He pushed away the guilt over the many jewels and family heirlooms he had stolen over the past year and a half. Callum pacified his conscience with the knowledge that the rich could afford to buy new pieces, if they wished—bigger and grander jewels to surpass anything he'd ever stolen, but he could not replace his daughter. After the bastard money-lender in London had shown him just how easy he could get his hands on his daughter, Callum had understood he would have to do as the man bid. There was no choice between the life of his child and a bauble that a matron of the *ton* wore. Becoming the Surrey Bandit had been his only option.

In time, he no doubt would harbor guilt, but not when his thieving kept his daughter safe and out of the clutches of a money-hungry madman. And thanks to the beautiful green jewel that sat snug in his pocket, his bandit days were over. He patted the gem as his horse came out of the forest and gave him a clear view of the fields that sat before his estate.

Green stretched for miles, along with a small stream that ran west of his home, and eventually, into the Thames. He pulled up Bandit and took in all that he now owned and lorded over. It seemed absurd that an estate of this size was for one man. Callum doubted very much that he would ever understand the Society in which he now circulated. It was a sphere in which he wasn't comfortable, and even less so after he started to steal from them.

The estate shone like a beacon under the afternoon sun. A home made up of different architectural designs—too many for it to ever be termed magnificent, unlike his neighbor's estate, Dunsleigh. The only asset, he supposed, was the woodlands that came right up to the home's lawns—it gave the place a sense of mystery and privacy, something he welcomed. Now more than ever.

Kicking his mount into a gallop, he headed home, enjoying the sun on his back and the wind on his face. He wished to see his daughter and tell her that he'd join her tonight for tea in the nursery. Just as he'd promised.

"ou were robbed! At gunpoint?" Josh bellowed behind the mahogany desk from which he sat, his eyes wide with alarm and his mouth agape with shock. "When? Where?" He stood, his chair flying backward and landing on its back. "Are you unharmed, Mother?"

Alice started at his obscenely loud voice, which threatened to deafen her. "Yes, we're fine. It was the—"

"We were robbed by the Surrey Bandit," their mama blurted, coming up to the desk and partaking of her brother the duke's half-drunk brandy. "He took the family brooch. The one I received from your father on the announcement of our betrothal." Her mother's voice wobbled with distress, and she poured herself another glass of the amber liquid. "I can't believe it's gone."

Alice clasped her mother's hand and hearing her sniff, she passed her a handkerchief. "It's all right, Mama. We are unharmed and that is the most important thing. Now," she continued, ushering her to a chair, "you sit. I'll tell Josh the rest." Her mother did as she bid, because now that the adventure was over, the woman was showing signs of distress. Perhaps she ought to call the local doctor to ensure she wouldn't have a fit of the vapors.

"Alice. Tell me what happened."

Her brother's question pulled her from her musings and she met his eyes, reading the burning anger that simmered in their depths. "The highwayman stopped us not two miles from the gates of the estate. He knew our names, used our titles when speaking to us, and demanded what he wished to steal. Poor Tony was knocked to the ground, but he's resting now in his room and promised it was a slight ache in his head."

Josh strode across the room to the mantel and pulled the bell cord. "We'll have tea and discuss this further. I think Mama needs a medicinal drink that doesn't contain alcohol." A footman walked in and bowed. "Please bring us some tea and whatever cakes or biscuits Cook has, thank you."

Alice watched the footman leave and went to sit on a

chair beside her mother. Her mama was very pale, and she hated the thief for making her parent ill with worry and sadness. Alice vowed she would find out who the fiend was and ensure he had the full force of the law brought down on his head that housed such lovely blue eyes.

"Did you get a look at the robber—his horse or what he wore? Any marks that could help the authorities recognize him and issue punishment? I'll send a note straight away to the local magistrate and have him come out to the house. He needs to hear that the bastard is close to our county and wreaking havoc."

"Josh, watch your language please," their mama stated, throwing her brother a stern glance.

"I'll do more than swear in situations such as these," he said, sitting down behind his desk. "How dare the fiend take what doesn't belong to him. To think he can terrorize innocent women, and in our home county, no less, is beyond acceptable." Josh paused, a deep frown forming between his eyes and giving him a wild look that Alice hadn't seen before, well, maybe once, when her sister Beth had been kidnapped and he had been determined to get her back before her reputation was ruined.

Josh looked up and pinned her to the spot. "Did he do anything else to you? Make any other demands or threaten you in any way, should you seek retribution against his attack?"

Alice stilled under his piercing eyes that seemed, since becoming a duke, able to read minds. Gosh, she hoped not, but she quickly squashed the thought of lying to him. To do so wouldn't help the situation. He'd only end up learning the truth, and then she'd be the one in trouble. Of course, it was best that he know everything that had happened out on the road, even if it did put a cheeky thief behind bars, or worse. "He put Mama in the carriage and pulled me behind the vehicle." She ignored her brother's growl of temper and continued. "He tried to barter with me, said that if I gave him a kiss he would think about taking my earbobs and giving me back the brooch. I agreed and—"

"You what! You kissed a highwayman. Lady Alice Worthingham, the Duke of Penworth's daughter, kissed a felon. Why I—"

"Stop, Josh, and listen to your sister. She hasn't finished telling you what happened." Her mama's authoritative tone cut through her brother's harangue, and his mouth settled into a displeased line, but he didn't speak again.

Alice stood and walked to the hearth, a cold chill making her seek the warmth of flames. "I made out I was going to kiss him. I allowed him to hold me close, as if to kiss me and then I kneed him in the groin. Quite forcibly, I might add. He fell immediately and didn't get up, didn't even sit up once I had the horses moving at a good pace. He continued to lie there." Alice frowned. "I hope I didn't hurt him too much. It's one thing to be expecting an assault, and it's quite another when it comes out of nowhere. He wouldn't have thought a lady would do such a thing, I'd think."

Her brother's bark of laughter brought her out of her musing. "Wonderful," he stated, slapping his desk. "I knew that your gumption was not for nothing. I hope the bastard suffers and his balls swell up so he finds even walking difficult."

"Josh," their mother said again, her voice stern. "We do not use such words in this home."

Josh shook his head but did not disabuse her.

"I ran for the carriage and returned home immediately. There is nothing more to add." Alice shrugged and again the feeling of melancholy washed over her. How odd that a man who should've terrorized her, only intrigued her. For all she knew, his childhood may have been hard, an orphan child, his life rife with trouble and misfortune. What else could lead a man to do what he'd done? The whole situation really was very cheerless. Maybe, once she did find him, instead of sending him to Newgate, she should help him? Turn his life about to have some meaning and purpose.

Her brother nodded, reaching across his desk and pulling a piece of parchment before him and dipping his quill in ink. "I'll write straight away to the local magistrate. If you could tell the staff, we'll have one extra for dinner, Mama."

A footman knocked and entered, placing tea on her brother's desk, before bowing and leaving. Alice came back over to the desk and poured the tea, placing one rout cake on a plate and handing them to her mama and Josh. "It seems there are no biscuits today."

Her brother looked down at the little cakes that were really biscuits, but everyone had become so serious, so thoughtful, Alice would do anything to cheer them up.

"I should imagine the magistrate will be out within an hour or so of receiving this." Josh stood and walked to the door, and yelling out to a footman, handed him the missive with orders to make haste to Ashford and deliver it as soon as possible.

"Will you need Mama and me to tell him what happened or will you do it?" The day had been very long, and her mama was still shaking, if the rattle of her tea cup was anything to go by. Alice hoped her nerves would settle and she would soon be set to rights.

Josh shook his head, finishing off his biscuit before reaching over and taking another. "Now that I know what happened, I'll take care of it from here. I'm beyond glad you are both unharmed from the whole experience." He took a sip of tea, shaking his head. "And I want neither of you to worry about what happened today. We will catch this fiend, and then we'll watch him hang for his misdeeds. I can promise you that."

Alice frowned. The thought of those dark, mysterious eyes being closed for eternity made her stomach churn uncomfortably. Thinking back over the situation, it really hadn't been so bad. Yes he'd stolen, but perhaps he was desperate. "I think we need to find him, yes, but I also think we should ask what has made him lead such a life. If given the opportunity, maybe he would stop his misdeeds and turn his life about."

Josh looked at her as if she'd turned into Medusa. "Are you mad? We will do no such thing. He will pay for what he did to both of you, and I'll not allow anything less for the blaggard. If I have to single-handedly take down the Surrey Bandit, I will. His life of crime cannot continue, no matter what has led him to do what he does. Even the poorest child can choose not to follow the path to which he was born. It may be hard work and difficult, but it is possible. This fiend has chosen to thieve and terrorize people, and now it is time to pay the price for such a life."

Alice nodded and hoped her attempt to look agreeable was working. "Of course, let him hang." But should she find out who the Surrey Bandit was before her brother, well, there was no harm in trying to help him, before all hope was lost.

With a little aid, maybe he could be redeemed, start afresh, and never have to face what her brother was so determined to see happen to him.

CHAPTER 2

*T*he following afternoon, Callum cantered up the long drive to the Dunsleigh Estate and his neighbor, the Duke of Penworth. He pushed away the nerves that the two women he'd stolen from, one whom he'd manhandled more than he ought, lived at the house. Would they recognize him? Would his voice give him away, or his eyes, which he'd been told by many an admiring female, were quite memorable?

He cringed, wiping away the light sheen of sweat that broke out on his brow. The best thing for him to do was to act like the neighbor he was, not the bandit everyone was hunting and wanted to see swing at the end of a noose.

Callum thought over the events of yesterday, and his heartbeat returned to its normal pace. The coachman was old and, as unfortunate as it was, he'd had to tie him up face down on the road, so surely *he* wouldn't recognize him.

As for the mother, a woman getting along in age, he could only hope the events had scared her enough that she could only remember fragments, not specific details. Only the Lady Alice might prove troublesome. He'd been so close to her, had seen her so clearly, that surely she would've seen certain characteristics of him. And damn it, never before had he wanted to kiss a woman who'd shown so much bravery. The little minx had stood up to him bravely. She'd had more courage than any he'd come across in this particular folly, and he couldn't help but respect her for it.

He looked down at the nondescript tan mount beneath him, and his outing into the lion's den became less worrisome. The horse he'd used the day before, Bandit, was happily stabled back at Kester House and having a well-earned rest. Should Lady Alice think to check on what he was riding, she wouldn't see the same mount. He would have to do something about keeping Bandit hidden, at least until everyone in this county forgot about his thievery.

No sooner did he have the thought did he come upon Dunsleigh. Callum stayed in the saddle a moment, before taking a deep, calming breath and dismounting before the large double doors to the house. He knocked and waited for the door to open before giving his card to a footman, dressed to perfection in his blue and gold finery, much nicer than his own staff were able to wear.

The grandeur of the house hit him like the knee to his nether regions had yesterday, and his pitiful lack of wealth settled heavier on his shoulders. The Worthinghams were amongst the wealthiest in England, any of the daughters would've been appropriate as royal brides, should their lives have taken them in that direction. From what he'd gathered, they were well sought out and liked among the *ton*.

He sighed, kicking his heels in the entrance foyer, before the servant reappeared and ushered him toward a front room. "His Grace will see you in the library, my lord."

"Thank you," Callum said, preparing to enter. He pushed away the niggling bite of jealousy that an estate that only sat a few miles from his own was eons apart when it came to riches.

As he entered the library, he realized that it couldn't have been more opposite to his own. Here there were books on every shelf, upholstered furniture, and a roaring fire. His had few books, a roof that needed repairs, and wallpaper that was peeling and falling off. The thought of his home and the disgraceful state it was in washed shame over him, and again hammered home how important today's meeting was to not only his estate's future but that of his daughter's well-being.

A month's pay was due to his servants, and soon, should he not gain some funds, they would have to start rationing food, or at least, be very careful with what they ate. As it was, they ate a lot of soup, bread, and pudding. They only meat they ate was what his staff caught in traps or the chickens in the coop.

The duke stood and came around his desk, holding out his hand and welcoming him with a smile. The gesture made his conscience prick since, only the day before, he'd been the one who'd caused distress to the duke's family.

"Your Grace," Callum said with a bow, shaking the duke's outstretched hand.

"Good to see you, Arndel, it's been too long. Please, come have a seat and tell me why you're so desperate to see me. Your missive last week seemed as if it was of some great import." The duke motioned him toward a chair, before taking his own.

Callum waited for His Grace to sit, then got straight to his pressing matter. "I do have some business that is important to me. I would like to sell the land that adjoins your estate and is not entailed."

The duke raised his brow. "But that's some of your best holdings. It also occupies most of the waterway your livestock require to drink from. I wouldn't think you would wish to sell, for that reason alone."

It was true. Callum was losing some of his best land, but when needs must. And those words couldn't be any truer than they were right now. "I know it's prized farming land, but I must sell, and since you're my neighbor and will be impacted by whoever purchases it, I thought it only right I should give you the first offer. Should you not wish to buy, I will have my man of business advertise and see if any bids are received."

The leather creaked as the duke sat back in his chair, his fingers steepled before his nose. "Well, I must thank you for the offer and, of course, I'm willing to purchase the land at an agreed price. But I am sorry that matters have come to such a point that this is what you're made to do."

Callum breathed a sigh of relief and smiled, the weight of his lack of funds dwindling somewhat upon his shoulders. "The estate will still be profitable even a hundred acres short and with the sale of this parcel of land, Kester House will be a step closer to solvent."

"Before we settle this matter," the duke said, frowning, "and please, with what I'm about to propose I mean no disrespect. I'm merely suggesting this as your friend, but perhaps, I could loan you the funds. Would you be open to such an arrangement? You would be required to pay the amount back, of course, and with interest, but I will match the interest rate of whatever financial lender has offered you, and it'll at least allow you to keep what the estate has owned for years."

As tempting as the offer was, and generous of the duke, it was not something Callum could agree to. He wanted to make this transaction a legal one where he'd not stolen to gain the money that would be the outcome to it. "No!" he said, a little too forcefully. Callum cleared his throat and tried to sound reasonable. "Thank you for the kind offer, Your Grace, but I do not wish to be beholden to anyone, if I don't have to be. I'm sure, as a fellow gentleman, you can understand."

The duke nodded. "I do and, of course, the decision is yours, but I wonder what your grandmother would think of you selling off the estate. She's not known in Society for her kind heart, if I may be so bold."

That was too true, and Callum, more than most, knew how hard and unforgiving she could be. After his mother had married a man not befitting the family name or connections, his grandmother had cut her daughter from the family. Refused to acknowledge her daughter even after she'd borne the old tyrant her first grandson. His selling of the parcel of land would no doubt bring forth either a visit in person, to include a setdown, or a very tersely worded letter.

"I stopped caring what my grandparent thought or did a long time ago. The dowager countess has no say in this," Callum said, meeting the duke's inquisitive stare.

"You may tell me to mind my own business, but is it true that your father was a lawyer, and that your mother married him without the family's permission?"

Callum nodded. "It is true, and my upbringing was not as affluent as it may have been had my mother stayed in the bosom of the family, but it was a comfortable childhood, full of love and support. More than what my cousin, the late viscount, endured. As you well know."

The duke leaned back in his chair. "Too true. They allowed the late viscount Arndel to live without censure, which undoubtedly led to his early demise and a legacy you now have to repair as best you can."

And a terrible legacy it was, with a crippling debt he'd rather not have inherited. Worse than even the duke could ever imagine. "Which is why I must act and do all that I can to ensure its survival."

"I commend you for it. And do remember, until the papers are signed, the offer of a loan is on the table." The luncheon gong sounded somewhere deep in the recesses of the home and the duke stood. "You're more than welcome to stay for lunch. We can continue this discussion after the repast, if you wish."

Callum stilled at the thought of seeing Lady Alice again, of being but a few feet across a mahogany table after their interlude the day before. To speak with her so soon, to give her the ability to study him at length had its own problems, some of which had nothing to do with him thieving from her, but his own nervousness about the chit. But his desire to see her again, even at the risk of discovery, overrode any common sense.

"I would welcome luncheon. Thank you, Your Grace."

"Please, call me Worth or Duke."

Callum frowned, knowing neither were the correct form of address. "Worth?"

"Short for Worthingham. I find being called Penworth a little too much, even if I am a duke."

They made their way out of the library, toward the opposite side of the home and a dining room where Callum could already hear the chatter of women and laughter. His own home was always so quiet. The servants went about in silence and disturbed no one, including him. Whether it was due to his late cousin and his hardness toward the help and they thought him cut from the same abusive cloth, he'd yet to find out.

Either way, the atmosphere here at Dunsleigh was what he wanted for his home. There was a feeling of happiness, of security and love that wrapped about you the moment you stepped in the door and it was one thing he wished for above all else, and he'd stop at nothing until his own life and that of his daughter's was as peaceful and secure.

"I haven't seen you much since you took up the viscountcy. I hope, other than these few monetary teething problems, all is going well?" the duke asked, filling in the silence as they continued down the hall.

"Very well, thank you." Callum pushed away the thoughts on how he'd treated others since coming into the title. For another to show interest and wish him well as the new Viscount Arndel made guilt prick his soul with its pointy little dagger. Yet, he'd had little choice, he reminded himself. If anyone should feel guilt about his current occupation as a thief, it was his deceased cousin and the moneylender who had no scruples when it came to those he clawed into debt. Callum had been innocent of any crime, until his daughter had been threatened. But soon, very soon, he would put this despicable lifestyle behind him and start afresh.

The staircase loomed to the side of him and movement at the top halted his steps. Callum looked up as a vision of beauty personified glided down the stairs. The blood in his veins pounded fast and fluid at seeing Lady Alice again.

Gaping at her, he snapped his mouth shut and wiped his sweaty hands against his pants. Of course, he'd seen beautiful women before, had married one, but the duke's sister, with her golden locks that would make the sun weep with jealousy, and her clear, intelligent eyes, had him thinking all sorts of things that he'd promised himself he wouldn't think again. Not after their interlude when he'd stolen from her, and had wanted so much more than family heirlooms.

"Good afternoon, Lord Arndel, are you joining us for luncheon?"

Callum swallowed at the sound of Alice's sweet, welcoming voice that could also be defiant and hard when required. He pulled at his cravat, too tight about his neck.

She came to stand beside her brother and took His Grace's arm, looking up at him expectantly.

Callum cleared his throat. "Yes, my lady. Your brother was good enough to invite me." One delicate eyebrow rose and he had the oddest feeling that she was aware her presence made him awkward. Little did she know it wasn't awkwardness that he endured, but desire, a need that was as strong and undeniable as air.

"Wonderful."

She pulled her brother forward and past him and the scent of jasmine teased his senses. He took a deep breath, not entirely for fortitude, and followed them into the dining room, the whole time trying not to take in her delectable swaying hips.

After today he could declare himself totally insane, for there was something wrong with his mind. Lady Alice was not, nor ever would be, for him. She was cultured, accepted within Society, whereas he was looked on as something the family had dragged up to keep the estate within their reach. She was rich. He was poor, and no matter how much her dowry could save his financial ass, he refused to marry Alice under such circumstances. The only course left for him to save the estate and care for his daughter, who needed him more than anyone, was to sell the unentailed land and finish off the tasks that the moneylender had blackmailed him into doing. There was no time for courting pretty ladies, not when he struggled daily to keep his tenants housed and fed.

"Lord Arndel, how lovely to have you here." The duchess welcomed him, gesturing to a chair across the table from her. Her eyes were a deep blue and sparkled with warmth, reminding him yet again of Lady Alice and where she received her inherent beauty.

"How are you settling in at Kester House?" the duchess

asked, placing a napkin on her lap and motioning for the servants to begin serving.

Callum followed suit and took a sip of water. "Very well, Your Grace. I'm happy to be part of the community of Ashford. This area of Surrey has many beauties." His eyes met Lady Alice's and he quickly turned his attention back to the duchess, but not before catching the grin that lifted Alice's very kissable lips.

He shook the thought away that her kisses would be lovely. If only to allow him to forget his worries.

The duchess nodded, thanking a footman as he poured her wine. "I've loved Surrey from the moment I was brought here all those years ago when I first met the Duke and Duchess of Penworth. The rolling hills and hedge groves, beautiful estates, and welcoming people make this one of the finest and friendliest counties I know. Although," she said, distaste clouding her eyes, "I'll be glad when the Surrey Bandit is caught and tried for his crimes."

Callum choked and coughed, placing down his water before he spilled it over the tablecloth. A glass of wine was placed before him. "I agree," he said, gaining his equanimity. "This fiend is troublesome, to be sure." He kept his head down, hoping no one noticed his fumble at the mention of the highwayman.

The delicious scent of chicken soup wafted up to him as a bowl was set down. His mouth watered at the thought of a good meal. He couldn't remember the last time he'd eaten anything that wasn't served cold or days old. Of course, as lord of the house, he only thought it right that he would miss out on the best meals, and leave them for his daughter and staff to partake in. But very soon that was set to change, and he looked forward to that day with vigor.

Looking down at the three different spoons he had to choose from, actually managing to eat this soup was another thing altogether. His survey across the tabletop slid to Alice and he watched to see which piece of cutlery she used.

Her hand went to the one at the top of her bowl, her hand halted on the spoon and she didn't pick it up. He frowned, looking up to see her watching him. Heat stole up his neck that she'd caught him and understood the reason for his staring. But instead of the censure he expected at not being well versed in dining etiquette, she smiled, understanding dawning in her eyes before she looked back at her meal and started to eat.

They ate in silence for some time, before Callum cleared his throat, hoping what he had to say was looked upon favorably by the ladies present. "I understand my cousin each year held a ball for the local gentry and working families of the area. Unfortunately, I must be the bearer of bad news and will not be able to hold it this year." Three pair of female eyes bore down on him. Callum chose to ignore their surprise and merely continued to chew his chicken, hoping against hope they wouldn't ask why he wouldn't hold the event.

"But it's tradition in the area, my lord. The late lordship always hosted the pre-season party. As much as we were disappointed last year that you did not hold one, we thought due to you only being new to the title that we should not impose on you too soon. But surely, this being your second year as Lord Arndel a ball cannot be too much trouble?"

"Well, as to that," he started, struggling to find the words without coming outright and saying he was near penniless.

"Before you give Arndel any censure over not holding the ball, it was in fact what we were discussing before luncheon. I've decided that we shall host the ball this year instead of his lordship. We haven't held one for the local gentry since father's death, and I think it's time we did."

Callum nodded to the duke in silent thanks before taking a sip of wine. Even with the sale of the land now secure, he couldn't spare any funds for a ball. It would be still too much for his coffers to stand, even if it weren't extravagant.

"That sounds like a wonderful idea, Josh." Lady Victoria, seated two seats up from him, beamed at her brother. "I do prefer not having to leave Dunsleigh, outings can be so wearing. Not to mention always having to travel to London can be such a bore. But a ball at home is just the thing."

"You don't like Town?" he asked, having not thought a young lady would dislike the atmosphere and parties that the bustling city offered. The theaters, gardens, and not to mention, the gentlemen.

Victoria shook her head. "Not at all. I prefer the country. I have my horses and my dogs here. There is not any other place on earth that I enjoy more."

Callum studied Victoria and wondered if she were older or younger than Alice. They were similar in looks, to be sure, both had golden locks, but where Alice had lighter shades running throughout, Victoria had a reddish kiss to her hair. She smiled at him when noting his attention, and he quickly turned back to his meal, hating that Victoria's eyes were as green as the emerald brooch he'd stolen. Perhaps staying for lunch had not been such a good idea.

The placing down of a crystal glass harder than was necessary had him looking across the table. Lady Alice watched him with an intensity that had him shifting in his seat. She plopped a grape between her lips and his mouth dried.

Had she recognized him of a sudden? Would she declare him the thief who had stolen from the family and have him shot by the duke before he could hightail it out of the house? Time ticked by and such a declaration never came. She continued to eat grapes more erotically than he'd ever seen before, while taking in his every move.

What had come over her?

"Do not worry, Lord Arndel, for we shall throw a ball that is as sought after as your late cousin's was. We shall not disappoint, I promise you." Victoria paused. "In fact, if you wish it, you could help organize it. There are many things that I'm sure your staff has noted down that is required for us to replicate your cousin's event. Maybe we could even hold the ball in your honor. Celebrate the title going into such capable hands." Victoria looked at the duchess. "Mama, what do you say? Do you think my plan is suitable?"

Callum swallowed and tried to mask his fear over such a thing. Not that he minded the duke hosting an event, instead of him, but never would he wish to have so many eyes on him. Many of them he'd stolen from. Awkward didn't begin to stress how such an honor would make him feel.

"I don't see the problem, my dear, and Alice may also assist you. Of course, this is only if Lord Arndel wishes to be guest of honor." The duchess took a sip of her wine, her eyes twinkling with pleasure.

Callum nodded, smiling to tamper down the conundrum that was coursing through him. *What do I do?* "I would welcome any ball that the Duke of Penworth holds, but it isn't necessary for me to be so singled out with such an honor. I inherited a title, I didn't solve world poverty." He took a sip of wine, needing the fortitude.

Alice turned to her mother. "When should we hold the ball, Mama?"

"Whenever you wish, my dear. Although I do believe before the Season commences would be best; otherwise, most people will be away in Town. If that suits Lord Arndel, of course."

He nodded, wishing he'd not stayed for lunch after all. "I will not be attending Town this Season, so whenever you hold the ball will be agreeable to me." He met Alice's eyes and cursed that he reveled in the disappointment he possibly read in her sapphire gaze. With his dubious actions over the last year, he was certainly not husband material for a duke's daughter. He shouldn't like the fact that she might pine for his attendance in Town.

"Oh no, we shall miss you in London this year, my lord. Will we ever have the pleasure of your company outside of Surrey?" Alice asked, sitting back as the main meal of roast beef was placed before them.

"In time, I'm sure I'll attend the Season, but I have other things that occupy my time at present."

"Like what?" she asked, her question bringing him up short.

"Alice," the duchess said, "don't be impertinent."

Alice studied him a moment before turning back to her meal.

"Before the Season will certainly work better for those attending," Victoria stated matter-of-factly.

Alice threw him a determined smile, one he recognized from when he'd had her hard up against the carriage and at his mercy. The memory of her supple and soft curves made him shift in his seat. "That gives us three weeks to organize. Plenty enough time, since those being invited are local to the county, and I'm sure very eager to know our new viscount better. Don't you agree, Victoria?"

Victoria nodded. "I do agree with this plan. We'll have to have the invitations out before this week's end."

Both sisters' eyes were alight with excitement, whereas Callum couldn't think of anything worse than being the center of attention. *Oh for crying aloud, why did I ever mention the damn ball to them?* He tried to calculate a way to not attend and came up blank. At this point in his life, the ability to pay for a new suit was a stretch and one he could ill afford. But how to tell them that when their ducal allowance was much more forgiving than his own? He could not, without looking more desperate than he already was.

"With the Season so close, I don't believe a ball is really necessary. Do you not agree, Your Grace?" Callum asked, hoping the duke would back him on his statement.

Alice ignored his words. "We shall make your honorary ball the grandest night you've ever seen. We'll invite all our acquaintances and friends and you will get to know who your neighbors are, as you should, now that you're the new viscount. You, Lord Callum, will be propelled into the Society in which you were born and with our brother's backing, we may manage to have you married, before the Season has even begun."

Callum choked and coughed, taking a sip of wine. "Forgive me for my lapse of manners. The drink went down wrong," he gasped out, punching the middle of his chest.

"Are you well, my lord?" Again, Alice watched him. She was forthright, so bold and confident as she looked at him. He was sure he'd never met anyone like her. From what he remembered of the limited events he'd attended last year, Lady Alice Worthingham was a much sought-after young lady, but with a will that would take someone extraordinary to endure for more than an evening out.

"Very well, thank you," he said, diving back into his meal, his need to finish what was on his plate overwhelming the determination to leave. "In regards to the ball—"

"We could have ice sculptures and foreign foods cooked up, the likes of which Ashford has never seen before."

This was beyond bearable. Stuffing the last of the beef into his mouth, he chewed quickly, wanting to go. Now. He checked the time and tried to think up a reason why he had to depart before luncheon had even ended.

"May we call on you in a day or so to speak to your cook about what was always served by the late viscount? I believe she always made the most delicious dry cake, and we'd so love for her to replicate that for the ball here," Victoria said.

Callum washed down his meal with the last of his wine, wishing it was something much stronger. "No need for that. I can send my cook over to Dunsleigh to attend you."

Alice chuckled, a knowing smile on her lips and his heart thumped to a stop. "We love a little jaunt every now and then. We shall visit you, Lord Arndel. It has been two years since we've visited Kester House. We would enjoy seeing any improvements you have completed since you inherited the estate, my lord."

The phrase *my lord* was uttered unlike anything he'd ever heard before. It was full of sensual implication and sweat broke out on his top lip. All thoughts of money and his lack thereof vanished with the saying of the two words. Before the threat from the moneylender against his daughter's life reminded him he needed to keep his head and not lose it to a pretty face. Or the sensual mouth that had been haunting his dreams and woken him restless and unfulfilled.

Realization struck like a hammer that he wanted her. Not at a ball surrounded by other guests, or here among her family. But alone. Just the two of them, if only to see if the attraction he had for the chit was wholly one side only.

His attention, without heed of who was about them, moved to the creamy, perfect flesh that graced her neck and below. The blue gown hugging the bountiful attributes that Lady Alice would one day share with her husband made his hands clench, and something comparable to jealousy shot through him at the thought of someone else laying claim to her body.

The duke cleared his throat and Callum prayed he'd not seen his blatant study of his sister. The duke wiped his mouth, seating himself back in his chair, seemingly pleased with his meal and having no inkling that his sister was being ogled by the worst gentleman guest they'd ever had.

"Shall we finish our discussion in the library, Lord Arndel?" The duke stood. "I'll see you at dinner, Mama."

"You will not be long will you, Brother? We have a meeting in Ashford. You have not forgot, I hope."

Callum pushed back his chair and a sharp piercing sound rendered the room into silence. "Apologies, ladies," he said, gritting his teeth at his ability to always draw inappropriate attention to himself.

"Is that today?" the duke asked, running his hand through his hair.

Callum frowned, wondering what the meeting was about. Whatever it was, the fierce determination on Alice's face looked like it was important to her.

"Yes, you said you would look over the buildings with me and ensure the quote from the carpenters isn't excessive. You know how important those cottages are to me. You had better say you will come."

The duke sighed. "Lord Arndel, I did promise and so I can only spare an hour or so before familial duty must take precedence."

"I understand, of course. And an hour will be most adequate." Callum faced Her Grace. "Thank you for having me to lunch. Good afternoon to you all." He bowed and left the dining room, welcoming the hallway's solitude and cool air on this warm afternoon.

The duke joined him and they headed back to the library.

The meeting went well, and today forward his life would settle for the better. As soon as he returned to Kester House he would send for his lawyer and have him draw up the appropriate papers to sell the land. Then he would organize a date for when he'd travel to the capital and be rid of the last jewel he'd ever steal for the moneylender.

Soon the Surrey Bandit would be no more.

It was not an occupation that had brought him pride or honor. The opposite, in fact. He was riddled with guilt, with remorse and anger, but people did things out of desperation, and his daughter's safety was paramount. He'd learned a long time ago how precious life was and how easily it could be snatched away. Amelia was one jewel he would never risk.

Callum stepped out into the bright midday sun and breathed in the warm, fresh air. For the first time since inheriting the estate and all the troubles that came with it, his spirits lifted. Marvelous.

CHAPTER 3

*A*lice followed her mama out and into the drawing room, frowning. What an odd luncheon they'd had. And most assuredly, Lord Arndel was the oddest of all. What was the man about? And why did he need a lawyer to draw up papers for Josh? What did that mean?

Of course, he was as dashing as ever and way too handsome for his own good. She had not missed his interested glances nor that her body didn't feel like her own when he threw such looks her way. Alice and the duchess walked upstairs to her mama's private parlor and she flopped onto a settee before the unlit hearth.

Her mama sat in her sewing chair and picked up her needlework. "What an enjoyable lunch. I do believe that Lord Arndel is smitten with you, Alice."

Alice scoffed, although a small part of her loved that idea. To have a suitor so close to home would be fortunate. Although, unlike Victoria, Alice did enjoy London and all its entertainments and distractions. There had been a time when she had abhorred the place. But she loved the city and the friends she'd made there the last two years, and it wouldn't trouble her should her main home be situated there.

Victoria picked up their small pug, Dash, trying to make the fat little puppy sit on her lap without squirming. "I agree. And I know I shouldn't be so forthright, but golly, he's handsome. If he'd not already taken a liking to you, Alice, I may have tried to gain his attention myself."

"Do you really believe so?" She was grinning like a fool. He was one of the most handsome men she'd ever met. And the fluttering in her stomach each time he looked at her had to mean something. The reaction she'd had to Lord Arndel was similar to the one she'd had with the Surrey Bandit, and it gave her hope, for she'd truly thought she was losing her mind reacting to a fiend in such a way.

Victoria made kissing sounds to Dash and the little dog licked frantically, trying to reach her face. "I do. I had the impression that he fought the attraction, though. I'm not sure why and I demand you find out. I would so love to attend another of my sister's weddings."

"Do not get ahead of yourself, my dear," their mama said, looking for different shades of cotton. "I'll accompany you to Kester House. I should've paid a visit after his lordship took on the title, and it was remiss of me that I did not."

Alice stared at the portrait of their father, which looked down on them from the mantel, the duke's passing the one reason why their mother had become a bit of a recluse. *God rest his beautiful soul.* "We will welcome your company, Mama." She sighed, thinking of Arndel. "I agree he's handsome, and while in London I did enjoy teasing the man whenever we met. And for a time, I thought myself enamored of him. But he was so skittish in Society and around women in general. I could never marry a man like that. And as much as I love you all dearly, I do not wish to be settled too near to Dunsleigh during my marriage."

"Why?" her mama asked, her eyes going wide with shock. "What is wrong with being so close to home?"

"Well, for one thing," Alice continued, "since Josh became duke, he has morphed into a stickler for rules and for everything that's boring. I know he'll marry someone who's just as boring, and I would have her on my doorstep at all hours, boring me to pieces. I would not be able to stand it."

Victoria's laughter rang out loud in the quaint room, and her mother threw her a silencing glare. "Even for me, that is too many borings in a sentence. And how can you say such a thing about your sibling? To be so close to your family when settled would be a blessing and far from a hindrance. Just think, you could visit me daily and ride out with Victoria whenever you pleased. And I'm certain whomever Josh marries will be as lively and beautiful as all my daughters." Her mother smiled, the delight of seeing such a situation come to fruition written clearly on her features.

"Well, it's settled then," Victoria said, huffing out a breath. "From what you say, I'm going to live here forever. The spinster of Dunsleigh. The one sister who never found someone to take her on."

Alice reached over and patted her sister's hand, which was being nibbled on by the pug. "Of course you'll marry. I'm sure, unfortunately, we all will." Alice winked at her and was glad to see a smile form on her sister's lips. "In any case, the Season will be starting soon and off to London we shall go. Hopefully, husbands will be found. But I can assure you, if only because his home is so close to mine, it will not be Lord Arndel." Alice held up her hand when her mama went to argue the point. "I know I've been particular in the past, but I'm determined. Anything outside of Surrey will be suitable."

Her mama put down her needlework and huffed out an annoyed sigh. "Really, my child? I thought you said, in this very room no less, the same thing about last year's Season.

And here we are again, about to partake on another jaunt to Town when we should not bother, because we all know you'll return here with me at the end of it."

Heat suffused her chest and Alice hoped it didn't spread to her face. She always became so blotchy when it did. "As I said, this year I'll not be so particular. I promise."

Victoria, unable to make the puppy do as she wished, placed him on the floor. "I forgot about your mooning over Lord Arndel last season. Why did you not pursue him? I thought you liked him."

"I did like him. I like him still," Alice corrected, thinking back on the previous year and her attempts to gain his interest. All of which had seemed to go unnoticed and certainly not returned. He'd been forever occupied and distant, so she'd given up.

That he was back in the county, calling and having lunch with them, looking at her with more interest than he'd ever shown before, meant nothing at all. He was simply doing business with her brother and being a good neighbor. Although she would love to find out what that business was exactly. "Last Season, he looked at me like I had the pox, so now, I'm not interested in his courting, should he start to do so. To be seen as a disease that could take one's life is not flattering, I assure you."

"Alice! You are a daughter of a duke! Do not use words such as pox and courting in the same sentence." Her mother threw up her hands in despair.

Victoria merely chuckled and opened a copy of *Belle Assemblée*, flicking through the pages distractingly.

"Well, he did, Mama, and I cannot forgive him for it. No matter how much he is startled anew with my beauty." Alice laughed at her own joke and stopped when her mother found no mirth in her words. "But in all seriousness, what do you think his business is about with Josh? Do you think he's finally ready to look for a wife?"

"I think he is. And if I'm not mistaken, which I rarely am, he's finally seen what was before him all those months ago and wishes his choices had been different." Her mother pursed her lips. "But you must remember, my dear, his family are not the easiest people of our acquaintance, and if you were to marry into them, they would not be as present as you may wish. From what I know, they did everything for the estate to go to another, more suitable, member of their set, before it was bestowed on Lord Arndel, who was the rightful heir all along."

Alice didn't like the image of a family disregarding someone so callously, especially when none of it was his fault that he was the heir. Lord Arndel certainly didn't ask to be born, and he'd certainly had no choice in who his family was. So for his kin to treat him with so little respect annoyed her more than she thought it should.

Thinking back over the previous Season, his first as viscount, perhaps she'd been too hard on him. With a family breathing down one's neck, waiting for him to create a scandal or monetary mistake, it was any wonder he'd not looked at her as anything other than another woman searching for a husband. An annoyance he'd had little time or interest for.

How absurd she must have seemed to him, teasing him, following him about like their puppy, who was now sniffing at the Aubusson rug. "I think Dash needs to go outside."

Victoria lunged from her chair and scooped up the pup. The duchess threw the dog a cursory glance before packing up her needlework. "I'm off to look at the weekly menus with Cook. I'm sure you girls can amuse yourselves for a time. It's a beautiful day, why not make the most of it and go for a walk?"

"Come, Mama is right, let's take Dash outside," Victoria said.

"We cannot be long. Josh is taking me into Ashford soon to meet with the carpenter to supply us with a quote on the cottages."

"We will not walk long."

Alice followed her, and making the ground floor landing, they headed toward the back of the house, through the music room, and onto the terrace. The little dog flicked about in Victoria's arms, clearly sensing freedom, and she set him down. His bolt toward the lawn was a little uncoordinated at first, but he soon got the hang of it and they followed at a more sedate pace.

"Would you really not look at Arndel as a possible suitor?"

Victoria looked at her, and Alice wondered if her sister read the uncertainty in her eyes. Damn the man for bringing forth the rioting emotions within her. "There is something that I haven't told a soul, and you must promise me if I tell you, you will not either."

"Of course," her sister agreed readily.

"Very well, it is true that last season I thought myself in love with the viscount. I'm sure you noticed that I followed him about, like your dog is now following that bee."

Victoria's attention turned to Dash and she clapped her hands, startling the puppy from trying to catch the little insect, which he, no doubt, would be stung by. "I recall, but I certainly don't remember you being obsessed."

"In any case, I feel like a fool for doing so, for he made it perfectly clear, and in no uncertain terms, he wasn't attracted to me."

"How so?" Victoria pulled her to a stop, taking her hand. "Tell me, dearest."

"I came upon him one night with a group of gentlemen,

and they were discussing us. All the Worthingham girls, in fact, and how Josh had his hands full trying to gain us husbands. Which is very untrue and absurd, as we're most certainly not desperate and really, if we wished, we needn't marry at all."

Victoria chuckled, nodding. "And what else did he say?"

"My name in particular, and I listened behind a potted indoor palm like my life depended on it. It's so embarrassing to think back on, but some of those men had courted me and I was interested to hear what they really thought." Alice watched the puppy for a moment, as it dug madly in the lawn. "They were joking about our estates being so closely situated and that I should be easy to secure, due to, what they termed, neighborly love. And do you know how he replied to such teasing?"

"How?"

"He said, and I quote, 'Lady Alice is most definitely not for me. Too much work for my taste and budget.'"

Her sister gasped. "He never. Did the other gentleman agree with him? And pray tell me who they were, for I'll not associate with any of those fools when we're in Town."

Alice rounded off some names but the truth was, they had all agreed with Lord Arndel. Each and every one had thought she and her sister would be expensive to keep and hard work to tame. Yes, they had flattered their looks, had gushed in the faces of the daughters of a duke, but Alice hated the fact they'd used the word "tame" as a term for them. Like they were pieces of horseflesh that needed breaking in.

How humiliating.

She was not an animal that needed to come to heel. She would be a wife, a lover, and possibly a mother one day, and no matter how much the men of their acquaintance may wish it, none of the Worthingham girls would ever be *tamed*.

"I find, and I'm sure you agree, that no matter how handsome Lord Arndel is, he is beneath my notice after such a statement. To be so rudely termed, and before other men of our set, was too much to bear. I could never marry him now, no matter how handsome his eyes are, or how succulent his lips look."

Victoria grinned. "'Succulent' is another word Mama would dislike you using, although I concur, his lips are very appealing." Her sister frowned. "I cannot understand him saying such a thing, but I believe you. I thought better of him. Since he's taken over the Kester House and the estate, he's kept the most beautiful stallion. Have you seen it?"

Alice fought not to roll her eyes at Victoria's change of conversation. Her sister loved animals and was often jealous of others when they possessed a great horse or sought-after breeding dog.

"I haven't taken any notice of his cattle, now back to our discussion—"

"I only mention it," Victoria interrupted, "because he wasn't riding the stallion today." She bit her lip. "I wonder why?"

"I don't know, perhaps it's lame or…something."

"*Hmm*, perhaps you're right, but I'll ask him about it the next time he's here. I wonder if he'd be willing to sell. I shall ask Josh to enquire about it."

Dash barked and ran toward the small stream that ran the eastern side of the house. They followed the little pug and noticed the crunching sound of cantering hooves on the drive behind them.

"Lord Arndel has left." Alice looked toward the front of the house and caught a glimpse of his lordship's back as he headed down the gravel drive.

Victoria sighed. "I should've asked him about his stallion before he left."

Alice took her hand, laughing at her sister's obsession.

"I'm surprised Mama allowed us to walk the grounds. Since the Surrey Bandit has been gallivanting about, she's been so worried he'll escalate and kidnap a virginal miss, also known as her daughters."

Victoria nodded in agreement. "As to that, I know why we're allowed out again. Apparently, there was a robbery in Kent. The local magistrate believes he has moved to another county, so we're safe from possible theft."

The little stream came into view and they both sat. Alice took the opportunity to take off her slippers, mostly ruined from the outing as they were only meant for indoors. She slid her silk stockings off and paddled her feet in the shallows.

"We should go for a swim. It's hot enough today."

Victoria contemplated the water for a moment before grinning. "Josh will tell us off for not acting as ladies, if we strip off down to our undergarments and swim."

Determined to cool down and enjoy the last few weeks they would have here before the Season commenced, Alice started to unbutton her gown. "We're not doing anything wicked by swimming. I'm sure he wouldn't mind, given the unseasonably warm fall."

"But what about your meeting?" Victoria picked up the pug that sniffed the ground beside them, and using a ribbon she carried, tied him to a nearby tree in the shade.

"I have time." Alice bit her lip, wondering since they were being so honest if she should confide in Victoria. Her sister smiled and Alice decided it wouldn't hurt. "Talking of Lord Arndel, I have another confession."

"What is it?" Victoria asked, stripping off her stockings.

Alice pursed her lips. "His lordship makes me nervous. I neither like nor approve of the emotions."

"Maybe deep down you do, though, and that's the problem," Victoria said, wading into the water.

Soon they were both stripped to their unmentionables and floating in the stream that was both cool and refreshing. "I'm so glad we learned to swim as children. Could you imagine not being able to enjoy such a pastime?"

"It would be the veriest of torture," Victoria said, looking up at the sky. "Before Lord Arndel had said what he did at the ball that evening, did you like him? Not as a friend, but as a possible husband?"

Alice had hoped her sister, always one to seek out a truth, wouldn't ask her that question. For she *had* liked him. Desperately so. Had, even for a time, thought herself in love with the man. What a foolish twit she'd been. "I like him, but no more than anyone else of our acquaintance. If I ever had more feelings than those, they have long left me."

The knowing chuckle from her sister irked, and Alice flicked water at her. "What are you laughing at?"

"Anyone with eyes could see you two were throwing looks at each other with a whole raft of conflicting emotions behind them. Certainly they were not glances you would bestow on a passing acquaintance. I think you like him still. More so than even you know, for let's face facts. He's titled, available, and if what Mama says is true, looking for a wife."

Alice thought over her sister's words, knowing she'd wondered the same thing a million times since luncheon. Were her feelings still engaged with the gentleman? She had promised herself she would hate his arrogance and easy dismissal of her after last season, but then, seeing him again, being reminded of his warm cultured voice and kind eyes... stormy blue eyes that inspired a longing that rioted within her...

Alice stopped swimming and stood up. How odd that his lordship's eyes were the same shade of blue as the Surrey Bandit's...

"I can tell, you know."

"What?" Alice asked, her sister's words pulling her from thoughts of the Surrey Bandit and how handsome Lord Arndel was. In fact the handsomest gentleman she'd ever met.

"When you lie."

She dove under the water to hold off the blush that fought to cover her face and give her away to her sibling. Coming back up to the surface she met her sister's expectant gaze. She wouldn't get out of answering her question. "I have no interest in the man. None whatsoever."

"You're lying again, sister. I can tell."

"How so?" Alice stood, crossing her arms over her chest.

"You're blushing."

She tried to cover the telltale sign that always occurred when she fibbed. Damn it. With all this water about, she'd not thought a blush could form. "Well, I don't know what to tell you other than I do not. You may choose to believe me or no."

Her sister swam farther out into the pond, her laugh echoing off the trees that surrounded the stream. "You'll get a pimple on your nose for saying such falsehoods."

"I will not."

"Ah ha! See. I was right, you do like him still."

Alice swam out to the middle, glaring at her too-knowledgeable sister. "I will admit I still find him uncommonly handsome, but I do not wish to marry him." She didn't mention the true reasoning over her anger at Lord Arndel. That the night he'd said those things about her and her siblings, he'd seen her skulking behind the ferns and had still continued with his damaging take on them all. A little piece of her had died that night, knowing gentlemen, no matter their rank or position in Society, were playing a game more often than not. She'd never thought Lord Arndel to be one of them. Why she'd imagined such a thing, she couldn't say, for she hadn't known him well before the Season had commenced. But she'd thought him true—a man with morals, a friend even.

And yet, friends did not treat or speak about the other in such a manner, and now going forward, no matter how handsome he was, or how diligent on acting the gentleman around her, neighbors and cool acquaintances was all they'd ever be.

---

*C*allum trotted down the drive, the crunch of gravel underfoot loud in his ears. His head pounded after the solid hour of negotiations on the size of the parcel of land he wished to sell and at what price the duke was prepared to pay. It had made his mind hurt, not to mention his pride.

It was a worthwhile sale, and all he had left to sell that wasn't entailed. The debt his late cousin had afforded him had left nothing for the estate to run on. A situation not easy to stomach and with the funds he'd gain from the duke, and careful budgeting, he could get the farm back to a profitable balance sheet within a couple of years. The sooner he traveled to London and rid himself of the jewel that would bring an end to his cousin's debt, the better. If the menacing missive he'd received only last week was any indication, the moneylenders were growing restless, so much so that his daughter's well-being had been mentioned once again. A subtle hint that they'd stolen her once before and that they could do it again, if they wished. He would die before he allowed anything to happen to her again.

He looked up at the old oaks that ran down either side of the driveway and welcomed the occasional shade the trees brought. Sweat beaded his brow when he turned off the road and headed toward his own estate.

In only a few weeks, Callum would be a free man, the noose of debt about his neck, and his lifestyle as the Surrey Bandit over. He spurred his horse forward. Today may have been tiring and challenging, but it had been worth every pain inflicted on his soul.

He cantered across the fields, happy to let the horse decide its own course. He followed the local stream that had once marked the two different estates. But no longer. Once the legalities were finalized, the stream would sit on the Worthingham's property line, and he would have the cash to prove it. Callum laughed, feeling joy and sensing a light at the end of the long, dark tunnel he'd traveled these past two years.

He slowed his mount to cross the small wooden bridge that passed over the stream and the muffled sound of laughter and splashing water came from a little ways upstream. For a moment, he stopped to listen and in doing so, had an inkling of who it might be.

Urging his mount forward, he rode through the thicket of foliage and jerked his horse to a stop when the vision before him became apparent. His horse flicked its head, not appreciative of his roughness on the bit, but Callum was too preoccupied to care once he saw what paraded before him in the water.

He ought to be ashamed of himself, hiding in the trees like some desperate youth, but he was not. To see Alice swimming, enjoying the cool water and the company of her sibling was something he could watch every day, even if she was a hellion most of the time. They were so innocent, unlike himself, who was as far from innocent as one could get; being the Surrey Bandit eliminated him from such virtue.

He swallowed hard when Alice floated on her back and

her transparent shift was all that stood between him seeing her true form. Not that he couldn't make out what delights lay hidden beneath her attire. Even fully clothed, Callum was aware of what assets Alice had to offer the husband she would one day acquire.

Dismounting, he pulled the reins over his horse's head and allowed his mount to graze before walking out into the open. The sisters continued to swim, both of them unaware he'd come upon their outing. Alice floated with her eyes closed, her lips in a contented smile. He cleared his throat, wanting her to notice him, for by God, he'd noticed her. Had in fact, noticed her from the first moment he'd seen her in London last Season. Not that he could have acted on his attraction back then—asset rich but cash poor—so much so that he'd been stealing from the very people she called friends.

But now, it was a different matter entirely.

Alice's golden hair flowed about her face, a halo of sorts when the dappled sunlight hit the water's surface. Callum forced his eyes to close and remembered to breathe. Where were his manners, his ability to act a gentleman? Not here, it would seem.

"What an odd man you are, Lord Arndel. Are you praying?"

With a start, he opened his eyes, cringing as both sisters stood in the shoulder deep water, staring at him. He shouldn't have followed the sound. He'd known damn well where it led—to nothing but trouble and a woman named Alice.

"I um—" He cleared his throat, looking away from the water droplets that fell from the most delectable lips he longed to take possession of. The thought of kissing her sweet mouth brought a mad flush to his cheeks, and he looked up to the sky for salvation.

"Well, are you going to answer my question, my lord? It's very rude. Don't you agree, Victoria?"

Victoria snorted. "I most definitely agree."

Only then did he look at Alice. "I apologize for my intrusion. I was on my way home, when I heard a sound coming from this direction. I thought an animal may have been injured or some such."

The raised eyebrow Alice bestowed in his direction made it perfectly obvious that she thought him a liar. And so she should, for he spoke bullocks that even sounded like bullocks to his own ears.

Idiot.

"Are you saying that our voices mimic that of an injured animal?" Her arms ran through the water before her, the movement distracting him from all sensible thought, before she said in a voice as sweet as sin, "My lord? Is that your opinion?"

Adjusting his too-tight cravat, he took off his hat and fanned his face. He looked to his horse and it, too, stared at him, as if waiting to see what answer he would come up with.

"No. Of course not. I was riding past, and over the sound of the horse I couldn't hear very well, you see. I apologize if I caused offense."

She shrugged and submersed herself deeper in the water. Definitely a good idea, in his estimation. "Victoria and I decided to go for a swim. I hope you don't mind, since we're on your land and haven't asked for permission."

That was the least of his concerns. The water glistened off her chin and dripped toward breasts that he refused to look at. There would be no turning back if he succumbed to such temptation. Callum shoved his hat back on his head and ignored the merriment in her blue orbs. "No, not at all. But." He looked about. "Where is Victoria going?"

Alice looked toward the direction her sister swam and smiled. "There's a shallow pool around the corner of the stream. The water is always warmer there. I should imagine that is where she's headed. Here in the center of the pond it can get quite cool."

"Ah, I was not aware of that," he said, losing his own battle and looking where he'd sworn not to. Damn it! Alice would think him more of an ass if he kept up such antics. And after last Season and what she'd overhead him saying, the chit didn't need any more inclination to hate him.

"Not that it matters any longer what hidden gems the water holds, for soon I'll no longer be the owner of it."

"You're selling?" She looked at him, shock clearly written on her features.

"Only some acreage to your brother, which I'm sure you and Victoria will be happy about." Her smile lit up the grove and he sat on a nearby log, not delving too far into his psyche as to why he was making himself comfortable before a near-naked woman. A virginal, unmarried miss and sister to a powerful duke.

"I cannot say I'm not delighted by this news, although I hope you've thought through the sale and are not making a hasty decision." She swam closer and he adjusted his seat. "I fear you will miss this swimming locale. It's such a beautiful spot to own."

He couldn't agree more and he supposed she had a point, but he would enjoy the funds for the estate more than a swimming pond. "I have enough land to keep me well occupied, I assure you." She chuckled and he laughed. When animated, Alice was one of the most handsome women he'd ever beheld. Over the past year, he'd watched her from afar, a woman of her rank, even with his new title, was so far above him he'd dared not court her. That he'd been atrociously rude last Season was all due to his own insecurities about his position in Society. He'd attended most balls only for the sake of identifying a certain ring, brooch, or necklace that the moneylenders wanted for the cache. He had not wanted to muddy the waters by courting a woman who clearly liked him a little. To be close with anyone could've thrown them, too, into danger, to be used as a pawn for him to do more than he already was as the Surrey Bandit. He'd not been able to risk it and, in turn, had hurt Alice without wanting to.

"Lady Alice, I must apologize for my reprehensible words and actions last Season. It was not a good time for me, and I fear you received the brunt of my harsh words. Each one of them an untruth that you did not deserve. I've wanted to say that I'm sorry from the moment I spoke them, and now that I can, I truly wish for you to forgive my ungentlemanly actions."

A slight smile tweaked her lips and he was lost. How he wanted her, with a desperation that didn't fathom thinking about.

"Apology accepted, Lord Arndel, even though it is shockingly overdue."

He smiled, a great weight lifted from his conscience. "Thank you for being so agreeable."

"Had your apology not been heartfelt, I wouldn't have accepted it, I can assure you, but it was, so you're forgiven." She paused. "As for the lake, I'll be happy to call this place my own from now on." She looked up at him, shading her face against the sun. "We learned to swim not far from here, you know. Our father taught us how to ride and swim, as well as any boy."

"I never knew your father, but from what your brother has told me, he seemed like a great man."

She nodded, looking away for a moment. "He was wonderful. I think you would've liked him."

Callum wasn't so sure the late duke would've liked him, if

he ever found out his neighbor was the Surrey Bandit. He pushed the thought aside. The point was moot, as the gentleman was dead and so, too, would the bandit be—very soon. "I think I would've, too," he agreed.

The wind chose that moment to pick up, leaves floating into the water as they scattered from the trees. "Well, I suppose we should head back."

For a moment, Callum didn't comprehend her words before she raised her brow and comprehension struck.

"Could you turn about, my lord? I need to get out and unfortunately, my shift isn't appropriate wear for you to see me in." She grinned. "Once I have my gown back on you may stop admiring the foliage."

"Forgive me." He turned and looked at his horse, rolling his eyes at his own stupidity. His mount stared at him as if he were a simpleton, something Callum certainly thought he was turning into. It snorted and lowered its head to eat the grass. The sound of Alice dressing behind him tormented him, and the urge to peek almost overrode his gentlemanly behavior. Victoria spoke as she joined Alice after dressing themselves.

After a little while, seeing him kick his heels in the grass, Alice came up from behind and tapped him on the shoulder. "You can turn about again now."

———

*A*lice went and sat on the small log that Lord Arndel had occupied and patted the wood for him to join her. She picked at the knot of her bonnet ribbons as he did as she bid.

After the cool water, seated this close to his lordship left her shivery, her skin prickling in little bumps. Perhaps this was a bad idea. She pulled hard at the knot and inwardly swore when it refused to give way.

"Here, let me have a go." He took her bonnet and the sight of his large, capable hands working delicately against her hat made her think of what they would feel like against her flesh, running across her lips after a passionate kiss, or replacing a strand of hair gone astray.

He removed the knot and looked at his work with pride. "There. Gone." He passed it back to her and she laughed a little.

"Thank you. You're quite handy to have about." Alice studied him for a moment. His eyes reminded her of the bandit's when he'd asked for a kiss. Hot and full of longing. But unlike the rogue thief, Lord Arndel was a gentleman, who many would think suitable for courtship. Not that she wished for such a thing, for she knew only too well what he thought of her. A rich spoiled child, to be precise.

"Where is Victoria?"

"She returned home. Something about letting her hunting dogs out for a run. She has a new little pug puppy that's forever taking up her time. The sole reason we came on our walk today, in fact. The little terror was well on the way to destroying Mama's favorite rug."

He laughed, a loud guffaw that was carefree and genuine, and she liked the sound of it. "I can understand your escape."

"Yes." They fell into silence for a moment, both watching the flowing waters go by and listening to the leaves crackle as they floated on the wind.

"I'm to have further meetings with your brother tomorrow. Maybe you will be generous enough to take a walk about the gardens with me?"

"I have a better idea. Since the ball is in your honor, let me show you about Dunsleigh" She placed her bonnet on her head. "We have many ideas for the gathering already, and I'd welcome your opinion on our plans. There is nothing better than a ball at home, I feel. As much as I've grown to love London, I do prefer assemblies here, to anywhere else."

"Here, let me help you with your bonnet," he said, taking the ribbons out of her hand and commencing to tie them about her chin.

Alice sat still as his fingers brushed her neck, and a shiver stole over her. He was so careful with his ministrations, concentrating quite a lot, that a little frown line formed between his eyes.

She shouldn't take so much interest in his visage, but being this close, it was impossible not to do so. Lord Arndel was handsome, there was no other word to describe him. Incandescently, delectably roguish. With the man sporting a dusting of stubble across his jaw and a serious brow that sat above the most perfectly shaped eyes she'd ever seen—who could not phrase him so?

He met her scrutiny with blue eyes that in parts looked almost gray, and the breath in her lungs hitched. Arndel took in her features, and unconsciously she bit her lip. Was he going to kiss her? She'd sworn never to look at him again in a romantic light, so would she allow him to kiss her, should he try? He did apologize and she said she'd forgiven him, so…

"Perfect," he said, finishing the bow and letting his hands drop from her ribbons.

Disappointment stabbed at her that he'd not tried, but she stopped that thought from going any further. She'd not wanted him to kiss her. Although looking at him again, she couldn't help but wonder at the softness of his lips. They were, after all, a lovely shape for a man.

His sigh, tinged with frustration, made her look up. "I should head back to Kester House. My servants will be wondering where I am."

Alice grinned. "Do you always worry about what your

servants are thinking?" She studied him a moment. Lord Arndel hadn't been in the position of lord and master for very long, so she supposed it was possible he saw his servants more as friends instead of employees.

"I suppose I do in a small way. I know I should not."

"I'm glad to hear that you do, for I share your ideals. We may have been born to privilege, or in your case inherit it, while others are not, but it does not make us any better than anyone else." From the first night she'd seen his lordship at the Haversham's ball, she'd sensed he really had no idea how to act or go about in Society and she'd liked that about him.

She had fallen a little for the male wallflower that he'd been.

Lord Arndel was the opposite of what one would term a "lofty lord." He'd gone about the ballroom looking like a lost kitten among a pack of wolves. He'd had no idea of what it was like in Society, to be a part of the *ton*, how to play the game, and master it, better than anyone else.

Most people in the *bon ton* were better actors than those who treaded the boards in the theaters. Looks could be deceiving among their set.

"I shall take that as a compliment, Lady Alice."

The wind chose that moment to pick up further and she shivered. "You should." Alice pulled her slippers on quickly, needing to return home and get out of her damp shift. "Has anyone ever told you that you smell like lemons, Lord Arndel?"

He ran his hands through his hair, looking a little self-conscious that she'd said such a thing out loud.

"My cook has perfected a soap that has a touch of the scent."

Alice made a noncommittal sound. "Seems everyone I meet these days has use of lemons. You may want to ask your cook if she's selling it." She stood and dusted down her gown.

Arndel followed her suit, stepping back a little. "I look forward to our meeting with you tomorrow, my lord."

He bowed. "Until tomorrow, then."

With one last glance at him, Alice strode through the foliage and headed toward home. Coming into the clearing, she stopped and took in the grandeur of Dunsleigh, sitting in the background like a magnificent beacon of comfort.

Bending down, she picked up a stick and whacked the grass that tickled her legs. Lord Arndel was a confusion she didn't require, especially now that she was about to embark on a Season where she was determined to make her mama happy and find a husband.

Not to mention, within only a few days—if the meeting today with the carpenter went well—she would be the proud owner of ten cottages in Ashford that she would have the repair and refurbishment of to oversee. By next winter, all the tenants who agreed to remain with her would be far happier in their more comfortable dwellings.

Arndel paying so much attention to her again wasn't something she'd envisioned, nor could she be excited about, no matter how much she thought him handsome, or how curious she was about his kisses. Apology or not, he'd said he wouldn't wish for a Worthingham sister as a bride, and even after his retraction of such a statement, a small part of her still stung at the thought of his words.

Alice was determined to find a man who was kind, truthful, and shared the same ideals as she did—one could change the world for the better with hard work, kindness, and understanding.

She sighed, swiping at the grass harsher than she ought. Over the last couple of Seasons, whenever she'd brought up such sentiments to the gentlemen who courted her, they'd laughed, or changed the subject entirely to fripperies or the latest Town gossip. Alice had taken each such occurrence as a sign that the man was not for her and hadn't pursued the suitor from that point on. So, to hear that Lord Arndel enjoyed the company of the common man was a conundrum.

Alice walked past the orchards her father had planted many years before, the branches hanging low, heavy with ripening fruit. The air smelled good enough to eat and her stomach rumbled. Upon returning home, she would see if Cook had baked any biscuits for their ride into Ashford. And she would make a mental list of everything she wanted to discuss with Arndel tomorrow regarding the ball.

CHAPTER 4

"*W*hy can I not come to the ball, Papa? I'm almost seven now. Please, I'll be the best daughter in the world, if you let me go."

Callum smiled at his sweet little girl's declaration and lifted her onto his lap. He welcomed the chubby little arms that banded around his neck, knowing all too soon she'd grow up and such cuddles would disappear. He sighed, wishing he could keep her this age forever with the magical hugs she bestowed.

"Now now, I explained that when you're of age you shall attend as many balls and parties as you wish. And," he declared, his tone serious, "I may consider gentlemen to court you, but right now I'm keeping you all to myself and therefore you're not going to attend this one."

Amelia pouted and he thought quickly on how to make it up to her before the tears followed. "If you promise not to get upset, we shall get your pony out tomorrow and resume your lessons. And today I'll have Cook make up those little tarts you like so much, and you may have a tea party in the nursery."

She grinned. "The ones with the cream in the middle, with a sprinkle of chocolate on top?" she asked, her eyes wide with excitement.

"The very ones." He nodded. "And I will check on you before bed." She smiled and hugged him again. How he loved this little being in his arms, more than he'd ever thought he'd love anyone in his life. Other than his wife, God rest her soul.

He tickled her and her infectious giggle made him laugh. He'd been so close to losing her. The memory of the carriage accident was as vivid as his daughter before him. Of them rolling into a slow flowing river, the scream of the horses, the sickening crack as his wife was thrown from the vehicle. That Amelia had only broken her lower leg had been a miracle, but that is where his luck had ended. After resetting her break, a fever had wracked her little body and she'd almost died.

Amelia rubbed her shin and he frowned, reminded anew of her injury. "Is your leg troubling you? I shall have Cook bring in a pot of tea."

Callum went to stand, but Amelia shook her head, her curls bouncing about her shoulders. "I shall be fine, Papa. It is only a little ache."

He set her on her feet, loathing the fact that she had to face such trials when others had no trials at all. His dubious actions against those of his own set paled to the fact that he'd almost lost his entire family in one day. That the bastard moneylender would threaten her life over a debt that wasn't even his left ice running through his veins.

"May I be excused? We're learning about animals today, Papa. Cats and dogs, actually."

Callum pushed her toward the door. "You may go, but walking pace only, if you please. I'll be up to see how your lessons are going in a little while."

He smiled as she came back over to him, her two little

hands clasping his cheeks, and bending her head to kiss his forehead. "Very well, Papa. But don't be too long. I want to show you how well I'm doing learning."

"Now that's what I like to hear. How will you help me with the estate if you're not educated?" He kissed her cheek. "Now off you go, or you'll not have time to spare this afternoon for playing outside."

Seemingly satisfied with his plan, Amelia walked out into the entrance hall, the light patter of her slippered feet heading in the direction of her schoolroom, which overlooked the rear gardens.

Callum's smile faltered once the only light in his life disappeared from view and he was left with a room that reminded him of what his cousin had passed on to him. Brick, mortar, and land, but nothing else. If the duchess did call with her daughters in tow, however would he explain the bare walls and worn furnishings? To see Lady Alice look at him with pity would be the veriest torture.

He stood and walked to the window and wondered how soon the Worthinghams would arrive. A mirror to his side caught his attention and he looked at himself, studying the man he'd become. Would his neighbors and friends ever look behind the mask of the gentleman to see the man beneath, a man with a belittling past and more secrets than simply being the Surrey Bandit?

He turned away from the mirror, his stomach sick with the sight of himself. He would have to hire some help, if the house was to have visitors going forward. Perhaps Fanny at the Angel Inn knew of anyone looking for work. And if all else failed, he would ask his butler, or groom, depending on the day and his requirements, if he was aware of anyone suitable for such employ.

Callum scribbled a short note to Fanny—no time like the present—and rang the bell.

His butler, John, entered. "Could you take this missive and deliver it directly to Fanny at the Angel, John? And be prepared that some staff may arrive over the coming days for an interview for employment. The Duchess of Penworth may be calling, and I cannot expect the skeleton staff I now have to be appropriate for a woman of her rank."

He grimaced at the sight of the peeling wallpaper in his library. "Also, should Kester House receive such callers, please have Cook make up an afternoon tea suitable for such elevated guests."

The silence that reigned after his command was loud. "Do you not wish to carry out my commands, John?" he asked, meeting the man's ashen face.

John shuffled his feet. "We'd not thought to trouble you, my lord, but the oven is smoking and requires the chimney to be cleaned. I'm not sure what Cook can come up with that's suitable for a duchess."

Of course, there are problems. There were many things wrong with the house: the roof leaked in the east wing, mold seemed to be eating some bedroom walls on the third floor, and now the kitchen chimney was in need of maintenance. *Whatever next?*

His servant shuffled his feet.

Callum muttered, rubbing his brow. "Have our gardener attend to the yard. I can't leave them in such a state under the circumstances."

His servant worried his hands together. "Ah, my lord, you don't have a gardener."

Callum walked over to the decanter of brandy and poured himself a generous glass. "I don't? Whatever happened to him?"

"The late Viscount Arndel removed him from his employ after disagreeing over when the roses should be pruned, my lord."

He blinked at the absurd reason for dismissing someone, but his cousin, the unpardonable fool, was wont to do something so garish. "Is the man still located in Ashford?"

"Yes, my lord. Although he's fallen on hard times since his dismissal."

Callum sighed. Damn it. If his cousin wasn't already dead, he would kill him for such disregard of his staff. "If you would see that the man calls on me, I'll ensure his employment recommences."

"That is very kind of you. Thank you, my lord."

He waved the thanks away, not wanting thanks for something that should never have been forced upon a required servant in the first place.

*lice and Victoria dismounted and laughed when Benny, a young lad from the village, and another man from the stable, came about the house to take their horses. The little boy smiled in delight at seeing Alice. She fluffed his hair a little in greeting, having always been fond of the boy. "I'm so glad to see you here, Benny, and you look like you're enjoying your new position. How have you been settling in?"

Benny's eyes lit up with pride. "Oh very well, my lady. They're ever so nice to me, and I'm always kept busy with his lordship's horses. Ma is now working in the kitchen, as well. I bet they're cooking up something right nice for ye while you're here seeing Lord Arndel." He patted her mare. "Did ye want to go see Mama? She'd love to see you, miss."

Alice smiled. "I can't at the moment, but tell your mama that I'll call on her tomorrow, at home, if that's agreeable. I have something I wish to discuss with her that's quite exciting."

"Oh aye, I wills miss." Benny led her horse away, his chattering to the other stable hand clear to hear as they rounded the side of the house. Their mama's carriage pulled up a moment later. Alice and Victoria waited for her to alight and join them.

"Oh my dears, what a rut-strewn driveway that was."

Alice looked about the yard. Its overgrown lawn was riddled with weeds and gardens that were once cultivated and well kept, now resembled nothing but chaos.

"If you would follow me, Your Grace," a deep voice said from the doorway. Alice met the sour face of the butler and smiled at him, noting with pleasure that he blushed.

The moment she entered, their steps faltered. The house was not what Alice had imagined for a viscount. Victoria's gaping mouth also showed her surprise. The walls were bare, unless you could count the staining on the wallpaper that showed where paintings had once hung. There was no carpet on the staircase, and there was a distinct smell of dust in the air. Victoria came up beside her, raising her brows.

"His lordship has no money," Victoria whispered, taking her arm. "Did you suspect?"

Alice shook her head. "No. Never, but it would explain why he's selling land to Josh." They followed the butler into what was once the library. Now it resembled a shell where books went to die. Lord Arndel saw her appraisal of the room and something inside her twisted that he might be ashamed of the lack of niceties.

His lordship bowed. "Your Grace, Lady Alice, Lady Victoria, welcome to Kester House. Please, take a seat. I apologize for not greeting you myself. I did not expect your visit so soon."

Alice ignored the veiled chastisement of their early arrival and did as he bade, watching him as she gained her seat.

"You have a lovely home, Lord Arndel," the duchess said, smiling a little.

Victoria stared at her with widened eyes. Alice shrugged. Their mama obviously didn't wish to be rude, and one always complimented a home when seeing it for the first time—flush with silk wallpaper and tapestries or no. But still, the comment did make the situation between them all a little awkward.

"I'm in the process of remodeling."

Alice didn't believe that for a moment. But if what his lordship said was true, she hoped local builders had been given the opportunity to tender for the work. "It is good to hear the house is getting some well-deserved attention. I'm sure it'll be beautiful when you're finished."

He nodded and sat, tidying up the missives that sat on his desk before he stood back up and rang the bellpull beside the mantel. "Afternoon tea for us, I think. It should be along shortly."

The library sported wallpaper stained with yet more missing portraits of ancestors and landscapes. A small spiral staircase sat at one end of the room, leading up to another floor where the bookshelves were, too, bare of books. "What a shame that the redecorating of your home would've required all the books to have been packed into storage. It must have taken you a great deal of time to put away all of the tomes."

Did his lordship suspect what she was thinking? That there were no books and hadn't been for some time.

"I have no idea how long the process took. The servants packed them away. And as for putting them into storage, I thought it best under the circumstances. I would not want any of them to be damaged with the work going on about the house."

"Of course," she agreed, but where were these builders, if

so much work was being carried out? Certainly there was no sound of hammers or tradesmen talking and shouting about orders. "Are the tradesmen having the day off?" she asked, regretting her nosiness the instant she asked the question. It was a character flaw she'd been trying to tamper.

"I sent word that today was too hot for manual labor. They're working on the roof at present, you see. I could not, in all good conscience, have them laboring under such harsh conditions."

"I didn't see any scaffolding upon our arrival..." Victoria said, looking out the window.

Alice laid a hand on her sister's arm. "We have not ventured around the back, my dear. And in any case, we have more important things to discuss today than renovations." Alice met Lord Arndel's eye and hoped he could read the apology on her face at starting the interrogation in the first place.

"They are yet to commence." He sat back in his chair, his smile strained. "Now, what do I owe for this impromptu visit? Did you not tell Her Grace that I would be back at Dunsleigh this afternoon, Lady Alice?"

"She did not." The duchess considered her daughter a moment, before she said, "But I thought it time that I paid my respects to the new Viscount Arndel of Kester House. It is long overdue and I apologize for it. Since the passing of my husband, I have been remiss in some of my duties, but I hope this visit will put paid to my shortcomings."

"I thank you for your call. You are all very welcome here."

At that moment, tea was brought in by the butler and placed before them on his lordship's desk. He stared at it with a look akin to horror and Alice took pity on him. "Would you like me to pour, my lord?"

He visibly relaxed. "I would be most appreciative."

They sat for some time talking of inconsequential things,

gossip from London, the Surrey Bandit, and their own hold-up by the fiend.

"I was shocked to hear Your Grace and Lady Alice had an unfortunate encounter with the highwayman. I understand he tied up your driver?"

The duchess fluttered her hands. "It was the most single terrifying experience of my life. The fiend manhandled us most inappropriately, and I've never been more frightened for my child as I was that day. I'm fearful every time we travel, that he may strike again."

Alice placed her cup of tea on the desk. A funny fluttering in her stomach commenced when she noted Lord Arndel watching her.

"And you, Lady Alice. Were you scared?"

She muddled over the question. "I had heard stories of the Surrey Bandit never harming anyone, other than perhaps, their hearts after stealing baubles of sentimental value—like the brooch stolen from Mama. So I did not think he would hurt us, so no, I was not scared." *More curious if anything*, not that she could say those words aloud.

"I'm very sorry you were accosted so."

For the life of her, Alice could not tear her attention from his lordship. He was being so very sweet, worrying and apologizing for a situation that was not of his making. It was very comforting having him so attentive, so concerned about her person.

The duchess put down her tea, the rattling cup pulling Alice from her thoughts. "Would you be so kind as to show us about your home, my lord? Tell us in more detail what you have planned with the renovations."

"Of course. I would be delighted." He stood and Victoria and Alice followed suit.

One by one they followed his lordship out into the foyer, Victoria sidling up beside him quickly. Alice frowned, not liking the smile Arndel bestowed on her sibling. Was she jealous of Victoria? She shook the thought aside, an absurd notion.

She followed slowly with her mama, taking the opportunity to look into the rooms they passed as they walked toward the ballroom on the opposite side of the foyer and toward the back of the house.

"I've always thought the ballroom at Kester was its best asset. I think you girls will agree once you see it," the duchess remarked, her attention going from one dilapidated wall or piece of furniture to another.

Alice had to concede that the one thing that did look very well today, was his lordship. His tan buckskin breeches sat on his muscular frame quite snugly, and it was a nice view from where she walked.

Victoria checked on her whereabouts, and Alice wiped the grin from her lips, hoping her sister's questioning frown wouldn't lead to an inquisition later. Alice shook her head, not willing to tell her sister everything that went on in her mind, things that no sister to a duke should be thinking regarding a certain viscount and neighbor.

The passage was wide, the parquetry floor in need of a little wax, but certainly nothing a little hard toil wouldn't bring up to snuff. At the end of the hall was a large window giving them a view of the north-facing vista and turning left they finally made the grand ballroom.

Her mama was right, of course, the room was the best she'd seen so far, and reasonably unscathed from lack of care. It was beyond perfect, with the Jacobean fireplace center in the room and the musical galley above, so no floor space was lost to the hired entertainment. It was in one word, lovely.

The walls were covered in yellow silk damask with a floral motif for decoration. It opened the room and somehow made it look larger than it was.

"I do believe this is Kester House's finest room, do you not agree?" said Arndel, pride coloring his words.

"It's a beautiful room," Victoria said, walking farther into the space and looking about, taking in the whole area.

The ballroom was long and narrow and would be perfect for dancing, while still allowing room for those who liked to socialize but not partake in any activity. Already she could envision a ball here, matrons looking over their charges at either end, while others danced the night away under the chandeliers.

Alice caught his lordship's eye, hoping he would ask her to dance on the night of the ball at their estate. A taller than average woman, she would fit perfectly in his arms. What wonderfully strong-looking shoulders he seemed to have— ideal for waltzing, for holding a woman close.

Victoria mentioned the lighting, and Alice looked up, inspecting the four massive chandeliers that ran the length of the room. She couldn't really see if any needed repair as white sheeting was tied around each one, keeping the dust at bay. At least the late viscount had thought to do that, before he left for London and forgot all about his estate.

His lordship joined Victoria, who was inspecting one of the two fireplaces and he laughed, a deep, gravelly sound she'd like to hear more often. Fluttering took flight in her belly and heat rose on her cheeks when he smiled. That it was aimed at her sister wasn't what she wanted, but then, if Lord Arndel's heart turned in her sibling's direction and not hers, she would be happy for both of them.

She would never begrudge Victoria happiness, not even if the gentleman was someone she herself had feelings for. Not that she had any grand, earth-moving emotions toward his lordship, but there was certainly something between them whenever she looked at him, a nervous buzz in her blood that left her breathless and a little muddled. But of course, it could all be she and his lordship might feel nothing at all.

Alice paced to the windows and raised the sash, welcoming the breeze against her skin, cooling her a little on this hot day. How absurd that seeing her sister gain some attention caused her to feel jealous. For that was exactly what it was that had raised its pointy dagger in her mind. Maybe the heat was addling her mind. It was quite hot in here, after all.

"Does the room meet your standards?"

His knowing grin made her warm yet again, and she leaned against the windowsill, needing all the cool air she could catch. Her mama watched them a moment, before joining Victoria. "The ballroom, although in need of a good clean and polish, is gorgeous. What a gem you have here, Lord Arndel."

He looked about, and pride shone in his eyes. "I think so, too. I plan to look after the home much better than the late viscount. The legacy I leave to my children will be better than what was left me."

"Since you've already started renovating the estate, I'm certain you will meet all the standards you have set against yourself."

He frowned. "How do you mean?"

Alice gestured toward the roof. "By the builders you've already hired to fix Kester House up. That's what I meant."

His lordship blushed, his cheeks tinged with embarrassment. "Of course," he blustered. "You must think me a gentleman without wits. Maybe I should get some fresh air to stop my muddling mind."

"You may share my window, my lord." It was very forward of Alice, but right now she couldn't think of anything nicer than to share a window with him.

He stalked toward her, his absentmindedness soon

forgotten as he headed in her direction. Never had Alice reacted to a man in this way. Even now, her heart beat too fast in her chest and the butterflies fluttered about in her belly.

He came up beside Alice and leaned against the window surround. Arndel caught her eye, and the look he bestowed upon her left her hot and flustered. Was she imagining his flirting with her sister? The darkening of his blue orbs that watched her with such intensity left her in no doubt he was as attracted to her as she was to him.

How very delicious.

"I do hope that in time I shall have the estate back to its rightful beauty. I know there are certain elements of it now that are shockingly ill kept, but I'm looking to remedy that soon."

Without thought, Alice touched his lordship's arm, the muscular strength beneath her gloves making her breath hitch. *My, oh my, he feels lovely.* "Once the roof is repaired you'll be able to start on the inside of the property, and no doubt you'll find that everything will fall into place. It may not happen overnight, but it will happen. We have faith in you, Lord Arndel that you will set this place to rights."

He chuckled. "I thank you, my lady."

"My dears, we have kept his lordship long enough. It is time to take our leave." The duchess gestured for Victoria to follow and reluctantly Alice turned to Lord Arndel. "Thank you for showing us your home today. I know it was an impromptu visit, so I hope you're not too cross with us."

"Never." He smiled. "Now, if you follow me, I'll see you out."

They walked in silence toward the foyer, and again, Alice couldn't help but see his lordship's fine behind. It was probably a blessing that the Season was about to commence. If her reactions toward Arndel were any indication, she was long past due finding a partner in life.

Her sister chuckled and Alice realized she'd noticed her fixation on the gentleman's nether regions. "Behave Alice, or Mother will notice and we'll both be scolded."

Alice shushed her, unable to stop the grin from forming on her lips. "Be quiet or they'll both hear you."

Her sibling merely grinned and, thankfully, the front door came into view. Freedom beckoned away from his lordship's perfect derriere and not a moment too soon. One day her ogling of him would be caught by the man himself, and then she would have reason to blush.

The next day, Alice submersed herself in doing her rounds of Ashford's poor. A job she would miss, if she truly meant the words she'd spoken to her mama, and marry by the coming Season's end. But then, wherever her husband's estate was located would surely have people in need, so she wouldn't have to give up her charitable pursuits.

She walked down an alley between terraced houses, distraught by their weathered appearance. The decayed wooden walls, plaster and windows broken, and rushes missing from their roofs allowed the elements to penetrate the cottages, leaving those huddled within cold and miserable.

Even from the outside, Alice could see that the walls were moldy and the whole area was not fit to live in, nevertheless to raise a family. Rubbish piled up in some parts of the road, in some areas as high as the ground floor windows. The dirt-lined streets and footpaths would be a sodden muddy track come winter and none of it was acceptable.

Alice waved to Benny, the boy who now worked at Lord

Arndel's estate. Every week since she'd taken over this role from her mama, the little boy had waited on the street to meet her before his employ. He was the sweetest little man, and she was beyond thrilled he'd found a job that helped contribute funds to his mother's household.

Tony, her groom, stood only a few feet away as she knocked on Mrs. Davy's door. And within the customary two minutes it opened and the village's former and converted lady-bird—as her mother would say—welcomed her inside.

On it went for the next few hours. Alice handed out food parcels, tended as best she could to their concerns and worries, and helped out with menial tasks that some of the tenants could no longer handle. Her attendance at their homes was only of short duration, but it was better than nothing at all, and as much as sometimes the visits were sad and upsetting, Alice always returned home feeling as if she'd accomplished something of import. Not just another day sitting at home sewing or learning how to paint. How boring.

Then finally, the family she always left for last, as it gave her the opportunity to stay and chat. After the unexpected death of Bess's husband the year before, the family had fallen on hard times, but with Alice's support, the family of three had survived and their future was looking positive once again.

"Lady Alice, we're so glad you've come. I thought ye'd never get here, as ye took longer than ye did last week."

Alice took Benny's hand, letting him lead her inside. "I'm sorry I'm late. Today was busier than normal. And I have not forgot, for I have a gift for you. It's not every day a young man has his birthday." She smiled and watched as Benny's eyes alighted with excitement.

"I'm nine tomorrow, my lady. And soon I'll be old enough to start courting ye. Will ye wait for me?"

Alice ruffled his hair, never had she known anyone as sweet and honest as this little person. "By the time you're old enough to marry, dear sir, I'll be old and gray. Much too old for you. I'm sure you can do much better than me," she said, smiling at Bess and taking a seat at the kitchen table.

Alice passed the food hamper to Rose, Bess's eldest daughter. The young woman smiled in delight at seeing the small cake Alice had brought for the family. "I had Cook bake a cake for Benny's birthday. I hope you don't mind."

"Oh, Lady Alice, you're so kind. I don't know what we'd do without you," Bess said, her eyes filling with tears. Alice clasped her hand, squeezing it a little.

"No more Lady Alice when we're alone. Just Alice will be fine."

Bess nodded, blushing a little at her kindness. Benny squealed with joy at the sight of the vanilla cake with chocolate icing.

"As I won't see you tomorrow, Benny, I hope you have a very happy birthday and enjoy your day immensely."

"Oh, I will, miss. For guess what? I get to help saddle up Lord Arndel's horse and possibly take it out for a ride on the morrow. He never lets anyone ride the stallion, and he's a beauty, miss. I would think he would rival any of the duke's cattle to be sure."

Alice started, reminded anew of the stallion everyone, including her sister, was gushing about. "I have not seen this horse. You do not mean the brown gelding he rides all the time?"

Benny shook his head, frowning. "No, he has the stallion stabled up most of the time. You should see the beast. At least sixteen and a half hands, to be sure. In the dark he's monstrous looking and can have a temper."

Alice thanked Bess, as she placed a steaming cup of tea and some biscuits before her.

"Well, you just be careful, my boy," said Bess. "Don't do anything you're not comfortable with. I'll not have your safety placed in jeopardy, no matter what financial cost to the family."

"And I agree," Alice said. "If you feel uncomfortable about anything you're asked to do, please let me know and I'll see that it doesn't happen again."

"You're too kind to us." Bess smiled. "Truly an angel."

Alice waved away the compliment. She was no angel, and she doubted that, should Benny have a problem while working for Lord Arndel, the viscount would be pleased if she stuck her nose into his affairs and right the wrong handed to the boy.

His lordship would probably send her packing, right smart.

"Lord Arndel wouldn't place me in danger, miss. I can assure you of that. I love working there. Even Rose has started working there as an undermaid."

"Wonderful." Alice took a sip of tea, so thankful that the family were happy and comfortable, well, as comfortable as they could be living in a house that was less than hospitable.

"His lordship said, with me working in the kitchen and Benny full time in the stable, and Rose now as a maid, that we could move to the small cottage east of the estate. It's a quick walk to the main house and would make the hour-long journey we must do each day from here a lot easier on us all. And I must say, I'll not be sad to leave this house, not only because of the memories that are always so fresh in me mind, but also because of the condition of the building. I cannot believe all this damp is good for me children's health."

"So you're leaving?" Alice looked about the small room, seeing the tattered linen on the bedding that sat behind a makeshift screen. The fireplace with bricks missing from its sides, and the air held the distinct smell of smoke, as if it was not drawing correctly. As for the tables and chairs, they were nothing but discarded crates from the shops. Alice couldn't agree more that the cottage was exactly what the family required and above all, deserved.

"You're not upset by our choice?" Bess asked, concern tinging her voice.

"Only in that we'll see less of each other, but I'm beyond happy to hear you'll be settled so near to work, and I know the house you're going to is sound and quite lovely inside. You'll be happy there, I'm sure."

Bess sighed her relief. "You're Lord Arndel's neighbor. I'm sure we'll see you as much as you can spare us the time. And of course, you're always welcome."

Alice took Bess's hand. "It sort of makes my news for you moot now, for I had some exciting information that I wished to share with you all."

"What was that, miss?" Benny asked, pulling up a stool to the table and looking at her expectantly.

"Well, I'm going to purchase these ten cottages along this road and fix them up for my tenants. The rent won't change. These houses are, by far, the most neglected in the town and I'd like to change that."

"Oh, my lady," Bess said, her eyes filling with tears. Alice watched as she grappled for her handkerchief and dabbled at her eyes. "I stand by my words earlier. You are a true blessing for this town and county." Bess sniffed. "I can't say I'm not a little jealous that another family will move in here and be living in such fine comfort, for I'm sure whatever ye do to the cottages will be the very best for those who live here."

"I hope so." And Alice truly did hope that was the case. Having been born without a care in the world, never being hungry or cold, she couldn't allow another person to suffer such a fate, if she had the means to change it. Of course, Ashford was only a small town, and there were many homes across the country that suffered the same fate, but one must start somewhere. And it was best to do something, even if small, than nothing at all.

Bess's daughter Rose started chopping up vegetables for the evening meal. "And I've stayed much later than I ought, so I'll take my leave. But please, let me know when you're making the move and I'll have the cart sent round to help."

"Oh, we couldn't impose. That's too much, Lady Alice."

"No it's not," Alice said, linking arms with Bess and walking to the door. "I will always look out for you. And remember, I'm Alice to you."

Bess laughed, shaking her head. "Well, in that case, we would be well pleased to borrow the cart two days from now, if it's no bother."

"It's no bother at all. And I'll call once you're settled at Lord Arndel's estate."

Alice bade good-bye and walked toward Tony who leaned against one of the abandoned terrace house's windows. The air had chilled with the evening sky settling over the town.

"Are you ready to return to Dunsleigh, my lady?"

Alice nodded. "Yes, thank you, Tony." Climbing up into the carriage, she looked down the street and vowed there would be no more cold winters for her tenants. Once the title settled into her name, the suffering under the old owner, a man who preferred Town life and the whorehouses that were stationed there, would be nothing but a bad memory.

What was the point of being born a Worthingham if one couldn't do something with it? She could hardly wait to start.

CHAPTER 5

"*A*bsolutely not!"

Alice sat forward in her chair and leveled the scariest frown she could form toward her brother. It was probably not the best glower he'd ever seen, but this was one argument she would win against the duke. "What I do with my inheritance is up to me, Josh. I have already spoken to Mama and she agrees. In fact, she stated to pay the amount Mr. Otis wants and be done with it. He won't compromise on price, and I won't compromise on my plans."

"He's robbing you blind! Or," he continued, wagging his finger, "perhaps he's the Surrey Bandit everyone wants to serve justice upon."

Alice fought the urge to roll her eyes but lost the battle. "Oh for heaven's sake, it's in the town you already own half the buildings in. What does it matter what I purchase the Pitt Street cottages for? Mr. Otis doesn't care about his tenants, never has, and if you took the time to look at the condition of the buildings, you would see that. And I refuse to see the unfortunate people suffer through any more winters. Now is the time for the repairs to be carried out, and that's exactly what I shall do. But I would like your approval, nonetheless. The price is what he wants, and that is what I'll pay. I have the men hired already for restoration, just sign off on the contract—that you agree to release my inheritance to purchase the buildings." Alice sat back, folding her arms across her chest.

"When Mama allowed you to take over her role visiting the poor it was only a matter of time before it gave you even more ideas to…well, have more ideas."

"You're so amusing, Josh. Maybe you should join the theater."

He glared, and a muscle ticked in his cheek. "You're about to embark on a Season, where I might add, you've promised Mama you'll look for a husband—seriously—this year. If I allow you to buy the properties for that absurd amount, how will you find the time to do all this work, to oversee what needs to be done and focus on your upcoming Season?"

"Don't be an ass, Josh. I never knew you didn't have a heart beating in that tiny man chest, for if you were a man at all, you would never have said such a thing."

"How dare you speak to me in that way!"

"Very easily. I'm older than you, if you remember, and you may be the duke, but you do not control my life. You cannot take away what Papa left me, or the house I own in northern England, so you may bluster all you like about what I'm going to pay for those cottages, but it'll change nothing. For I will do it and you will sign that piece of paper allowing me to purchase it at the agreed amount."

He sighed, running a hand through his hair, a trait her brother only ever did when he was livid. "Oh really?" he said, his brow raised. "Why would I?"

"Because I'm your sister and you love me."

Josh threw up his hands, leaning back in his chair. "I give

up when it comes to you. There is no sense or thought of respectability when Alice Worthingham is involved."

"Oh please, do stop with the dramatics. There is nothing wrong with me helping the poor, nor would anyone in Society see anything untoward. They would more likely commend me for it." She gave him her sweetest smile, which only brought forth a scowl from him. "So you will chaperone me into London Friday so I can sign the papers and proceed with the handover of the titles?"

"I'll agree to the new amount, but Mother can attend you. I hadn't planned on traveling to Town until the Season commences."

"Mama refuses to go, unless you're with us, and she said if you go, then she need not attend on this occasion. She's scared the Surrey Bandit will strike again. We'll only be gone a night, and then you can return to Dunsleigh and bury yourself in all this estate work you love so much."

"You do try my patience." Her brother stood and poured himself a glass of brandy. "Be ready at the crack of dawn. I may travel up and back in the one day."

"I have no problem with that, but I'll have my maid pack a small valise in case you change your mind."

He shrugged. "Do whatever you wish." He sat back down, studying her a moment. "Ever since you were little I remember you always helping people and animals. Even the little ant that was in the path of your slippered foot you felt the need to aid. Why?"

"Because I can. We're so well-to-do, born into privileges some people can only dream about. How can I not try and help when I can? How can I go through my life and trample all those beneath me, through no fault of their own? Just as I didn't ask to be born the daughter of a duke, neither was an ant born only to be squished under my foot. These people are truly in need, and I care for each and every one of them. They're good people, Josh. You should not judge so harshly."

"You cannot save everyone, Sister."

"I know." Alice looked out the window to a garden more manicured than her fingernails. "We are so blessed. We have everything we could ever wish. We need wood, our gardener cuts it for us. We ring a bell and magically a servant arrives to do our bidding. And yet, not five miles away, people huddle together under lice-infested blankets to keep warm in winter. They have to scavenge the surrounding lands for wood in the dead of winter, only to come home and cook nothing but watered down food not worth eating in the first place."

Alice took a steadying breath. What she was about to do was right. It may not be what Josh wanted her to pay for her plans, but what was that when people were in need? "I want to help these people. I'm going to rebuild those cottages and refurbish them. And I'm going to ensure that during the summer months, wood is collected from our lands and deposited in a building I'll have built at the end of the lane for them all to use. And then, should I have any money left, I'm going to get the road cobbled."

"You have thought of everything, it would seem. And pray tell, what if your singular attempt at being a vigilante makes you poor? Unmarried and poor. What then? You'll only have your dowry upon marriage, and do you really want to be beholden to your husband for the rest of your life? Josh raised a pointed brow. "I cannot see such a situation being to your liking."

Alice stood, walked to the side of the desk, and, bending over, she kissed Josh on the cheek. "I will never be beholden to my husband, silly. For I have a brother who's the Duke of Penworth. A brother I saved from a tree many years ago. Mama still doesn't know about that. If I ever need more money, I know who will save me. Just like I saved him."

Josh looked up and a smile teased the edge of his lips. "Does Mama know who got me stuck up that tree in the first place?"

Alice laughed and walked toward the door. "Well, you shouldn't have followed." She paused. "Will you approve the amount? No matter our differing opinion on the matter, I would so love to have your support on this."

He sighed. "I suppose a trip to London would give me a chance to call in at my club," he mused. "So I will set aside my thoughts on the price and support your plan. To enable the build to begin and end in a more prompt manner, I'll write to our solicitors today and ensure all will be ready for transfer on Friday. I won't hear any excuses as to why you have to cry off attending the Season due to a leaking roof or warped wood, though."

Alice smiled, relief pouring through her like a balm. "Thank you, Brother. I'll not forget your kindness and because of your charitable behavior, I shall introduce you to all my friends this year. Perhaps if we both have a successful Season, we could have a double wedding."

"I recommend you leave before I change my mind, minx."

She laughed, doing as he bid, but not before she heard a resounding chuckle from the duke.

---

*A*lice let Juno have a free rein and urged her mount into a gallop. She laughed as the mare, on her first run out since birthing her foal last year, took off at a blistering speed. Alice looked behind her. Victoria coming up fast on Pan, Josh a close second on the horse's hooves. Her sister's determined visage to win the impromptu race easy to read. Alice bent low over Juno's neck, but it was no use, Victoria's mount could not be outrun.

The wind whipped at her hat, the speed which they traveled made her eyes water and her vision blur. Alice looked up and, all too soon, the forest that surrounded Lord Arndel's home grew ever taller in their view, and she eased her horse into a canter, and then a trot.

"Juno seems much pleased being out and about again," Victoria said, waiting for her and Josh to catch up.

Alice patted the mare's neck, pulled her into a walk, and allowed the horse to regain its breath. "She does, doesn't she?" Alice reached up and pulled a leaf from a passing tree. "This is the first time I've ridden her without her foal. She seems to be handling it well."

"She loves and trusts you, and why wouldn't she want to be out with her favorite human."

Alice smiled, knowing the feeling was mutual. All the sisters had been given horses on their coming-out and all were named after mythological gods. It was a little joke between them, and one their brother, who didn't wish to play along, never understood.

"Did your business in London on Friday go all to plan? Mama said she thought so."

"It went very well, and although we ended up staying the night in London, I took the opportunity to have Josh attend a meeting with an architect who'll draw up some new plans for the houses to make them more efficient for the families. The last design wasn't quite right. He's a brilliant man, and young, but full of ideas."

Victoria threw her a curious look. "Such praise. Somehow, I think you purchasing and renovating those houses will be all that Brother can handle this year."

"I agree," Josh mumbled, sardonically.

Alice frowned. "What do you mean?" Her siblings

chuckled and finally Alice understood. "Oh, don't be absurd. I'm not looking at the architect in that way, no matter how handsome or smart he is."

"I'm glad to hear it." Josh adjusted his seat. "I'm going to go for another run. I shall meet you at Kester House where we shall ask about this famous beast of a horse Victoria refuses to let go."

"You make it sound like I'm obsessed, which I am not."

Alice smiled, watching as Josh cantered off. They walked along in silence for a moment before she said, "I want your opinion on something that I have been wondering about."

"What?" Victoria ducked as they went under a low hanging branch.

"I was curious as to what you thought of Lord Arndel? I noticed last week you seemed quite happy when speaking to him, and he in turn, you."

Her sister grinned. "He's handsome to be sure, but other than that, not much is known of him." Victoria shrugged. "It's hard to form an opinion of a man who hides himself away from local Society as much as his lordship does."

Alice nodded. It was strange that Lord Arndel, having come into the title of viscount, would keep himself at arm's length from Society. Since the few balls she'd seen him at in London the beginning of last Season, by the end of the Season, he'd all but disappeared. She'd always put it down to his lordship enjoying himself elsewhere in the city, much like his cousin had, prior to his untimely death, but perhaps she'd been wrong. If he was looking to marry, to start a family, keeping oneself out of the sphere in which you should circulate to find a suitable partner wasn't the most logical thing to do.

"He is a little secretive, don't you think?"

Victoria shrugged. "He was nice enough in Town last year, until your altercation with him, and then we didn't see him at all. But I gather he's trying to make amends of that faux pas, and is now sorry for his hurtful words."

Alice conceded the point, for Arndel had apologized for his insult last season, even though she had yet to fully forgive him. "I did hear Josh mention to his man of business that Lord Arndel never had anything to do with his family prior to taking up the title of viscount. Which is odd, don't you agree? One would think he'd be bosom friends with them all, considering he was next in line."

"I'm not acquainted enough with the family to know how any of them interact with each other. They may merely be a family who are not close, unlike our own." Alice smiled.

"I suppose that could be it. And in any case, he seems determined to be more a part of the community, which is welcome. There are many suitable women among our set who'd settle well as his wife." Victoria threw her an assessing look. "Don't you agree, Sister?"

The question rattled Alice more than it ought, and she pursed her lips in thought. That Arndel might marry someone whom she knew well had never entered her mind. Of course, she'd thought about him becoming married, but the person had always been faceless, a woman from Town that she didn't know. The idea that one of her friends might become his wife, walk up to him at any moment and ask for a kiss, go to bed with him each night... She swallowed. How disturbing.

Alice didn't like the vision it created. She cleared her throat before answering. "Of course, yes."

Victoria pulled Pan to a stop and Alice, too, paused at the edge of the forest and looked across the less than well-kept lawns of Kester House. "I have noticed that he looks at you a great deal, Alice."

Alice's mouth popped open and she closed it with a snap, hating the fact her stomach fluttered at the mention of him doing so. "If he does, it's only to find fault, I'm sure." She laughed, wondering if the heat on her cheeks was actually visible. "You should not say such foolishness, in any case. It'll only bring embarrassment to both me and his lordship."

"It's no foolery, I assure you. I've seen him sneak glances at you when he thinks no one is watching. Every time he does, he looks like he's been deprived of something, or is longing for the very object of his desire." Victoria smirked. "In fact, his actions remind me of how you used to act around him last year before *he* acted like an ass."

"Don't swear." She looked toward Kester House, studying a home that seemed more majestic than she'd ever thought before. "And please don't remind me of what a silly fool I was last Season. I practically groveled at his feet before I heard exactly what he thought of me."

"He didn't mean that and he's said sorry. You should forgive him." Victoria paused. "And if you keep frowning like that you'll get wrinkles."

Alice scoffed. "And you're wrong about Lord Arndel. While I do believe he may be truly sorry, I don't think it's me he's interested in, no matter what looks you say he's turning my way."

"Oh, he's looking. Why, the other day, when you were inspecting his ballroom, I'm amazed you didn't feel the burn of his attention. He likes you, more than you think, and I do believe that if you were to give him the idea that his feelings may be returned, he would act on those emotions."

Act on his emotions? What did that mean? And if it meant what Alice hoped it did, it certainly explained why a nervous fluttering took flight through her body whenever he was around. Did she like him more than a friendly neighbor? Did she still admire him, as she had at the beginning of last Season? Did she want to?

Victoria chuckled. "Come, we cannot dawdle here in the trees all day; Josh is expecting us."

Alice allowed Victoria to canter ahead as she followed behind. After her sister's words, she had the absurd desire to grin like a debutante partaking in her first dance.

Taking a deep breath, she fought to pull herself together and not arrive at his lordship's home all blotchy from embarrassment and with a nervous stutter to her words. She was a daughter of a duke, more than capable of conversing with a viscount.

She beamed. How very delicious if Arndel did like her more than a friend. It would certainly make living at Dunsleigh more interesting, and as for the coming Season, something to look forward to, even though he'd said he wasn't attending. Perhaps Victoria was right and forgiveness was best, and what happened after that could be very agreeable, too.

CHAPTER 6

*A*lice jumped down from her horse and handed the reins to a waiting stableman. Victoria did the same, and within a moment they spied Josh cantering toward them from the west of the property. He stopped, showering them in gravel.

"Really, Josh, was your dramatic entrance necessary?" Her brother merely chuckled and alighted, coming to stand beside them. "Shall we see if Lord Arndel is home? We have a stallion to view, I believe."

"Let's be off." Victoria rubbed her hands together in glee and started toward the home.

Alice spied Benny coming from around the side of the house, and she waved to the small boy. He smiled and came running over.

"Lady Alice, you're back. Mama wanted me to say thank you the next time I saw ye. We're moved in right nice at the cottage and I even have me own room."

"That's wonderful, Benny. I'm so glad you're all settled. Tell your mama I'll come and visit very soon."

"Aye, I will, my lady." He started toward the stables, but

paused, turning about to look at her. "Ye look very pretty today, miss."

Alice laughed, thinking that Benny would be a favorite among the ladies when he became of age. "Why thank you. That's very kind."

He nodded, seemingly pleased with himself. "Well, it's true. Ye are."

"We're here to see the famous stallion you told me about."

"Oh aye, miss, he is the finest horseflesh that you ever beheld. There would be few, I'd imagine, who wouldn't think him the best of beasts."

Alice was more intrigued every second. "I should imagine if you think so, then he surely is."

Benny's face turned to brooding. "Oh, he is, my lady. Would ye care to come and take a look where I work and where the horse is kept? I keep all the stalls clean for the horses, not a steamer to be seen. You'll be right proud of me, ye will, miss."

Alice ruffled his hair. "I'm already proud of you, have been since the day you were born. And I'm certain you'll keep up the splendid work for his lordship, and one day it will pay off for you. I can promise you that."

"Then you'll come. Come and see the stables, miss."

Alice inclined her head. "We will come as soon as we've paid our regards to Lord Arndel."

"Thanks, my lady."

Alice followed her siblings toward the door, smiling. The footman stood waiting, ushering them inside and into the foyer.

Alice idly chatted to Victoria while they waited for his lordship. Josh paced before the front windows, and after some time with no sign of his lordship, Alice found a nearby chair and sat.

She turned at the sound of pounding hooves and looked

out the window. Her mouth fell open at the sight of Lord Arndel cantering past the front of the house, the black stallion on which he sat, frothing at the mouth, heaving with the effort of a long run.

"That must be the horse Benny had been talking about." Victoria sighed. "Well, the little boy wasn't overexaggerating. The thoroughbred is magnificent."

Alice had thought Benny may have been overzealous in his praise, but that wasn't the case, for the horse was truly magnificent, much like the man who sat atop it.

She started at the thought and shook herself. She did not want to turn into a simpering fool over this man who'd just ridden past her like Adonis.

Moments later, footsteps sounded deep in the house and Alice settled her riding skirts more evenly about her legs. Wanting to look busy, she made a ploy of taking off her gloves and fiddling with her hat. The last thing she needed was for Arndel to think they'd been anxiously waiting for him.

She need not have bothered. Lord Arndel, so lost in thought, strode straight past them, his direction toward the library clear and Josh cleared his throat to gain Arndel's attention.

"Lord Arndel?" her brother said, amusement written across his features at Lord Arndel's lack of awareness of those who graced his home.

"Your Grace?" He skidded to a halt and turned startled eyes toward them.

"I hope you don't mind, but Lady Victoria wished to view your fine horseflesh, namely, the horse that you just rode past on, and I said I would accompany her."

He looked about the foyer, clearly shocked. "Ah—of course you're welcome here. Anytime."

"Maybe we should've called at another time," the duke said, taking in Lord Arndel's less than immaculate attire.

He stood with his hands on his hips. How tall he seemed when standing so. Not only that, but he looked a little disheveled after his ride, and it gave him an air of danger that, Alice had to concede, she liked.

"Did you not receive our note of our intended visit? We can come back at another time, if it's more suitable." Alice hoped he wouldn't send them away. She wished to meet with him, talk with him again, as they had done the other day when here with her mother.

"No." He relaxed his stance and waved them toward the front door. "Come, I'll take you to the stables directly and you may see my horses."

"I understand you used to breed them?" her brother stated. Alice started at the information, having not been aware Lord Arndel had done so. What else did she not know of this man?

"I did, yes, and it's something that I wish to continue, once I have the estate back to its former glory."

Victoria walked ahead with Josh, and his lordship ended up beside Alice. The smile that had formed on her lips would not dissipate, no matter how much Alice tried to refrain from showing what being beside this man did to her resolve.

"We should organize a race," said Victoria. "Just a lark between our acquaintances. Dunsleigh has a long, level field that would be perfect for such an event."

Alice assessed Lord Arndel and was pleased to see he seemed interested in such an idea. "The few horses I have left in the stable would welcome a run. If you can arrange such a day, Your Grace, then I would be pleased to have my cattle take part."

"Were your horses bred for racing?" They continued, heading toward the side of the house. She breathed deep, his lordship's scent smelled divine, like fresh country air mixed with lemons. It had also not passed her notice that his cravat was loosely tied, showing off a lovely tanned neck that left her breathing erratic.

"I saw your horse on your return. It's a beautiful animal." Alice stole a glance at him. He didn't meet her eye, but only fiddled with his gloves. Was he as nervous as she was being near to him again?

"I don't ride him often, not nearly enough as he'd like." He took the little notebook she held tight in her hands and opened it. "What is this you carry?"

Alice snatched it back, hardly believing he'd done such a thing. "You do know that you should wait for a lady to hand you any notes she may be holding. For all you know, I could've been holding a lover's tale or a private missive to someone."

"A lover's letter..." He grinned and she was pulled under his spell. "For me?" He took the notebook back, holding it out of her reach. "Then please, let me read, for I'm more than interested," he drawled in a tone that was deep and full of meaning but only for her to hear. He skimmed it quickly and no matter how she tried to clasp his arm, she couldn't take it back.

He sighed dramatically. "I cannot tell you how disappointed I am that it's blank. I thought you'd written a tome about how you really feel about me."

"You wouldn't like to know. Trust me," she whispered, taking back the book and leveling him with a glare.

He barked out a laugh. The sound, carefree and true, not fake and practiced like she'd heard in Town by so many gentlemen.

"Maybe I would."

Heat bloomed on her cheeks, and she checked to make

sure her siblings were unaware of their antics behind them. Thankfully, they were.

"Trust me, you would not," she quipped, her tone one of calm assurance that she was far from feeling.

"So what have you brought your notebook for, if I may ask?"

"I was hoping that I could write down the recipe for the dry cake that your cook used to make for the late viscount's entertainments."

He leaned toward her, a sardonic lift to his lips. She should push him away, let him know in no uncertain terms that he was being forward. To have him this close, his cheek but a slight lean away did nothing to help her situation to remain indifferent. From here she could see his dark, long eyelashes that swept over his cheeks like a fan. In all truth, his lordship had lovely features and skin. Alice doubted there was much to find fault with.

He bit his bottom lip and looked up, catching her fixation of him.

"I think I can arrange for you to meet with my cook." He studied her a moment, not trying to move back and give them space, but if anything, tempting her to close the gap between them and see where it would lead. Alice swallowed, having never been in such an intimate situation with a man before but liking it nonetheless. Liked it a lot.

At some point, they had stopped walking. A restless longing burned to know what his lips would feel like. Were they as soft as she imagined them to be, did he kiss well, did he want to kiss her? "Thank you, my lord. That would be most useful." Her words came out as a whisper and his attention swept to her lips.

"Anything to please you, Lady Alice."

Her brother hurried them along and Alice jumped back, her heart hammering in her chest.

Alice strode forward. What had she been thinking only a moment ago? And in front of her brother no less! She looked back at Lord Arndel and read the simmering desire in his eyes.

He slowly caught up to her, his stride slow and predatory. *Oh my...*

"I understand you have two sisters that are married, do you not? I hope they've settled well into their new positions."

"Yes, very well, thank you," she said. "Elizabeth, or Beth as we call her, married Lord Muir, an earl from Scotland. They live in the Highlands, in a castle, no less. It's quite beautiful there and not far from Avonmore, our family's Scottish estate. Although that was left to Isolde after our father passed."

"You like Scotland, then, and have spent some time there." He studied her and she sighed. "Like" wasn't a strong enough word for how much she adored England's northern neighbor.

"I do. Very much so. It is truly a magnificent place and one I wish to explore more. So much history there, and not always the best, considering England and Scotland's past, but times have changed since then, thankfully."

"I've not been there myself, but I would like to go. Perhaps, when I'm married, my bride will like to travel there, instead of the continent." His stare turned primal and Alice couldn't seem to tear her eyes from him. Was he hinting to her as to what he wished? To bring up marriage before an unmarried woman wasn't what any well-bred man ought to do, but his lordship didn't seem to care about that.

She cleared her throat. "My other sister, Lady Isolde, the second eldest in the family, is recently married to the Duke of Moore."

"Another duke. And here I am, a mere viscount."

Alice laughed, hearing the humor in his statement. "A

viscount is not *mere* at any time, and you, Lord Arndel, are certainly not mediocre, if that was your meaning." Alice stopped speaking as the words left her mouth. *Now I'm flirting? Whatever next?* She cast a horrified look at his lordship, relieved to see nothing but genuine affection is his blue orbs. Even so, Alice really ought to learn how to control her wayward tongue.

"I like that you think so." His scrutiny was disconcerting to say the least, but look away from it she could not.

"Tell me what you do with your time. I have an inkling that you like to keep busy." He smiled and her feet felt like they were on unstable ground.

If he thought her a spoiled child who only embroidered cushions and sang in the gardens all day, he was quite mistaken. "I keep myself quite busy. There are many things to keep me occupied most days."

"Such as?" he smiled, helping her step over a small puddle.

"Well, I recently purchased the cottages on Pitt Street in Ashford. I'm about to start renovations on them."

He gaped at her. "You are? And your brother allowed such a thing?"

Alice rolled her eyes. "Of course. Although we may have disagreed about the price, at first, but I made him see the sensible side of my agenda. It truly is a great idea and I can hardly wait to start."

"You're going to oversee the build?" He sounded shocked.

"Of course. How else will I ensure that the best outcome is reached? The cottages in Ashford will be the talk of the county and make all those who live in the community green with envy." By the time she finished the build, everyone will wish to live there. She met Arndel's stare. Clearly, he was a little taken aback.

"I can see you're stunned."

He smiled a little in awe. "I am. I've never heard of a

woman doing such a thing, and certainly not a daughter of a duke."

She shrugged. "We must all do what we can. I'm able to help, I wish to, and so I will. It is as easy as that."

He didn't smile, merely stared at her a moment. "What a remarkable woman you are to do such a thing for those less fortunate than yourself."

Never in her life had Alice received such a heartfelt compliment and that it had come from Lord Arndel only made her more discombobulated. "Thank you," she said, unsure of what else to say.

They came up to the stables, and a stableman, an older gentleman with graying hair and glasses, greeted them.

"Bill, can you please bring out Bandit. Lady Victoria wishes to view him."

His head stableman pulled off his hat, bowing a little. "Of course, my lord."

Within a few minutes, the beauty they had seen just after their arrival walked out of a stable block that was away from the other horses. Victoria *oohed* over the animal, and without hesitation walked up to it, first letting the horse smell her hand before patting his nose.

"Oh, he's beautiful. How lucky you are to have such an animal. I must admit that I'm utterly jealous of you, Lord Arndel."

The duke, too, went up to the horse and patted its neck. "Did you breed him yourself?"

His lordship remained with her, which pleased her more than she liked to admit. "No. Although I will breed from him if I can. Bandit was left here on the estate after the late viscount's passing. I suppose even Robert knew when to draw the line at selling such a fine specimen of a horse."

"I'm glad of it," her brother said, running a hand over the mount's back.

Victoria came back and joined them. "I assume because he's a stallion that is why you keep him in a separate stable from the other horses."

"I do yes, he can be…let's say, a little temperamental at times."

Benny, seeing them inspecting Bandit, ran over and bowed. Alice chuckled, loving the fact the little boy was such a character. "Lady Alice, did ye want me to fetch Juno for you? And Lady Victoria," Benny said, before spying the duke. "Oh, and His Grace? No one sent word that you were here. I'm sorry I don't have ye horses ready for you yet."

Alice waved his concern aside. "Never mind that. Perhaps while the others are looking at Bandit, you can show me where you work."

"Really, my lady? I would love to, if his lordship doesn't mind."

Alice looked at Lord Arndel and was relieved to see only mirth directed at the young stable hand's request. "You may show Lady Alice where you work, Benny."

They headed to where the other stable block was situated. It was full to brim with horses; two other stable lads walked from one stable to the other, busy with their tasks.

Benny pointed out each horse, their age, and height as they made their way through the building. The stalls were clean and well kept, and Benny explained how certain stalls were kept for his lordship's horses and those of guests.

"Since I'm here, I may as well help you saddle up Juno, shall I?"

"Oh no, my lady. Ye can't do that. I won't take long, if ye can wait a wee while."

"It's perfectly fine, Benny. My sister, I should think, will be with Bandit for a little time yet." She walked farther into the stable block, taking in the horses that leaned over their gates and nickered to a new face.

Unlike the lawns and gardens that surrounded the property, the stables were completely the opposite in appearance: clean stalls, fresh-smelling hay, horses that were groomed until they shined. Lord Arndel obviously loved his cattle very much.

"Lord Arndel had these horses prior to coming to Kester House, or so Bill told me. He used to breed them. Sold some at Tattersalls, too."

Another tidbit that Alice had only just become aware of, thanks to her brother. The fact that he believed his past was not worth discussing, or discussing with her, made her wonder. Was he ashamed? Did he not like people enough to let them know him a little better?

"His lordship certainly seems to have many horses stabled here. Where is it that you've placed Juno?"

Benny strode up to another stall not too much farther along and opened the stable door. Juno gave a neigh and walked over. Alice patted her neck.

"You have a beautiful horse, my lady. She's similar in size to his lordship's Bandit." Benny placed the saddle on her mount and quickly tied up the girth, pulling both front legs to stop it pinching. Alice smiled at how quickly and efficiently the lad did his job, and she was pleased he was so confident with his work.

"I suppose she is a similar height."

Benny leaned on the wall as if an old hand at his job. "What did ye think of his lordship's horse? Isn't he as dark as the night and as tall as the sky?"

She smiled at the boy's wayward imagination. "I think Bandit will father some very beautiful foals." Alice gestured to a stall further along. "I see his lordship has a small pony. Do you use the little gelding to learn how to ride on?"

Benny laughed, leaving Juno for a moment and moving on to her brother's horse to saddle. "No, my lady. That's

Whiskers. He's his lordship's daughter, Amelia's, horse. She often rides him about the yard, although she's not allowed to go any faster than a trot. I'm able to canter, since I'm older than her by two years."

Alice started at Benny's words and looked at him quickly. "Lord Arndel has a daughter?" How did she not know this? Alice snapped her mouth shut, sure she was gaping like a guppy fish. And then a more dreadful thought occurred to her. Was he married?

Oh no…

"Aye, my lady. She's only seven."

Alice slumped against the stable wall, utterly blindsided by what she'd just been told. Lord Arndel was a father? Did that mean he was married? But that didn't make any sense. If he was, he'd never flirt with her. Would he? "I did not know his lordship was married." What had become of her? She paused, not certain how she should word her next question, but dying to know the truth of the situation, she questioned the boy. "Do you know what happened to her ladyship?"

Sadness replaced the warmth on Benny's visage and he sighed. "Carriage accident from what I've heard. Lady Arndel, God rest her soul, was thrown when it rolled down a hill. Lord Arndel broke his daughter's fall and came out relatively unharmed, but Amelia broke her leg. It is believed the driver lost control of the horses and took a curve in the road too sharply. I would've sacked the driver had I been in charge."

How devastating. Alice couldn't imagine growing up without a mother. Her own was the most loving and kind woman she'd ever known, and to think they may have never known her was unimaginable. Poor Lord Arndel, too, losing the woman he loved at such a young age. "How terrible for them all. I'm so sorry for his lordship and little Amelia."

Benny nodded. "Aye, Cook says it was hardest for his

lordship. Before taking up the viscountcy, Cook worked for him in Northumberland, you see. His lordship had a modest home, nothing like this grand estate and was really in love." The little boy scrunched up his nose as if he'd said something distasteful.

Alice digested all that had been revealed and could hardly believe it. Arndel hadn't said a word to anyone, for she was certain her mama knew nothing of this disclosure. It made her wonder why he was keeping it all a secret. Was he still mourning his wife? Had they been a tremendous love match —one he'd never recover from? Alice couldn't imagine giving her heart to someone, only to lose it through such tragic circumstances. "Lord Arndel must still miss her dearly, since he's not remarried." It was terrible of her to question little Benny, but needing to know the truth, she couldn't help herself.

"They knew each other since they were kids, from what I heard Cook say."

Benny finished saddling the other two horses, and with her help, they walked the mounts out into the yard. He chattered away about his mama and sister, and Alice nodded when required, pleased the struggles in his home life, that only a few months ago had been difficult, had finally come to an end. Joy surged through her that she'd been a part of their life's change. That by stepping in, acquiring employment for Bess and her children, she had given them hope, something they'd not had for a very long time.

"Lord Arndel is the nicest master I've ever had. He often comes out here and teaches me all that he knows about horses and looking after them. I'm learnin' lots and I'm going to be the best groom in the world."

Alice ruffled Benny's hair. "Excellent. Then I can hire you to be mine."

"Will ye, miss? But…" he faulted. "If I was to work for ye,

who'd work for Lord Arndel? I'd feel guilty if I left him without a groom after everythin' he's done for me."

Alice took pity on the boy lest he go home and have nightmares. "Of course, the choice is yours, and you have plenty more to learn yet, so do not worry about your future now. Just remember, you may come to me anytime you feel the need to. My home is always open to you, no matter where I am. Now," Alice said, "run along and tell His Grace his horse is ready."

The duke and Victoria bade farewell to the horse, and even from where Alice stood, she could see Victoria didn't wish to leave the magnificent stallion. She smiled, admiring her sister a little more.

"Are we ready then?" the duke asked, turning back to Lord Arndel and shaking his hand.

"I believe so." She smiled at Benny's quiet whine of disappointment. "I will see you again soon, Benny. Don't forget I'm to call on your mama in a few days."

Lord Arndel threw her a curious look, and Alice knew what he was thinking. What was a sister of a duke doing visiting a kitchen maid? She didn't explain herself. After all the secrets he'd been keeping from her, he could muddle on that for a few days longer.

Benny smiled, but didn't reply, merely held Josh's horse as her brother mounted.

Alice led Juno to the mounting block, and with the assistance of Benny she climbed up and settled herself into the stirrups.

"Beg ye pardon, my lady, but you're not riding astride? Won't ye get in trouble riding that way?"

Alice grinned, deciding it was probably best she didn't tell Benny that she always rode like this and wore breeches under her dress to make the journey more comfortable. She'd never liked side-saddle, nor its restrictions. And out here in the country, no one paid any heed to what they did, so long as they didn't do it in Town.

"It's perfectly fine, I assure you." Alice turned to Lord Arndel who came to stand beside her.

"You haven't received the ingredient list to make the cake you wanted."

Alice waved his concerns aside. "It's not urgent, but if you could have your cook write up the recipe and have it sent over to Dunsleigh, I would be most appreciative."

His brow rose and he grinned. "Until we meet again then, my lady."

She studied him a moment. A man once married and in love, by all accounts. What had he been like as a husband? Passionate, caring, sweet and cajoling... Victoria trotted past, bidding his lordship good-bye. Arndel stepped back, bowing. "Safe travels," he said.

"Good day, my lord." Alice followed Josh from the yard, before trotting away from the estate.

---

*C*allum stood at his library's window and watched as Lady Alice cantered across an open field, but halted before the forest that surrounded his lands, and gave Kester House one last inspection.

What was she thinking? After seeing Bandit, did she suspect him at all? He ground his teeth, not at all pleased, knowing what an intelligent mind that pretty face hid.

Footsteps sounded deep in the house, before a light knock sounded on his library door.

"Enter," he barked out, watching as his head stableman, Bill, shuffled in.

"When Lady Alice visited the other stable block, do you know of what Benny and her ladyship spoke about?"

His stableman's eyes widened at the question and he stood still, clenching and unclenching his cap in his hands. "Inconsequential things, my lord. Lady Alice did enquire about Whiskers and Benny explained that it was Miss Amelia's mount, but other than Benny explaining his daily duties, not a lot was said."

Callum swore. So now Alice knew of his family, and he'd not been the one to tell her.

He sighed, running a hand over his jaw. Not that he was angry at Benny, but himself. He should've told Alice a long time ago that he'd been married. The moment they met in Town last Season he should have explained that he'd loved and lost his wife. Damn it.

"Did she say anything about Bandit to Benny, do you know? Anything at all?" Callum listened with trepidation that Lady Alice had recognized the mount that he'd been scurrying about the county on, as the Surrey Bandit. The day he'd stolen from the duchess, Alice had seen his horse, but being some months ago now, his only hope was that she'd forgotten Bandit's markings.

"Nothing, my lord. Only that the horse was a beauty and she wished Benny well, told the lad to keep up his good work." His stableman paused. "I apologize if anything the young lad has said or done has caused you pain, my lord. But I'm sure Lady Alice will not go about the district telling people of your horse or its value. The Surrey Bandit could never get away with stealing a gentleman's mount without giving up his identity."

Callum waved the man's concerns aside, hating that his staff, if they knew the truth about him, wouldn't care a fig of his feelings and would merely quit and never come back.

He took a calming breath, the first since Alice had arrived. She had a certain knack to discombobulate him at every turn. Even last Season when she'd followed him about, teasing, and taunting him to dance with her, he'd always been on guard as to what she'd say or do next. Not that he'd not enjoyed their interactions. He had, very much so. For the first time since losing his wife, Maria, he'd seen in Alice someone who would make him laugh, while also warming his bed, pleasantly so.

It was probably why he'd kept his widowhood and daughter a secret, not wanting anyone to like and care for him out of pity, but because of who he was inside.

Why he'd had to go and ruin it was something he'd never forgive himself for, and sometimes he wondered if Alice would, either. Even now, she guarded herself about him, protected her heart from falling for his.

He sighed. "Place Bandit back in his stable and keep him from view from any guests who may arrive. He's too valuable to lose to some highwayman."

"With all due respect, I'm sure if there are any thieving bastards, beg ye pardon, my lord, around, we would've heard about it by now."

Guilt pricked his soul, knowing he was the bloody thieving bastard who roamed the lands, and no one else. "Yes, of course." He walked back to his desk and sat. "No doubt the Surrey Bandit is long gone with all his jewels."

His stableman agreed, frowning. "There was just one more thing, my lord."

"Yes," he said, looking up at the man.

"Bandit was in a right mood when Lady Alice's mare, Juno left. It seems your stallion has taken a liking to her mare."

Callum scoffed. He could sympathize with his horse at least on that score, for he had a penchant for its rider. "And… this is relevant why?"

"Ye horse is kicking at the stable walls and trying to bite anyone who tries to pass too close to his stall. Did ye want me to let him out into the back paddock for a day or so? No one ever passes that side of the river and it's secluded enough with the surrounding woods. I think if we're to stable him again, he may do damage to himself or his stall."

"You may release him, or, as we know all too well, he'll be in a terrible temper." Callum pursed his lips. With the upcoming ball, the Worthingham's constant calling-in and his horse being known about, it was probably time he left for Town and rid himself of the brooch. The last item he'd acquired had sat long enough in his safe, and should Lady Alice realize who his horse actually was and where she'd seen him before, there would be no stopping her from going to the local magistrate and having him locked up in Newgate. Or worse, hanged.

Even though the damn moneylenders hadn't sent for the jewel, he needed to be rid of them—the jewel and the money-lenders once and for all. He would no longer wait for the say-so to arrive in Town. If Lady Alice happened to remember where she'd seen Bandit before, at least no evidence would be found on the property. And there was no proving that his horse was the very same the Surrey Bandit used. It would be her word against his.

"Two days hence, ready the carriage for London."

"Right ye are, my lord."

Arndel watched as his stableman turned about and left. He looked out the window to where he'd seen Lady Alice last, riding astride, wild and untamed, as usual. Would she be the same when warming her husband's bed?

Reaching over, he clasped some parchment and scribbled a note to the moneylenders that he'd be there in three days to make the transaction. He blotted the note closed without his family's stamp, relieved, to some extent, that all this would be over in only a few days. Three days and the estate would be debt free, no IOUs clamping down hard on his shoulders, threatening his daughter and his life. Threatening to go public with the debt.

Freedom beckoned, a fresh start with a future to plan. One that hopefully, included the delectable Lady Alice Worthingham and her natural charms.

CHAPTER 7

*A*lice sat against her headboard, idly staring into the darkened space. The images of Lord Arndel's horse Bandit clear in her mind's eye. A niggling thought that wouldn't fade, no matter how hard she tried to disbelieve what her memory had revealed to her. The horse was magnificent, there was no doubt, a memorable horse.

And that was the terrible thought… Had she seen Bandit before?

She reached over and clasped her glass of water, downing it quickly. More deliberation would be needed before she could make any sort of claim against his lordship. Or tell him that she believed his horse had been used by the Surrey Bandit in his nefarious thieving scheme.

Throwing off her blankets, she clasped the candle beside her bed, walked to where she kept the flint, and lit the candle again. Alice walked about the room, lighting all the candles she could find, needing to be able to see, to rid herself of the dark that haunted her dreams.

Lord Arndel had named his horse Bandit. What gumption to name his horse after the very trade in which he partook.

He must think them all simpletons, and it would certainly explain as to why no one ever saw his lordship on the black beast, for if they did, some would surely suspect. Just as she did now.

Ass!

Her door opened and she started, before recognizing her sister Victoria who peeped around the threshold. "I heard you walking about. Are you well?"

Alice nodded. "Shut the door," she whispered, "and come in. We need to talk."

Her sister seemed eager, and, going back to her bed, she gestured for her to sit beside her. "I had a terrible thought. One that I can scarcely believe myself."

"Oh no. Do you want to talk about it?"

"What I'm about to disclose to you mustn't go beyond us. You must promise me this. Swear it even on your life."

Victoria's eyes went wide. "Of course." She crossed her chest with her hand. "I swear."

Alice studied her a moment and sure she was being genuine, took a deep calming breath and stated, "I think I know who the Surrey Bandit is."

Victoria stared at her a moment before her sister's question squeaked out of her. "You do?"

Alice shushed her. "Quiet, or you'll wake Mama and she'll want to know why we're having a tête-à-tête in the middle of the night."

"Tell me quickly, then. I must know all that you suspect."

"I don't know if I ever told you, but on the day that Mama and I were robbed by the Surrey Bandit, I saw his horse. A beautiful, fine thoroughbred, and at the time, I thought it odd that a man of such ill-repute would own such horseflesh. Admittedly, I forgot about it and put the horse down to being stolen. But now, I'm certain that the horse is, in fact, owned by someone very near to us."

Victoria frowned, leaning forward. "Tell me more, quickly. Who do you suspect?"

Alice understood the moment she said the words she couldn't take them back. But she wasn't wrong in this. His lordship was, in fact, the highwayman who had been terrorizing this part of England. He had to be. "Lord Arndel."

"Don't be absurd." Victoria sat back, looking at her as if she'd lost her mind, which Alice may very well have, for such a thing as what she was thinking was surely mad.

"No I'm not. After seeing his lordship ride back to Kester House the other day, and then seeing the horse up close, I knew there was something about the animal that I recognized but couldn't place. But tonight, somehow it all became clear. I know where I've seen that horse before, and as absurd as the declaration is, it is true."

"So you have not confronted his lordship about this? What do you think he'll have to say for himself?" Victoria huffed out a breath, clearly shocked. Alice clasped her sister's hands when she kept wringing them in her lap.

"I haven't confronted him, no. When we were at his estate, the horse never triggered a memory, not until now at least. Like you, I only noticed its breeding and wondered, like you, of its fine lines. As to what his lordship will say, well, that is anyone's guess. He could deny it, of course, say his horse was stolen, but…"

"But what? Tell me what you're thinking. I can see you've thought of something."

Alice wasn't sure how she was going to say what she must; however, it had to be done. "I've never told anyone this before, and please do not think less of me after I tell you my most disgraceful secret."

It was Victoria's turn to take her hands. Alice welcomed the support. "I would never think badly of you. Ever."

Alice hoped that were so. "The day Mama and I were

robbed by the bandit, he pulled me a little away from the carriage, stood too close to be deemed appropriate, and asked for a kiss. I offered a trade for a kiss and he seemed in agreement."

"You kissed the bandit!"

"Victoria, quiet, you'll wake up the household." Alice listened for any ensuing footsteps, but hearing none, carried on. "I never kissed him and had no intention of doing so. I only allowed him to believe I would, but that's not the shameful part. The shameful part was that I *wanted* him to kiss me. I fell into his dark blue orbs and knew that, should he kiss me, everything would fall away. Or fall into place. My stomach was all a flutter behind that carriage, Victoria. I wanted to touch that bandit, clasp his shirt, and have him hard up against me, and now I know why."

"Why do you know this?"

"Because I have the same reaction to Lord Arndel. Always have. And never with anyone else. So if his lordship denies the claim, I will know he's lying. I trust my senses on this. That bandit was his lordship, and I know he wanted to kiss me as much as I wanted to kiss him."

"Oh my word. This is scandalous! Lord Arndel, our neighbor and friend, is the Surrey Bandit?" Victoria shook her head. "It cannot be true."

Alice nodded. "It is true, my dear." But now what were they to do about it? That was the biggest question of all. Alice slid off the bed and paced beside it, thinking back to that day and how his whispered words, his pleading eyes, had tried to seduce her at the back of the carriage. She glared at the landscape portrait above her mantel. What a wicked game he was playing.

"What will you do with this information?"

"I do not know." Alice sighed, hating the fact he'd put her in such a position, even if unaware of it. Damn him and his thieving tricks. "He's stolen from so many families, so many people that we call friends. Such actions are not acceptable. What do you think we should do?"

Victoria pursed her lips in thought. "We must go to the local magistrate and tell them what we know and suspect. They can do the appropriate investigation, and if it's proven that he is, in fact, the thief, well, he'll be dealt with as expected."

Alice cringed. Lord Arndel in prison, possibly hanged for his crime? The thought didn't bear thinking of. She did not agree with such punishment, no matter the social standing of a person. Oftentimes, people were desperate. It was quite possible Arndel had been more desperate than they thought.

"He has a child, Victoria. I don't think we should involve the magistrate just yet."

"This is too much." Victoria walked over to her and pulled her to sit before the fire. Her sister picked up two logs of wood and placed them on the smoldering coals. "How do you know this? He's never spoken a word about a babe."

"His lordship was married and fathered a little girl, her name is Amelia."

"Oh how sweet. I do like Amelia for a name."

Alice rolled her eyes. "Victoria, please concentrate on the problem at hand, but I agree, Amelia is a lovely name. His wife died after a carriage accident that involved them all. His little girl broke her leg! Having a child complicates this situation slightly, well, in my case it does. We know his family does not approve of him, would have liked someone else to inherit the estate and title, so imagine poor little Amelia being foisted onto them. I doubt very much they would be kind to her."

"True." Victoria nibbled her lip, a trait she had when trying to solve a problem. "Maybe we should confront him. Give him the option to explain his actions."

"I agree. I think this is how we should proceed, at present. Maybe the day after tomorrow? I'm meeting Josh in Ashford in the morning to go through the cottages and look through the plans before building starts."

Victoria stood, pulling her shawl about her shoulders. "We shall speak more on the subject tomorrow when you return, but I think we should both get some rest. There is nothing to be done about this now, and it seems the Surrey Bandit has halted his thievery of late, anyway, so maybe he's stopped altogether."

Alice could only hope, or was the reason behind the fiend's disappearance because they were more involved with his life and he couldn't so easily sneak away and steal… "I will see you tomorrow. Thank you for tonight. I needed someone to talk to and get all this off my chest. I'll sleep better for it, I'm sure."

Her sister bent and kissed her forehead. "I'm certain of it, too. Good night, dearest."

Alice bade her good night and watched her leave. She slumped into her chair and watched the lively fire flicker and lick the new wood on its top. What a predicament Lord Arndel has found himself in, and even if he could come up with a meaningful excuse as to why he had partaken in such underhanded means, it did not mean Alice would allow him to get off so easily. He may not face the hangman's noose, but he would certainly face her punishment, and after stealing her mama's precious emerald brooch, her penalty would undoubtedly be worse than anything the authorities could mete out.

*A*shford was bustling, each and every person busy with their business and trade. Alice rode through the main thoroughfare where houses and shops intertwined, a few of the locals looked her way and nodded in welcome. Alice smiled back and spoke to those who shouted out a greeting or remark. How she loved this town and wished only the best for the people who lived here.

Her father, a great believer in helping those less fortunate, would be happy knowing what she was about to embark upon with her little row of houses.

She continued through the narrow streets toward the local inn, where their lawyers from Town had sent the building designs and where, Alice hoped, her brother was now collecting them.

Her groom followed close on her horse's hooves as she came up to the inn, but she used the hitching posts outside the local butcher. Something told her should her mama find out she tied up Juno before the inn, the notion wouldn't be seen favorably. Even Alice had to draw the line at how scandalous that would be.

Looking across the gravel road, she dismounted. Her brother's horse dozed in the sun, its head hung low as it awaited Josh to claim him again.

And thankfully, within only a few moments of her arrival, her brother exited the inn's front door, a tubular container in his hand as he strode across the dirt-lined road. "There you are. I worried you had forgotten." Her brother halted before her, grinning. "I have gossip."

Alice gave her brother a quick kiss on the cheek and took his arm. "Sorry I was late, but it was such a beautiful day I thought to take the longer route into the village and enjoy the county a little. We'll be in London only too soon, and I'll miss all this beautiful green."

Josh nodded. "I agree. And I like going up to Town, but even I must admit, this Season I'm not as keen as I usually am."

"Why?" Alice studied him.

"I feel this Season both you and Victoria will marry and I'll be the only Worthingham left at Dunsleigh. As the youngest in the family, even if I am duke, I'll miss you and V."

Alice hugged him to her, her eyes smarting at her brother's words. And he was probably right, they would all marry, if not this year, in the not too distant future, and the life that they had lived as children would be no more. But then, one must grow up, even if one did not wish to. "We will miss you, too, but I promise should we marry and move away, we will visit often. So you will not be rid of us so easily."

Josh smiled. "I'm glad."

Alice sighed, looking about a village she knew as well as herself. "Now, what is this gossip you have? I can see by the parcel in your hand you have the housing designs. So what news?"

"I ran into your little friend Benny earlier today. He was waiting outside the inn."

"Was he with Lord Arndel?"

Her brother raised a curious brow. "Oh ho ho, what's this? Lady Alice interested in the whereabouts of a gentleman?"

Alice cursed her stupidity at sounding so eager to know if Arndel was in town. Now that she suspected him of being the Surrey Bandit, the eager beating of her heart in her chest really ought to stop. His lordship was a criminal, a thief, and one who had tried to kiss her while robbing her at the same time.

"Don't be absurd," she said, sniffing her disdain at such a stupid question, that wasn't so silly at all. "I was merely concerned for Benny's welfare. He's so young, he shouldn't be on his own." Alice didn't bother to mention the boy used to live in this very town and had run about often on his own or with his friends.

"We are talking about Benny, your friend Bess's youngest lad, who, I might add, is more street-smart than you are." Josh laughed, shaking his head as they continued their way toward where her cottages were located.

"Even so." She paused, not wanting to sound too eager to hear what news Benny had imparted. "What is your news? You were going to tell me something."

"Ah yes, well, apparently Lord Arndel is traveling to London. His house is in an uproar as only yesterday he's decided to go."

Alice frowned. "Did Benny mention why his lordship had to travel to London? He's leaving for Town only a few weeks before the ball. I wonder what would take him there?"

Josh shrugged. "Gentlemen, my dear, travel to Town often, with little or no excuse but to get away. I would suggest he's merely doing such a thing."

"And Benny's going with him, I suppose."

"He is." Josh helped her over a small rut in the road. "He's very excited about it. What with seeing London for the first time, even if only for a night or so."

"Only a night." Alice stopped. "Do you not think it odd that he's only going for one night?" She chewed her lip. "I wonder what the trip is about."

"You forget, Sister, we traveled up for only one night. Now come on, the builders are waiting for us," he said, pulling her along.

Alice's mind whirred with thoughts about his lordship's trip. Was he up to something? Was his trip linked to being the Surrey Bandit? When she returned home she would consult with Victoria as to what she thought of Arndel's spontaneous trip to Town. It was too coincidental that, after she'd seen his horse Bandit, he was now high-tailing it to London. He didn't know that she suspected him, but perhaps he was smarter than she was giving him credit for.

And Lord Arndel had to be particularly intelligent, for he'd been stealing for a while and authorities were not even close to knowing who was doing it. Come to think of it, whenever she'd seen the drawing likeness of the thief nailed to trees and shop buildings, none of them had even looked like Arndel.

They passed another coaching inn and Alice walked over to it upon seeing an image, weatherworn and torn, but still nailed up on the outside wall. She shook her head, the image did the Surrey Bandit no justice, and, with such pictures to go by, it was no wonder he'd not been caught. All but one of the features were incorrect, the eyes—that, at least, someone had drawn correctly—and it set in stone what Alice suspected. With such eyes staring back at her, she was, without question, right in her assumption that Lord Arndel was the highwayman.

"Alice, come. We'll be late." Her brother gestured for her to join him, and without hesitation she pulled the image from the inn and joined him.

"What are you doing with that?"

She shrugged. "Victoria wanted to see what he looked like, and this will explain it to her adequately." And it would give her something to confront him with when she met with him again, if she decided to do such a thing, that is. Nerves fluttered in her stomach at the thought of such a conversation and his reaction to being called out as the bandit. Although Alice didn't know what he may do on the occasion, something told her it would not be pleasant.

"You look pensive. You're not worried about the cottages?" Her brother studied her a moment. "It's a little too late to pull out of the escapade now."

Alice smiled up at him, if only to hide what was really bothering her. Josh didn't need to know what she suspected, for if he knew, if anyone were to find out, Alice hated to think what would happen. "Not at all. Everything's well. I'm merely worried about whether the architects have achieved everything that I wished them to."

Josh patted her hand. "I'm sure they've done exactly as you ordained. They wouldn't dare upset a paragon like you."

"Well, aren't we the epitome of hilarity today."

"I do try," he said, grinning as they came up to the first cottage on Pitt Street. "And here we are." A shining black carriage stood before the first house, the gray-matched pair quietly waiting. On the side of the door were the golden embossed letters that read: Brown and Co Master Builders.

For the remainder of the afternoon, with the guidance of the two master builders from London, they discussed the plans of the dwellings and how to make the best use of the space that was available to them. It was agreed that all homes would have the same basic layout with identical features like stoves and built-in furniture, where possible. They would use the central chimney to heat the upstairs rooms during winter and ensure the parents in the house would sleep separately from their children. All the beds would be built-in, a suggestion from Mr. Brown that Alice couldn't help but think was a marvel of an idea.

There were other cosmetic repairs, such as new doors and windows, to limit the weather from impacting those who lived there. The houses would be stripped bare and repaired and refurbished to an adequate standard, or at least the standard in which Alice thought appropriate.

"This is going to cost you quite a large portion of your inheritance," Josh said, taking her arm as they took their leave. "Are you quite certain?" He rolled up the plans.

Excitement rushed through her and she couldn't wait to

begin. "I am well aware of how much it will cost. Isn't it wonderful?"

Her brother shook his head, expelling a resigned sigh. They stepped out onto the street and started back toward the main thoroughfare of town. "These houses are going to be marvelous, Alice. If I haven't said it before, I'm proud of you and I know Papa would be proud, too."

Alice's eyes smarted at her brother's words. "Thank you, Josh. And thank you for helping me with it all, even though I know you had your reservations about it. I know it's going to be grand."

"You've inspired me to do more, and I think I may also look into a venture where I can help those in need."

As they turned a corner, Juno looked up and neighed at Alice in welcome. "I think that is the very best idea, and if you need any help, you know who to ask."

CHAPTER 8

*A*lice huddled down beside the blackberry bush, keeping her head lower than the surrounding foliage. She pushed away the absurd thought of how silly she would look if caught in this situation, a duke's daughter acting like a spy in the British government.

But she doubted even a spy would scamper about on the ground as she was doing.

Victoria slid in beside her. Her sister, too, dressed in boy's breeches and a shirt that had surpassed its public use. Their hair was pulled back in simple ribbons and neither resembled who they should. Just thinking about what their mama would do to them should she ever find out about this escapade sent her stomach to coil in knots. The duchess, a normally placid soul, would not see this at all acceptable. They would both be married off to the first gentlemen their mama saw.

They lay there for a time, watching the workers of Kester House. A gardener dug and raked a large garden bed that was waist high with weeds, his sweat-stained shirt evidence of the laborer's hard work.

Over the last few minutes, Benny had come and gone from the stables multiple times, busy with his chores, while other men had pulled a traveling carriage from a nearby shed and oiled the leather straps and polished the equipage until it shined.

"Well, what can you see?" Victoria asked, remaining hidden.

"Nothing yet. Just a few workers going about their business, but I do think his lordship will be traveling to London tomorrow."

"How do you know that?" Victoria lifted her head to look and frowned.

"Because the carriage is out, and his lordship never goes about the county that way. He's always on a horse." Speaking of which, Alice hadn't seen nary of Bandit. Furthermore, all of the stable doors that led out into individual pens were open, but there was no sign of the stallion.

"I think he's done something with the horse he used to rob us, but I may be wrong. We should look at the other fields to see if he's hidden him from view." Alice watched in silence for a moment, her sister Victoria gasping and hiding when a maid on the first-floor landing hung a worn floor covering out a window and started to hit it quite forcibly with a cane.

"Get down or she'll see you," Victoria hissed, worried that they'd hear them as well, even though they were quite a distance from the house.

"We're too far away for anyone to see or hear us here." Alice bit her lip, wondering if she should confront Lord Arndel before his trip to London or after. The weight of knowing he was the Surrey Bandit lay heavily on her mind, so it was probably best she spoke to him before.

"We should tell Josh. I know you do not wish to, but I think it would be best. We don't know how Lord Arndel will react to us knowing, and even though up until now the Surrey Bandit has never been violent, I'm not sure we should take the risk and find out if his lordship has a breaking point."

Alice sighed, knowing her sister had a point. But then an idea came to her—wickedly inappropriate but keeping them free from censure due to the nature of the plan.

"What are you grinning about?" Victoria clasped her arm. "Please remember the Worthingham name will only protect you so far, Sister, and by the scheming look on your face, I have a feeling whatever it is, I'm not going to like it."

Alice threw her the most innocent look she could muster. "Do not worry, for what I have planned will only ever be between you, me, and Lord Arndel. And no scandal shall ever darken our door because of it." Looking back toward the estate, she stilled when spying his lordship. Her attention fixed on the strong muscled line of his legs and broad shoulders that were on show as he strode his determined path.

"What is it?" Victoria asked.

"Stop being a ninny hammer and look for yourself."

"Just tell me," she pleaded.

Alice sighed. "Lord Arndel has entered the stable."

Out the corner of her eye, Alice noted her sister roll her eyes. "I fail to see how seeing the gentleman enter a stable proves anything."

Alice waved her comment aside. "Of course it doesn't prove anything, but we're not here today to prove anything absolute. We're merely observing the workings of an estate. From afar. Undetected." And should Alice find him guilty of the crime, he would pay for it dearly.

Regaining her gumption, Victoria looked. "We should go, before someone sees us and we're made to explain our presence."

"We don't have to explain anything to anyone." *Arndel*

certainly played by those rules and thought nothing of it, so why shouldn't we?

"What do you plan to do about this, Sister, if you're not going to tell Josh or the authorities?"

His lordship came out of the stable on his usual brown gelding and anger reverberated through her that he'd had the audacity to steal from them, his so-called friends, have luncheon with them and talk about the theft, while all the time being the low-bred whelp who'd orchestrated the whole thing.

How dare he...

Revenge coiled about in her mind as a plan on how to get back at his lordship outlined in her head. "Let's be off, and I will tell you all when we're ensconced safely in my room."

"*T*his is the most absurd, dangerous thing you've ever made me do."

Alice glanced over at her sister, and behind the brown bandanna that covered all but her eyes, a sheen of tears threatened to topple over.

"Don't you dare get upset. Nothing untoward will happen, and we're merely taking back what is ours."

"You cannot be sure he's even the bandit, and you're going to confront him! This is madness, Alice."

"Oh, I'm sure he's the thief, for no other gentleman has eyes like his lordship." Eyes that were as dark as the deepest oceans and as stormy as the high seas. That had looked at her with such hunger that she'd felt like the most delicious treat. "We know he's not traveled to Town for quite some time, so there must be a reason behind this hasty departure."

Victoria swiped at her eyes. "He might be buying a suit for the ball."

"It's too coincidental. He knows I saw the horse and he's going to London so he's not caught with all his plunder. He thinks I'm going to go to the authorities and is protecting himself by ridding himself of the jewels."

"What if he's not, Alice? What if he has no contraband on him at all?"

Alice shrugged. "We will worry about that, if it eventuates that way. But it won't. Trust me. I know to the very core of my soul that he's up to something." Lord Arndel was the Surrey Bandit and Alice would prove it.

"He could shoot us."

Alice didn't disagree with her sister's statement, for Lord Arndel could very well shoot them both, or his driver could, for that matter, but nothing ventured, nothing gained and all that.

"I wish you had never talked me into this." Victoria's grasp on her reins was brutal and her horse's prancing only paid heed to its rider's rioting emotions. "Relax, you're making your horse nervous, and I don't need him to bolt. I need you here, helping me."

Victoria glared at her. "Thanks for the concern."

Alice turned her attention back to the road. "You said you would help me. I don't understand why you're acting the princess. You've never been afraid of doing what you know is right. And this is right, no matter how nervous it makes you feel."

"There is a difference between stating your opinion, giving a set down to a too high-in-the-instep lord, and robbing one at gunpoint on the road."

Alice ignored her. Lord Arndel needed to feel what it was like to be stolen from, for his opinion and feelings to be trampled and ignored, all because money and fortune beckoned with pretty earbobs or emerald brooches.

"He may have nothing in his carriage besides himself and then what will you do?"

"We will go home."

Victoria huffed out a breath. "You will look like a fool and, by the way, these costumes are not adequate enough, and he'll see through my bandanna and your mask. This escapade of yours, which I truly do not think you've given enough thought, could ruin us."

"It shall not and you will see that I'm right and you're wrong and then, my dearest little sister, you may apologize."

"I shall do no such thing. This could kill me, and I refuse to act contrite to anyone who may put me in harm's way."

The sound of an approaching carriage rumbled down the lane and Alice smiled a little to calm her sister's startled visage. She adjusted her seat, ensuring the flintlock that was seated in her lap was ready. "He's going to London to sell the jewels. I'm certain of it. Now," she said, walking Juno to the side of the road and behind some hedge groves. "Join me here. We need to surprise him."

Victoria mumbled something about wishing she'd never had her as a sister and Alice smiled. Riding up beside her, they both sat in wait. Alice scratched her scalp, the men's short hair wig that sat atop her head itched terribly. "Nothing will happen to us, my dear. I promise you, although I cannot guarantee the same for his lordship." That she couldn't promise at all.

***

*C*allum frowned, looking outside the carriage window at the passing foliage, his mind a whirl with guilty thoughts. Under the seat opposite him, in a little nondescript bag, was the jewel he'd stolen from the Duchess of Penworth. By tonight, it would be in the hands of the moneylender near London's East End docks.

The carriage lurched to the side as they rumbled around a corner and shouting with a gunshot sounded loud in the air. He stilled, trying to see what was before the vehicle, and when his driver pulled up, dread coiled in his gut.

"What the hell." He clasped the leather handle above the window to stop himself from flying forward. He looked out the window and cursed the offending dust, which stopped him from seeing anything. "What's going on out there?"

No answer was forthcoming, and opening the door, Callum stepped out. It was an action he should have thought through more, before being so hasty to investigate. The cold barrel of a flintlock pressed against his temple and he stilled.

"We go there," the feminine voice drawled, a humorous tone to her words. "And I believe it would be best that you cooperated with us, lest I have the urge to shoot you."

"You wish to shoot me?" Why he asked such a question he didn't know, but there was something familiar and comforting about the voice that gave him the nerve to press his luck a little.

"Oh, most certainly, Lord Arndel. In fact, right at this moment, I don't believe there is another in this whole county that I would enjoy shooting more."

Now he recognized the voice and how this game would play out. "You wound me." He paused, wondering if he could make a go at clasping her gun and turning the advantage over to himself. He discredited the thought instantly. He couldn't do that to Alice, he would merely let her have her fun and then he would see what came next. "How will I ever recover."

"Shall your hand twitch again my lord, you will find my bullet in your nether regions, so it would be best to listen to the woman who currently holds a gun to your head." Callum looked toward the other voice. Lady Victoria sat atop a large bay gelding, her hair pulled back and a bandanna covering her mouth.

Callum jumped when a shot rang out, but as quick as he could breathe, Lady Victoria pulled a second gun from her saddle bag and aimed it toward his driver. His servant was holding his gun out to his side, the stark, shocked visage of the man making it only too clear to him that he'd tried to take control and failed.

"Put the gun down, John," Callum said, watching as his driver threw it to the side of the carriage.

"What do you want?" he asked, knowing only too well what the Worthingham women were after. He watched as Alice raised her brow and grinned.

"*Tsk, tsk, tsk*, my lord. Impatience is not something that I will take lightly, nor do I believe you should rush those who are holding up your carriage."

"What would you suggest, then? You've stopped us, and I'm curious as to why."

Alice took the gun away from his temple and keeping her attention fixed on him, walked to stand before him. "We're curious, of course, what our little robbery of you today will grant us. Tell us, dear lord, what treasures your carriage holds?"

The driver shot Callum a curious look and he ground his teeth. The last thing he needed was for his servants to know what he'd been doing around their own home county. Not that he ever stole from the poor, but still, they had morals and wouldn't look upon his thieving as respectable behavior.

"Let John go and we'll discuss this further."

Alice tipped her head to the side, thinking over his request. "Very well. John," she said, yelling out to his driver, but not taking her attention off Callum. "You may leave. Now."

His driver looked to Callum for confirmation and he nodded. Within minutes he was without help and alone with the two hellions.

"Now, Lord Arndel, don't make me ask my question twice."

"It's in the carriage, under the seat closest to the driver."

Alice smiled, her lips a deep red and as delectable as ever. With the mask over her eyes, he became more aware of how beautiful the other features on her face were. An overwhelming urge to touch her, pull her hard against him and kiss her, consumed him and he fisted his hands at his sides, lest he do exactly that.

"I'm so glad you've decided to cooperate. I do hate conflict." She waved her gun over toward Victoria. "Now stand over there so I can get on with the business at hand."

Callum did as she bade and turned to watch as she climbed up into the carriage, the tight-fitting breeches, an article of clothing he'd never thought to see on Lady Alice Worthingham, caught his full attention, not to mention the perfect round globes of her ass. He let out a relieved breath when she disappeared from view.

"I would suggest your attention be diverted to something other than my comrade's bottom, my lord."

Callum looked up at Victoria and grinned, liking how Alice's sibling's eyes narrowed further, and she aimed the gun a little lower on his person. "Apologies," he stated, not apologetic at all. In fact, it was one item of clothing he hoped to see her sister in again, if only to strip her of them and enjoy what pleasures lay beneath.

Alice mumbled something in his carriage and then jumped out, laughing, the sound mocking even to his own ears. She slipped her hand into the bag that held the jewel he'd stolen, and he cringed at the disgust that flittered over her visage. "Like what you see?" His tone was scathing, but more at himself than Alice or her sister. That he'd been forced into this life was no excuse. His actions as the Surrey Bandit were reprehensible.

She nodded. "I do, and I like this piece more than anything." Alice lifted out the emerald brooch that was the duchess's and he cringed. "I think I'll keep this piece for myself."

"That pin belongs to the Duchess of Penworth. Maybe you ought to gift it back to her," Callum said.

Alice's eyes held no mirth. "Do not get the impression, Lord Arndel, that just because we are thieving from you, that we will keep these goods for ourselves. On the contrary. We will do the right thing and ensure that what we take is returned to the rightful owners."

"How Christian of you," he drawled, hating that she was right, no matter how much her thievery from him would make his life hell. The moneylender would not be happy that the emerald brooch was lost. He would simply have to find an alternate way to raise the funds equal to the brooch's value. And in a way that would not raise eyebrows around the county. There was always the few mares and even Bandit could be sold. He must think of something.

Alice threw the bag to her sister and, amazingly, Victoria caught it one-handed. Callum shook his head, having never known women of such rank to be so capable. "What do you intend to do with me now?"

Alice placed her gun in the holder on her saddle and strolled up to him, smiling. "Oh, what will we do with you now?" Her words were low and not without a little flirtation.

Callum couldn't tear his eyes from her and he swallowed. "What will you do with me?" he asked for only Alice to hear.

Her blue orbs darkened with contemplation, but she didn't lose stride. "What would you like for me to do, my lord? I may be a thief, but do not be deceived, even I have morals."

"I'm well aware of those. Believe me." She laughed at his words and his lips twitched. That they could find the humor in this situation, and make light of it, said a lot about her character and he liked her more for it. Maybe if she knew the truth, she could forgive him.

"Perhaps," she said, sliding a finger across his chest and making his heart beat wildly, "I will go to my family and tell them what I know about the mysterious Viscount Arndel of Kester House."

Callum denied her a reply, not sure if provoking her would be wise.

She clasped his hand and pulled him toward the back of the carriage. It was uncannily reminiscent of what he'd done to her only weeks before, and fire ignited in his blood, hot and heavy.

"Do you want me to tell the authorities and have the full force of the law come down on your head?"

"No." Callum crossed his arms and leaned against the equipage. "I want only *you* to punish me." The words left his mouth and the moment he said them he wanted to rip them back. He was acting the cad and with a woman whom he shouldn't bait. By the gleam in her eyes, she understood his meaning.

Dammit he liked that look. A lot.

"Tell me if you need me," Victoria yelled from the front.

"All is well," Alice countered, her inspection of him lowering to his wrists. "What lovely cufflinks you have, my lord. Are they gold?"

Callum glanced at them. "Yes."

She smiled. "I may be willing to do a deal with you, my lord."

"A deal." He fought not to smile, hoping this conversation was going where he thought it might. "What kind of deal?"

"I believe you ought to hand over your gold cufflinks, and in return I may sweeten the sting of losing such a valuable bauble."

"Such as?" he asked.

"A kiss."

Without hesitation, Callum undid the small pins that held his shirtsleeves together and slipped them into her palm. In silence, she watched him, but he could see her mind was whirring at the thought of what she'd suggested. But then, when you poke a lion, what did one expect? No cufflinks, even if they were made of the finest diamonds or purest of gold would be worth keeping, if a kiss from Alice were on offer. "I'm all yours," he said, not moving but waiting for her to initiate the kiss.

Her fingers fisted about his cufflinks and she placed them into her pocket. "As a gentleman, I didn't think you would agree."

He laughed, shaking his head. "I may have been born a gentleman, but I did not grow up as one. And you should not offer such temptation, if you did not wish for me to taste it." A light blush rose on her cheeks and a jab of pity took hold. "But of course, as a gentleman now, if you do not wish to kiss me, I will not make you."

Her shoulders stiffened and her chin lifted. Anticipation throbbed through him. *I have her now...*

"I do not go back on my word, my lord."

"Very well, then." He waggled his eyebrows at her and her eyes narrowed.

"Having said that, Lord Arndel, do not push your luck."

He bit back another laugh and conceded. "Very well. I shall wait patiently."

When she didn't move, he said, "When you're ready, of course, so, too, am I."

With a huff, Alice stepped forward, clasped his jaw, and kissed him. The first thing Callum realized was Alice was quite tall for a woman, and it didn't take very much effort to lean down and deepen the embrace.

She was as stiff as a board in his arms before he wrapped his arm about her waist and hauled her in against him. On her gasp, he kissed her hard, just as he'd longed to for many weeks.

With each glide of the kiss, the slight stroke of his tongue against hers, she relaxed, became compliant in his arms and gave him what he'd dreamed about. And her kisses were what dreams were made of: sweet, explorative, untutored. Never had he been as intoxicated by an embrace as he was right now in Alice's arms.

The soft sigh that she released as she sank into the kiss sent his wits spiraling. For a moment, Callum grappled for control, but when her tongue lightly touched his, it all vanished.

With his free hand, he clasped the nape of her neck, feeling the hard, fake wig that she wore. He wanted to rip it from her scalp. He wanted to run his hands through her beautiful locks and hold her right as she was, for all time. Kiss her senseless for as long as she'd allow.

She pulled back and stepped out of his arms altogether. Callum let her go with regret and consoled himself with the fact that her eyes looked heavy with desire and, if he wasn't incorrect, a little awe.

"I shouldn't have done that."

"Why not?" He shrugged, the action in some way releasing his taut muscles. "You're not worried about your reputation, are you? I thought you were a highwaywoman and nothing else."

"I am, but I'm also a woman who should not have done *that*."

"Are you a woman of rank?" Callum watched as her eyes darkened in warning. He smirked. "Preferably, I would like you to come back here and do it again."

Her mouth opened on a gasp, and he strode up to her, clasped her face, and kissed her hard, quick, and deep, before pulling back and bowing. "I hope we see each other again."

Alice nodded and walking over to her horse in what looked like a daze, mounted quickly, and joined her sister. "I'm sure we will, Lord Arndel, and sooner than you'd like, if you continue this type of thieving lifestyle. Do I make myself clear?"

"Very," he said, watching as the women turned their mounts and cantered down the road before turning into the trees. Callum swore, running a hand through his hair.

For all his teasing of the little minx, she'd still run off with his portable blunt and now he would have to send word to London and notify those his deceased cousin owed money to, that the debt would not be paid. Not with the jewels that had been required, at least. Damn it!

The thought brought unease, and he wondered what else on the property and estate he could sell that might get him out of such a bind. All that came to mind were the horses. It was all he had left. Everything else had already been sold. The breeding program he'd hoped to rekindle to create extra income for the estate would no longer be possible. The whole situation he'd allowed the moneylenders to get him into was a disgrace. *He* was a disgrace.

Climbing up onto the box of his carriage, he clasped the reins of his matched pair and turned the vehicle about, heading back to Kester House.

The sound of approaching horses met his ears, and he looked up to see his carriage driver along with other men from the estate barreling toward them. They pulled up in a cloud of dust, looking about for the two thieves who had been there.

"Are ye all right, my lord? We came as soon as I could gather some men."

Callum pulled the horses up and waved their concern aside. "I've been robbed, but little else." *Other than a kiss that will occupy my mind for many years to come...*

"Are we to continue to London?" his driver asked, frowning.

"No. When we return to Kester House you may put the carriage away. It's no longer needed."

"Right ye are, my lord."

"You men may ride ahead. I'll not be far behind." They nodded and rode off, looking into the forest as they went, no doubt searching for the two hellions that were the Worthinghams.

He flicked the ribbons and the horses walked on. He didn't focus on anything at all, merely thought back over the recent events, wondering when he would see Lady Alice again. For he was certain the little minx was she.

But what would she do with the brooch, and how would she explain to her mama how the jewel came back into their hands? And worse, how was he to secure his future without the jewel the moneylenders wanted so badly? Under no circumstances would he ever take it from Alice's family again, so what would pacify the money shark?

Above all else, Amelia was his main concern. Her safety was paramount, and to keep her so, he would tell the few men who worked for him to remain on guard and armed, even if he had to tell them about his cousin's debt. Explain that men of ill-repute wished him and his daughter harm if he didn't pay what was owed and soon. After all Amelia had faced losing her mama, she deserved a future free of trouble or scandal. He wanted her home to be something to be proud of, not founded on a father who did as he was bade to men who deserved no respect. If the money from the horses would satisfy the moneylender, then Callum would have to learn patience, work the estate with what he had, and grow it from there. In time, maybe he could purchase more horses and breed them. He would make his daughter proud, if it were the last thing he ever did.

CHAPTER 9

The duchess gasped, tears springing to her eyes. "You found it where?" Their mama held out her hand, her face a mask of disbelief and happiness. "Let me see."

Alice placed the little keepsake into the palm of her hand and smiled at the love in which her mama looked down on the brooch.

"I cannot believe I have it back."

"We were riding home from Ashford and as odd as it is, Victoria and I noticed something glistening on the road. We stopped to see what it was and you can imagine our shock and delight upon seeing your jewel. We rode home as soon as we could, to tell you of our marvelous find."

Alice caught Victoria's gaze and smiled. On the way home, after they had changed in the hunting lodge a few miles from the estate, they had agreed on a story as to how and when they'd found the brooch. And if their mama's overwhelmed happiness was anything to go by, she believed them.

Their mama pinned the brooch to her gown and eyed it

lovingly. "I am overjoyed that I have it back. Oh, thank you, daughters. You've made me most happy."

Alice sat, pouring herself a cup of tea. "It was a lucky find, Mama, and nothing more."

"Even so," the duchess replied, "I'm in mind to treat you both for your splendid service to me today. On the morrow, we shall travel to Ashford where I shall buy you whatever you wish. Victoria, I know you admired that pink shawl in La Mariette's store."

"Thank you, Mama. I would like that very much." Victoria sat also, admiring the brooch as much as their mama.

Alice pulled her legs up beside her and settled back in her chair. "If you wouldn't mind Mama, I would like for my gift to be held off until we reach Town. I haven't found anything in Ashford that I desperately need."

Their mama raised her brow in surprise. "Truly, daughter? Are you sure there is nothing you would like me to buy or help you with?"

Alice noted her amused tone and wondered at it. Was she teasing her in some way? "I don't believe so." She frowned, wondering what she was missing in the conversation.

Her mama laughed. "I merely meant that if you wished for help with the houses you're refurbishing, I'm willing to donate. Just tell me what you would like me to do."

"Truly, Mama?" Alice leaned forward, excited at the thought of what she could further do to improve the small homes. "Well, there *is* something that I think the cottages will need, but haven't looked into it a lot yet, as we're a little away from being at that stage of the build."

"Tell me, and I will see what I can do."

Her mother's generosity was more than she thought returning a brooch deserved, but it seemed, when one did a good deed, sometimes good things happened in return. "As you know, the families who live there have very little, and

I'm having the builders make all the beds in the cottages as a permanent fixture in the rooms, but I have no linen. No straw or feather mattresses, for that matter. And as much as I would love them to sleep on feather, I know that is an extravagance, but would you help me fit out the cottages with bedding? That would be the best gift in the world, and I'll not ask for a new wardrobe again unless it's my husband who's purchasing one."

"As much as I'm thrilled you're still talking of marriage, preparing the bedding for your tenants will be my pleasure. Finding this brooch is something I could never thank you girls enough for. So, it will be an honor to help you."

Alice stood and hugged her mama. "Thank you so much. This is beyond all my expectations."

Her mama laughed. "That would make two of us, my dear." She paused, gathering her wits. "But speaking of your renovations, there is talk in the town of you taking control of the builders, being quite forthright and demanding when it comes to the work commencing and such. I can't help but think, no matter how fantastic your venture is to help the needy, that your brother would be much better suited to doing what is rightfully a man's employment."

"I disagree, Mama. And I'm sorry you're worried about what people are saying, but I am not. I will help the people of Ashford, and the old fuddy-duddies can go hang."

"You may be the daughter of a duke, but someone mentioned that your gown was covered in dust and your hair was gray with cobwebs."

Alice shrugged, taking another sip of tea. "The townspeople ought to be thankful their patron's daughters are not frivolous and cold-hearted, but wish to make the world a better place and help those who are less fortunate."

A resigned sigh sounded from her mama and Alice smiled, having won the argument.

"Very well, but try not to make so much of a spectacle of yourself. You are to travel up to London soon for the Season. And I do believe smooth hands would be better met by your gentlemen admirers than calloused ones."

Victoria chuckled.

"Talking of my cottages, I have another meeting in Ashford tomorrow with Josh and the cabinet maker, so I think I'll go upstairs and have my dinner sent up tonight. If you don't mind, Mama. I feel a little tired after today's adventure."

"Are you well, my dearest?" her mama asked, concern tinging her voice.

"I'm very well. I just want to relax and rest in my room." Alice ignored her sister's concerned glance and stood. "Good night."

"I'll come with you. I, too, am feeling a little weary."

"Will you be down for dinner, Victoria, or should I let the servants know it'll only be me and Josh?"

"I'll be down for dinner, Mama, I'm just having a little rest beforehand." Victoria leaned down and kissed her mother's cheek, and clasping Alice's arm, pulled her from the room.

As soon as their slippered feet hit the foyer tiles, Victoria rounded on her. "You said once we returned home and Mama accepted our story that you would tell me what happened with Lord Arndel? You went behind the carriage and were awfully quiet. I demand to know what you're playing at."

Alice scoffed and went to walk away, but her sister squeezed her arm—hard. "What are you doing, V?"

"What happened, Alice?"

"Nothing occurred." The lie, a betrayal to her sister, threatened to release every word, every thought, and action she'd done behind that carriage. To confess how much she had loved every moment of it. How much she longed to experience another such kiss.

"You're blushing brighter than Mama's favorite roses." Victoria threw her an assessing stare, before pulling her toward the staircase. "You kissed him, didn't you?"

Shame, mixed with excitement, ran through Alice, and heat suffused her face. "I didn't think my taunting of him would lead to such an action." But in truth, Alice had instigated the kiss. For weeks she'd wanted to see what it would be like to kiss a man, and not any man, but Lord Arndel.

The thought of his lips against hers, his slightly roughened jaw that told her all too well that the man before her was a virile, suitable gentleman. Not that she'd allow him to court her—he was a liar, a thief, and the Surrey Bandit— which she couldn't forget. But...maybe, if he redeemed himself in some way.

"Well, I can see it has. How could you? He stole from us."

"I know he did. I haven't forgotten, and I intend to make him pay for his crimes. And one kiss does not equal marriage. I merely trifled with him, that is all. No need to get your shift in a knot."

Victoria gasped. "My shift? Seriously, Alice. I know you've always been the wildest of us all, golly, even Josh isn't as wicked as you can be, but you cannot go kissing gentlemen on the sides of roads. Especially, not Lord Arndel. If Mama ever found out what he's done, and you marry him, well, it will kill her for sure."

"As I said, I don't intend to marry him. Stop worrying." They continued up the stairs, the frown line between Victoria's eyebrows becoming deeper with each step. "It won't happen again. I promise."

Her sister nodded but didn't look to be consoled by her words. "Now that I've scolded you, I hope you keep your word." Victoria bit her lip, a light flush marking her cheeks. "Will you tell me what the kiss was like?"

Alice laughed, hugging her close to her side. "All that I hoped it would be rolled into one. He kissed me with such passion I thought my stomach, which was full of butterflies, would float away."

"Wow," Victoria said dreamily. "I've heard men can kiss quite enthusiastically. Did he?"

Alice thought back to his strong arm that had wrapped about her waist, the other holding her head firmly against his. Their breath had mingled with each stroke and glide of their mouths, the delicious spike of her heartbeat that she wanted to feel again, if only one more time. It was any wonder her older sisters, who were now respectfully married, always seemed to disappear from balls and parties at the oddest moments. For, if what they were doing with their gentlemen admirers was anything like she had done with Lord Arndel, well, it certainly explained a few things she'd been wondering about.

"Yes, I do believe he did, but then," Alice said, smiling. "I have nothing to base the kiss on, for it was my first, so perhaps he was merely amusing himself with me."

Victoria scoffed. "I've seen the way Lord Arndel looks at you, and believe me, even if I don't know much about the opposite sex, he does not look like you're merely being trifled with to cure his own boredom. And that's why I feel I must caution you against teasing such a gentleman, for after what he's done and what we know as fact, you cannot marry him."

"I know that." Alice stopped outside her bedroom door, knowing only too well what her sister meant. "I will see you at breakfast."

Victoria smiled. "Good night, Alice. I hope you're feeling more reinvigorated come the morning."

"I'm sure I will." Alice walked into her room and rang for her maid, deciding that a bath was in order, too. Perhaps that would wash away the day's trials and like her sister said, come the morn, all would be better and life would seem less troubled.

Not that she could guarantee the same for Lord Arndel. She would have to think about his punishment. She did not like to be judge and jury to a fellow peer, but when one wanted to keep said peer from the gallows, due to the fact he was the sole parent to a child, exceptions must be made.

When her maid appeared, Alice ordered her bath, sat down at her writing desk, and pulled out a piece of parchment. She scribbled a short note for Lord Arndel, notifying his lordship of her intention to visit in two days and that she expected him to be at home. Alice didn't sign the note, but she had no doubt that he would know who the sender was nor did she need her mama to find out who she was sneaking out to visit, unmarried as she was.

She sealed the note and sat it where her maid collected all her mail from the little silver salver on her desk. Out the window, she looked toward where Kester House stood and wondered what he was doing right at this moment and what he was thinking.

After today's adventure, something told her tonight would be a restless sleep for his lordship and, even with all that she was aware about Arndel, the thought didn't fill her with pleasure, but sadness.

CHAPTER 10

wo days later, Alice found herself sitting in Lord Arndel's library, the gentleman unfashionably late for their meeting. She tapped her foot against the parquetry floor and stared out the window, watching as the gardener strode across the lawn with a wheelbarrow full of weeds.

At least the garden was looking a lot better than it used to.

The door opened and closed, the snip of the lock loud in the quiet room. Alice didn't bother to turn and greet his lordship. He was late and there was no hiding the truth as to why she was here today.

They had a lot to discuss.

Lord Arndel strode past her and much to her dismay, the gray suede buckskin breeches looked worn and a little tattered. How bad were his financial woes? He didn't bid her welcome, and her stomach twisted in nerves. For all her aplomb, even Alice understood the severity of their forthcoming conversation, and so it would seem, did he.

He sat, and with seeming reluctance, looked at her. He'd not slept, if the dark shadows beneath his eyes told her anything, nor did he seem pleased to see her. Which, she supposed, was understandable.

"I apologize for my tardiness and lack of formal attire. I was not expecting you until this afternoon."

Alice looked away, as he hastily tried to right his cravat, and, unable to do it without a mirror, left it loose about his neck, the top shirt buttons lay open and allowed her to see his too-lovely shaped neck. Had he been sleeping? The thought of him idle in his bed, half dressed or perhaps even naked, wasn't a helpful musing and she shook the deliberation aside.

"I must apologize for calling early. I have an appointment I do not wish to miss in Ashford. I hope you do not mind. Perhaps I should call another time, when you've had time to dress yourself appropriately." Alice raised her brow, narrowing her gaze when he chuckled, the sound deep and oddly, seductive. She'd meant her remarks to be cutting, anything other than this longing that had taken over her body and wanted nothing more than for him to take her in his arms and kiss her senseless. Just as he had a few days ago. What would his lordship do if she stood up and went and sat in his lap? Would his reaction be horror or hope?

"*Tsk, tsk,* my lady. You are all kindness this morning."

She sighed. "I think you know, and let's not pretend otherwise, why I am here today."

"I have no idea." He stared at her without a flicker of emotion, and Alice couldn't believe the gumption of the man. He wanted her to state it, to bring up what obviously he wouldn't. The cad.

"How old are you, Lord Arndel?"

He frowned at the change of subject. "Nine and twenty years, but I fail to see how this has anything to do with our discussion."

"I'm merely wondering if your lack of memory is due to

your ancient age, as it would seem that his lordship is nearly thirty, and so one could forgive you for your inability to remember as to why I would come."

He smiled and her stomach tightened. Alice adjusted her seat and fought to pull herself into some form of decorum. There was something wrong with her to be so out of sorts. It was most certainly not due to Lord Arndel and his ability to fluster her without even saying a word. She inwardly swore.

"You wish to discuss the ball you're hosting in my honor."

Alice ground her teeth, hating the fact he was baiting, teasing her to the point where she would lose her temper and say or do something she would regret. She nibbled her bottom lip and with a little satisfaction watched as his lordship's attention fixed on her mouth.

"Not the ball, no. Although that would be a much preferable conversation. Alas, due to your actions over the last few months, the ball and its organization will have to wait."

He didn't say anything, just stared at her with a stoic visage. "Go on, then. I wait with keen interest."

"You leave me with little choice and so I will be blunt. How long have you been the Surrey Bandit?"

"A while."

For a moment Alice didn't say a word, having not expected him to be so honest. "Is that all the reply I'm going to receive from you, my lord? *A while*. Are you not ashamed of your actions? I would've thought an apology was in order, since you stole from my family. But it would seem you believe this kind of behavior is acceptable."

"Would saying 'sorry' make what I've done to you forgivable?"

His eyes were no longer filled with mirth.

"No."

"Well then," he said, leaning back in his chair. "It is a wasted word that I do not need to say."

She gaped. Unbelievable, insufferable coxcomb. "Do you hear yourself? You sound, and forgive my language, like an ass. You ought to beg forgiveness from everyone. You have a home, land, and a daughter, although you keep her from everyone for reasons only you yourself know. And yet you would risk all of that to line your pockets with gold."

"You have no idea as to why I stole, and yes, it was wrong, but people will do what is required for those around them to live normal, healthy lives without danger or threat. And I would do it all again should my loved ones be threatened."

"Were they threatened?" she asked, wondering at his choice of words.

His lordship rubbed his jaw and looked toward the windows for a moment.

"You forget that you also stole from me, Lady Alice. Two wrongs do not make a right." He laughed, mockingly.

"Answer the question, dammit. Are you being threatened? Is there more to this thieving that you're not telling me?" Such a possibility hadn't entered Alice's mind, and on reflection, even she would consider such crimes, if her family was in danger. Of course, such thoughts were wrong, and in church next Sunday she would have to beg forgiveness for such views, but it didn't change the fact that she would still do what was required to survive.

"Language, my lady." Arndel stood and came about the desk, leaning against it before her. Alice sat back in her chair, not liking that being this close to his lordship did all sorts of absurd things to her body. It was not her own when around him, and as hard as she tried, she could not get her heart to behave.

"Your mouth is quite the dirty little fiend when riled."

Alice stood, coming up to stand almost eye level with him. "That's a lark coming from you, for as I recall, you enjoyed my mouth." Where the words came from, or the gumption to say them, Alice had no idea, but say them she did, and the heated turn of his demeanor left her knees weak and her stomach coiling in expectation.

He reached up and laid a finger against her lips, and her breathing hitched. "I wonder what else your mouth could do when tutored."

Alice frowned, not understanding the meaning behind his words. She should step away, she really ought. "And will it be you who tutors me?" His finger slid across her lips, and a heavy ache settled between her thighs. "After your kiss the other day, I find your technique lacking, my lord."

He smirked. Smirked! And Alice had the urge to swipe off such a delectable lilt to his lips. Lord Arndel was truly acting the rogue.

"I don't believe that for a moment. And no matter how much you may deny it, you liked my kiss. Admit it."

Heat suffused her face. "I did not. If anything, it only proved that you, my lord, are a debaucher and thief whom, after this ball, I shall have nothing to do with."

"Well," he said, standing and pushing her back by her shoulders before walking around to the other side of his desk and taking his seat. "How will I ever recover from the cut direct such as the one you intend to give me?"

Alice strode up to the desk and leaned over the mahogany. "This conversation is not over, sir. You must pay for what you've done, and I'm here to ensure that is the case."

"And what does the honorable Lady Alice Worthingham suggest? Please don't say you wish for another kiss, for the first one was torture enough."

Alice pushed away the flicker of hurt that his words caused. He had to be lying, for remembering back to their embrace, it had been anything but torture and he had seemed to enjoy it.

"As you know," she said, pacing before his desk. "I have a

row of cottages that are about to be renovated. I need a man on site who'll overlook all that I wish to be done. My mama has raised concerns over me doing it myself, and because I love her so dearly, I promised to be a little less…"

"In everyone's business?"

She glared at him. "No. Inappropriate, even though I don't believe doing something to help others could be deemed as such, but we must keep the upper ten thousand happy, mustn't we?"

He shrugged. "I never have, nor will I ever. And neither will I fall into your plans, so it would be best that you find another gentleman to do your bidding."

"I will not. And for two reasons," she said, holding up two fingers. "First, you have no choice. Second, I will sweeten the deal for you, even though you deserve no such appeasement."

He raised his brow. "How so?"

"Well, I'm glad you asked." He rolled his eyes and she sat back down. "The crime you committed, should I go to my brother about, would either see you at the end of a noose, or transported for life. Because of Amelia, and only because of your daughter, Victoria and I have agreed to hold what we know to ourselves. We will, and I can promise on my life, never break that promise of silence, but of course, it comes at a price."

Alice could see the muscle on his temple flex before he said, "And that fee is to help you with your cottage rebuilds."

"Yes." She smiled and he glared. "But that's not all. Gathering the only jewel in the bag was Mama's brooch, Victoria and I worked out an approximate value of £1200. Does that seem correct?"

*C*allum stopped grinding his teeth. Lady Alice Worthingham was clever, but even this went beyond what he ever thought her capable of, and he had held her in high regard. Well, until she'd come up with the absurd notion she was spouting right at this moment. "That seems correct."

"Well, forgive my rudeness, but—"

He scoffed and she paused. Forwardness, if not rudeness, was her second nature.

"What?" she asked, looking at him like an innocent child and not the devil's spawn she so obviously was.

He waved her concern aside. Something told him whatever Lady Alice had to say, he needed his wits about him. "Nothing, please continue."

"What I was going to say was that your home seems in disrepair. You're selling land, and you're stealing items from wealthy land owners. Forgive me, my lord, but your pockets are to let."

"My financial situation is not your concern, Lady Alice." He threw her a silencing stare, which of course, she ignored.

"I find speaking frank and to the point is best, and Lord Arndel, by the state of your library, anyone can assume what I've just stated. But it is here that I think I can help."

"You cannot save everyone, my lady. Now," he said standing, wanting the little minx out of his house. He'd had enough of being told what he already knew: that he was asset-rich but bloody broke. Not even able to keep his daughter safe from moneylenders hell bent on claiming their pound of flesh. "I think it best that you return to Dunsleigh."

"I don't," she said, not moving. "I will offer you a boon, and I think you should take the offer. I know you'll not see it favorably, but again, should you refuse, I shall have to think again about keeping your secret safe. For my solution will

TAMARA GILL

help you and your daughter, who is my main concern in all this trouble you've brought upon your head."

With each word out of her mouth, no matter how consuming or exquisite, right at this moment, were he not a gentleman, he'd throw the Lady Alice Worthingham out on her perfectly shaped ass. If only the solution he was sure she was about to disclose was as easy as that.

"I will, therefore, offer to pay you each week up until the equal value of the amount you stole. I'm sorry that money has caused you to act in such a way, but I believe you should swallow your pride, if not for yourself, most certainly for Amelia. No one need know of our arrangement. It'll be between you and me."

You and me. The words pulled him from the red haze he was starting to see her through. As much as she was trying to help, the thought of charity, when he'd grown up with nothing but second-hand goods and, sometimes, a peer's leftovers, made his fists clench at his side. He'd promised to find a way forward with this estate in the atrocious condition it had been left for him, but he'd be damned if he'd accept help from an interfering miss who thought too highly of herself. Not that her offer helped in the least. The money-lenders wanted the Duchess of Penworth's brooch, the last trinket in a long line of beautiful jewels that had paid off his cousin's debt.

"Forgive me for being blunt and not a little rude, but get out. Now."

She gasped and for a moment, he regretted speaking to her so, not liking the hurt that flickered through her eyes. But she needed to leave. Immediately. Before he picked her up and placed her outside, preferably on a rose bush with thorns or a freshly laid horseshit patty.

She gathered up her gloves, pulling them on vigorously while glaring at him. He marveled at her courage. Even in the face of his temper, she had a backbone. Callum couldn't help but adore her more for it. "Think about my offer. *All* of what I offer." She walked to the door and paused. "Work in Ashford commences tomorrow. I'll be there from nine."

Callum held up his hand, not wanting to hear another word. No gentleman should swear in front of a woman, but that was all he wished to do. "Good day, Lady Alice." Not that she was acting like one.

She curtsied. "Good day, my lord."

"Daddy?"

Alice stopped on the threshold and looked up to where his daughter stood at the top of the stairs.

Callum sighed, gesturing for his daughter to come down. "Amelia, this is Lady Alice Worthingham, the Duke of Penworth's sister. Lady Alice, this is my daughter, Miss Amelia Arndel."

Alice dipped into a curtsy and so, too, did Amelia. Callum smiled, knowing she'd been practicing for such situations for months. He winked at his daughter.

"It's very nice to meet you, Miss Amelia. I've heard so much about you."

Callum frowned, knowing Alice was lying to save his own rude ass at not telling anyone of his daughter's existence. Why he had not, he doubted he'd ever fathom. It wasn't like he was ashamed of her. He loved Amelia more than life itself, but perhaps he'd wished to keep her safe from people who would view her differently for not having been born a peer.

"You have?" Amelia clasped Callum's hand. "Papa, you told her ladyship about me? How exciting."

Alice chuckled. "He did and he told me you're doing very well in your studies."

Something in Callum's chest thumped hard at how kind Alice was being toward his daughter. And what a spectacular liar she was. And what a total ass he'd been.

"I am, my lady. I'm studying very hard and learning all my letters and I can count now up to one hundred."

"That's wonderful. How very proud your father must be."

Callum swallowed the lump in his throat and nodded. "I'm always proud of my poppet, no matter what she does."

Amelia smiled up at him and Callum lifted her up. Alice eyed them a moment, before she turned back toward the door.

"Alas, I must go, but thank you for seeing me today, my lord. And Amelia?"

"Yes," his daughter said, her eyes bright with expectation.

"I think we're going to be great friends, and so would you mind calling me Alice? Titles are so tiresome sometimes, don't you agree?"

"I would love to call you Alice. Thank you, my lady."

Alice chuckled at his daughter's lapse already. "I will call again, Amelia, and we'll have tea. All young ladies need to learn such etiquette if they're to host afternoons in Town when they're older."

Amelia turned to Callum. "Can Alice teach me, Papa? Please say yes?"

"Of course," he said, nodding to the woman wiggling under his skin more each day. What a truly remarkable soul Alice was, even if she was a meddler at times. "Thank you for the offer."

"It's no trouble. Amelia and I will have a jolly good time. I'm sure of it."

The footman opened the door and Alice turned to leave. "Think about my offer, Lord Arndel."

He glared at her departing figure, all good humor going at the reminder. "Good day, my lady, and thank you again for coming."

She waved a hand over her head but didn't reply.

Unable to control his ire, Callum slammed the front door

before she reached the second step. He strode back into his library, his footsteps like the drum of a war march before the battle. Various servants stopped to see what the ruckus was about, but with a steely glare, they soon went back to their employment.

He placed Amelia down on the chair before his desk, before pouring himself a whisky, swirling the golden liquid in the crystal glass before downing it in one swallow. How dare she expect him to heel to her rules? He would never, under any circumstances, be blackmailed again. Callum would sooner walk down the main thoroughfare of Mayfair naked before doing as she asked.

"Papa, Lady Alice had the loveliest gown I've ever seen. Did you see?"

Arndel looked up, having forgotten his daughter was in the room with him. He smiled and, picking her up, sat down with her on his lap.

"I must admit I didn't notice her ladyship's gown." Liar, he had noticed her attire, right down to the delicate fichu that sat across her chest that attempted to conceal the delicacies hidden beneath. He tweaked her button nose when she gave him a disbelieving stare.

"I hope she calls again. I would love to take tea with a real lady. She has lovely hair." Amelia sighed and Callum smiled. Alice did have lovely long locks, and he wished he'd managed to feel them the day they'd kissed. Not that that would ever happen again. 'Twas a shame, for no matter his lies to her, Lady Alice's untutored lips had been delightful. Another lie he'd told.

His daughter looked up at him, her normally perfect forehead furrowed in confusion. "Do all gentlemen slam doors after their guests have left? Nanny says gentlemen should always open the doors for ladies and bow in farewell, or perhaps even kiss their hand, so long as the lady has a glove on."

Guilt rolled through him at the thought of his crass, ungentlemanlike behavior. That his daughter had been privy to it made it even worse. He ought to be taken outside and horse whipped. "I apologize for what you witnessed, Amelia. I shouldn't have slammed the door behind Lady Alice. I was angry and upset over something we had discussed earlier, but even so, that is no excuse. I will be sure to apologize to her next I see her." Arndel inwardly shook his head at his own actions. *What was I thinking?* The woman, vexing as she was, held his little angel's future in the palm of her hand. He would be wise to think over her offer and meet her in Ashford on the morn, for he could never bear to lose or leave his precious girl.

"Papa, are you angry with me?"

"Of course not. What makes you ask such a thing?" he asked, pushing a lock of hair away from her eyes and meeting her gaze.

His daughter's little hand rubbed against his face and tried to pull his lips into a smile. "You look mad at me."

"Never at you, pet. I was thinking of how terribly I've acted. I promise it shall never happen again." And it would not. If there was one thing Callum honored, it was his word to his daughter.

"Will you allow me to ride Whiskers today? Nanny said I was free to play for an hour or two."

For all the years he would live, Callum would forever marvel at how changeable children and their thoughts could be. He hugged her for a moment, before swinging her up into his arms and onto his shoulders, eliciting a squeal of excitement from her.

"Well, we had better make the most of our time and get out to the stables straight away. And, when we return, would you like to have lunch in the dining room with me? I'll be all alone, otherwise."

"Oh, yes please, can I? I should practice, Papa, since I'm going to be a lady when I grow up, exactly the same as Lady Alice."

Callum walked toward the back of the house, ensuring his daughter didn't hit her head on the door threshold as they headed toward the stable. Her future was paramount, and, if for a time, he had to please the esteemed Worthingham daughter, then so be it. He would bow to her decree and ensure the little lady atop his shoulders was forever free of scandal. As for his cousin's debt and the final jewel that was due, well, he could only hope the sale of his horses and the money that would bring would be payment enough for the moneylenders.

To work for Alice for some weeks would be no hardship. Callum could only hope he could withstand the company of the little minx without strangling her...or kissing the hell out of her.

CHAPTER 11

*T*he carriage pulled up before the cottages in Ashford and Alice jumped down, not waiting for her driver to open the door. Already she could hear the hammering of wood and nails, and as she stared at the buildings, a cart full of timber rumbled down the road and stopped before the houses. The air smelled of pine and she breathed deep, liking the scent and all that it meant for the houses before her. New roofs, walls, and furniture. Wonderful things.

She watched the few men who worked. Scaffolding was being placed along the front of the dwellings and already some men were working on the roof, pulling down the leaking thatch roofing to be replaced with the new slate tiles Alice had chosen.

A man stepped outside and spoke with the cart driver, and it took Alice a moment to recognize him. Joy, unlike she'd ever known, shot through her and she couldn't stop the smile that bloomed on her face. Lord Arndel turned and nodded in welcome. Alice stared like a besotted fool. Dressed in laboring clothing that was the polar opposite to what he normally would wear, the sight left her speechless.

She'd not thought he could become any more handsome than he already was, and yet here was a man who would turn any young woman's eye. Not that she was looking at him as a husband. After his atrocious behavior, his lordship would be lucky if they ended up as friends. *Who am I fooling?* She liked him. Surrey Bandit or no.

He started toward her, and she sighed at the sight of his tan breeches and black knee-high boots that only accentuated his fine form. Alice ought to chastise herself for being so crass, but she did not. Her behavior was not that of a lady and she should be ashamed of herself, but she wasn't.

His lordship swiped off his hat and pushed back his unruly hair, that spiked a little, due to a sheen of sweat that covered his forehead. Her knees betrayed her and, for a moment, she fought not to faint.

"Good morning, Lady Alice. I hope you've come to work hard."

The glint of amusement in his eyes made her smile. "You changed your mind? I didn't think I would see you here today."

"I've conceded on a couple of your requests, but not all, and we'll discuss those changes a little later over lunch. I've booked the private parlor at the inn for our use."

Alice nodded, excited at the thought of dining alone with his lordship. Well, other than the presence of her maid. "I look forward to it."

He ushered her into the first cottage, Benny's old home, and headed to where the kitchen was located. They discussed at length the changes that would take place and going over the plans, decided the table could also be built into the house's design to save more room and additional cost for the families who would call these cottages home.

The builders nodded in understanding, but continued to work, every now and then talking to Callum and taking direction from him.

"I see you've settled in quite successfully as foreman."

"I came early, before they arrived. I suppose they assumed I was the one they should listen to when they saw a lord dressed, ready for work, and giving orders before they'd strapped their tools to their belts." He laughed. "It was a plan that seems to have worked."

They walked up the stairs and came to the children's room. "I thought the beds would be best beside the window, two bunks on either side so they have a view and sunlight, of course."

"Bunks? What are those?" Alice had never heard of such a thing, but they sounded interesting, and if the item was helpful to the family, she was grateful for any suggestions or advice Lord Arndel could give her.

"They're beds that stack on top of one another. We had them as children, due to our house being only a small cottage, much like this one. Space was utilized well."

The thought of Arndel growing up in a cottage seemed at odds to where he now lived and the title he claimed. "How is it that you grew up in such circumstances? You're a viscount now, surely your upbringing had to have been better than this," Alice said, waving her hands about the room.

"My mama, God rest her soul, married for love, which meant she did not marry for money. My father was the third son of a vicar who couldn't afford to send anyone other than his eldest to university. My father had to make his own way in the world. Mama's family disowned her and cut her off without connections or funds when she married him."

Alice touched Lord Arndel's arm as he seemed to grapple with saying such things out loud. "I'm so very sorry for her.

That must have been very hard and upsetting to lose one's family merely for loving someone not worthy in their eyes."

"Surprisingly, Mama bore it very easily, as I don't believe the Arndels were very loving to begin with, so she missed only the finer things in life. My grandmother, who's still alive, refuses to come to Kester House now because I'm a viscount. I wish Mama were alive to enjoy such theatrics. She would've relished having the upper hand on all the snobs."

Alice laughed. "I think I would've liked your mother, my lord."

He nodded in agreement, his eyes sparkling with mirth. "You remind me of her with your wild ways and spontaneity. And like my mother, you're always trying to make other's lives better. She did, too, although most of the time it was us taking charity and not the other way around."

They stood in silence for a moment, before Alice said, "So these beds, there would actually be two in total space, but four beds overall?"

"That's right," he said. "And you could make it that the beds could hold yet another on top, making six beds in total. Of course, the higher beds are for the older children, with safety rails to keep them from falling off."

Alice pictured the beds in her mind's eye and marveled at the ingenious use of space. It was brilliant. "I cannot wait to see them, and I know the families going into these cottages are going to burst with excitement at seeing what we've done for them." Without thinking, Alice hugged Lord Arndel in thanks, excited about the future prospects of these homes and his help in achieving those dreams.

*C*allum stilled the moment her arms reached about his neck, and his heart beat a crescendo that made his breath catch. The first thing he noticed was her scent—roses, rich and sweet, intoxicated him—and he chastised himself for the fool he was being. Next, he would be writing sonnets about the minx.

Her beautiful blue eyes widened at the realization at what she was doing. "Forgive me, Lord Arndel. I should not have done that."

A light blush rose on her cheeks but instead of letting her go, he pulled her closer. More surprising than her impromptu embrace was the fact she did not pull away. In fact, she met his forwardness with a little defiance, and the urge to kiss her into submission roared through him.

"There are other ways in which to thank a gentleman for his clever ideas." Callum hoped she understood that his meaning was not the one most innocent misses would conclude.

She laughed, tipping her head to the side in thought. "I will not kiss you again, my lord."

Callum barked out a laugh and let her step out of his arms. He shook his head, once again confounded by the Lady Alice Worthingham. She was much too smart for him, and, therefore, absolutely perfect. "You think scandalously," he said, teasing her. "That was not my meaning at all. I merely meant you could've thanked me verbally, or sent me a bottle of your brother-in-law's finest whisky from Scotland."

"Henry's?" she said, throwing him a teasing grin. "I'm sure he would, should I ask. He's most doting on Beth and would do anything to please her sisters."

Callum couldn't help but think to not please a Worthingham lady would not be worth your while, and should one be so lucky as to win their love and affection, one would give the world to ensure they were forever happy and content. "Thank you," he said, wishing more than he ought that her thanks had been a kiss.

His mama, although poor, had been rich in love and support from his father, and through their marriage, he had learned what it took to make such a union last and thrive. His first marriage had been one of love and affection, and he would forever love Maria and the beautiful daughter she'd gifted him.

But all things come to an end, and it was time for him to move forward and marry, find a woman who could guide Amelia through her future in the *ton* as a strong and independent woman, like the one standing before him.

"I will let you explain to the workers how to make these bunk beds, shall I?" Alice laughed, heading for the door and walking across the small hall to the parents' room. Callum followed her. The roof of this room was missing, and they could see up into the clear blue sky.

"So this is where the parents will sleep. I had thought to place the bed here," she said, pointing out a square on the wall opposite but facing the window. "What do you think?"

"I think that would be fine. The position does not hinder the door, and it gives them a pretty view of the sky first thing upon waking."

"I'm going to have doors placed on the upstairs rooms as well, for privacy."

Callum cleared his throat. "That would probably be wise." He walked farther into the room, assessing it. "You could also build in some cupboards for storage, should the families going in here not have much furniture. It wouldn't be a difficult task, nor expensive to do so."

Alice leaned against the window frame and studied him a moment. "Do you mean building chests of drawers?"

"No," he chuckled, "nothing as extravagant as that, but

merely shelving along one side of the room." Callum watched as she looked about, thinking on his suggestion before she nodded.

"I think that could work, and as the foreman, I'll leave the details of this in your capable hands, as well."

The following few hours were filled with similar conversations through all the cottages, as some were in worse condition than others, and needed alternate plans and ideas, although the original architect's drawings were always adhered to, they simply added extras to make life more comfortable within the dwellings.

Callum introduced Alice to the workers, having met some of them when he'd first inherited Kester House in its deteriorated state. A few of the men working for Lady Alice had fixed the most pressing jobs on his home—as much as he could afford, before he'd been saddled with his cousin's debts.

Alice seemed pleased with the first day's progress and by noon the roof of one house was off entirely, and the men were fixing the beams to ensure they could hold the new slate tiles.

They walked out onto the street. Locals stood outside their houses watching the building works, and some children yelled out questions to the men busy on the roofs.

"Well, I don't know about you, Lord Arndel, but I'm famished. Shall we have luncheon?"

Callum held out his arm and Alice took it. He was surprised at how comfortable she seemed to be with him, considering who he was and what he'd done. He'd thought after she found out the truth, his future would've held nothing but the walls of Newgate or possibly worse, banishment on the other side of the world in the penal colonies of New South Wales.

The inn was bustling with patrons, mostly men of all

kinds who took the opportunity to include liquor with their lunch. Upon entering, the barman nodded in welcome and waddled over, gesturing them toward the private parlor. The whole time it took them to walk from the front room to the parlor, the man expelled his gratitude the Lady Alice Worthingham had chosen his establishment to dine.

Alice smiled kindly at the older gentleman. Callum held out a chair for her to take and seated himself beside her. Although there were chairs on the other side of the table, he wanted to take advantage of the window that ran the length of the room and gave them a good view of the town's main thoroughfare.

That was what Callum told himself. It had nothing to do with wanting to be near her.

And yet, by the time the desserts had arrived, Callum had to decree that lunch was a diversion he had not needed. To watch Alice laugh, smile, and enjoy her food, licking her lips after devouring a delicious strawberry tart, was, in his estimation, too much to bear.

Again, her small perfect lips slid over the spoon, licking a drop of cream that sat at the side of her mouth and Callum adjusted his seat. Never would he eat with her again. He tore his gaze back to his own tart and demanded he get hold of his sensibilities.

"May I ask you a question, my lord?"

Her words pulled him from his inappropriate thoughts involving her mouth and he nodded. "What do you want to know?"

"You lived in Northumberland before Surrey. Do forgive me if I'm being too forward, but it sounded as if you had a comfortable life there. And yet, you've mentioned your parents struggled financially in their life."

"We were poor, that was true, but Maria, my wife, came from a respectable family. There was some peerage in her ancestry, but her father bred thoroughbreds for the well-to-do. Beautiful horses that the toffs of London fought to purchase. When I started courting Maria, and we fell in love, her father made me an equal partner in the business. And during the three years we were married, the business became more successful."

She eyed him a moment, a small frown line between her brow. "The debt of your cousin is surely not such a large sum, that with all these assets, how could you not have paid it off and be done with it. How is it that it's caused you so much trouble?"

The memory of what Maria's father had done chilled him, not to mention how the moneylenders had threatened his daughter to get what they wanted from him. He shivered. "On Maria's death, her father blamed me, cursed me to the devil, and tried to take Amelia away from me. Our agreement was not legally binding since no documents were ever signed over the partnership. He cut me off without a dime, and when I wouldn't allow Amelia to live with him, he had us kicked out of the house he'd gifted Maria and me. I fled with the few horses I had purchased with my own income and moved into Kester House when I inherited. It was not a good time."

"Is your father-in-law still living?"

"No," he said, regret churning his gut. And he would never forgive himself for not making amends with a man who'd been brought low by grief. "He passed away only last year."

She squeezed his arm and he nodded. "I'm so sorry."

So was he, and yet, there was little he could do about it now, all of that was in the past, and now he had to look to the future and figure out a way to get himself out of his current mess.

"You said earlier that you would not comply to all of my

demands. Would you care to elaborate on your decision now, my lord? We're alone as you wished to be when discussing the matter."

Callum looked over to where the maid sat before the window, where she, too, partook in the same luncheon, her attention wholly fixed on the goings-on outside.

Unable to bear the little bit of cream at the side of her mouth a moment longer, he passed her a linen napkin. "Before I start, I want you to know that my decision is final and not negotiable." And he hoped she would see sense enough to understand why and not fight him on it. After the wonderful morning they'd had with each other, he would dislike it very much if they fought now.

"Go on," she said, pouring a cup of tea while placing yet another tart on her plate.

He cleared his throat. "You wished me to help you with the cottages, and as you can see, I have agreed to do this. No matter what you think, I do wish to make amends to you and your family for what I've done, and helping to build these homes, giving what advice I can, will achieve that."

"Are you looking at this as a form of punishment?" Her bright blue eyes met his, and he read the concern in them.

"At first, I may have thought this a punishment, although, I must admit, that today has been nothing but enjoyable, so I no longer think in that vein."

Alice took a sip of her tea. "I'm satisfied that you're trying to right a wrong, even if only through manual labor. It is enough for me, and of course, Victoria agrees."

She leaned closer to him and the smell of roses met his senses, making him wish she'd move closer still. "You are in need of funds, my lord, and I've removed the asset that would've given you the blunt you needed," she whispered. "For the honest work such as you started today, as discussed, I'm willing to offer a wage in lieu of the goods."

"I cannot take money for goods I never owned in the first place. Furthermore, I don't want your money, although offering it is more than I deserve."

Her lips thinned and she sat back, watching him. "So it would seem you're a changed gentleman, a man who has seen the error of your ways." She paused. "Tell me why you stole, Lord Arndel."

He sighed, the sound filled with regret. "It's no secret my cousin had run up debts I could not pay. The debts were, frankly, beyond my reach, even if I sold what was not entailed. I refused to lose the estate under my control, but it was looking less likely every moment that I could keep it." He paused, not sure how much he should tell her of his troubles. "I will find a way forward, and in a legal sense, I promise." The way ahead would encompass him insisting the last amount due to the moneylender be in cash, not an emerald brooch. Would it be enough for the criminals who haunted his shadow? He didn't know, but he hoped so. It had to be, before the thugs arrived on his door, and made good on the threats against his daughter.

After thinking over Alice's proposal, he'd concluded he could not take anything for the work. It would be wrong, and if he was to prove himself not the cur on Society, he had to stick with this decision.

*A*lice didn't doubt that Lord Arndel had pride, but perhaps in this instance, too much was on hand. "So you have debts, why not marry an heiress and have her dowry settle your financial woes." Her maid seemed a little less interested in the street beyond, and more on their conversation. "You may go for a walk if you like, Mary. If you could call back for me in ten minutes, we will return home."

"Yes, my lady," her maid said, bobbing a quick curtsy and leaving.

"I don't want my wife to think the only reason I married her was to gain her money. And you cannot tell me that should a gentleman offer you marriage under such a guise and you became aware of the fact, that it would leave you happy."

"Of course not." Alice would hate such a truth becoming her reality, but it was common enough through the *ton* for those who had little option. "I know I'm lucky in that my brother is a duke and I'm forever secure in my position, married or not. And I know others are not so fortunate, but we still have a choice, if given the option, when truth is involved." His eyes narrowed and Alice wondered what he was thinking. If only she could be so forward as to ask him.

He cleared his throat, turning to look out onto the street. "Furthermore, I do not wish to be honored at the ball. Under the circumstances you're well aware of, I do not feel comfortable at such praise."

"Of course you are to be the guest of honor. Not only would not doing so seem odd now that the invited guests know why we're hosting the ball, but because you have repented. And...right at this moment you are trying to redeem your actions as the Surrey Bandit." He raised his brow and she frowned. "Your past career as a highwayman was a momentary lapse of concentration. Your neighbors wish to meet the new Viscount Arndel, and let's not forget, should you choose to continue your horse-breeding enter-prise, the connections you make at the ball can only help, not hinder."

"After all that I've done, you would still welcome my company?"

Was that trepidation in his voice? "We all make mistakes,

my lord. And I believe everyone is entitled to a second chance. Of course you're welcome."

"Thank you," he said, placing his hand over hers.

Alice stilled, having not expected such a thing. She pulled away, fussing with her napkin in her lap, before slapping it onto the table. "You may tell me to mind my business, as I know you've been more than honest with me today, but what will you do with the debt your cousin left you. How will you pay it?"

"That is not a concern I wish to lay at your door, but be aware that I'll not be marrying any rich miss for it." He finished off his drink and Alice watched as his throat worked while swallowing.

Her mouth dried at the sight of stubble across his jaw. Her fingers itched to touch him. Was it hard and prickly, or would it tickle her lips just as it had the last time they kissed?

"Very well," she said, standing to distract herself.

His lordship followed her lead. "There is one thing I wish to know, Lady Alice."

"Just Alice would be fine, my lord. I think we know each other too well for such formality."

He laughed, nodding. "I believe you may be right."

She looked up at him, smiling. "What is it you want to know before I bring this delightful day to an end?"

"What story did you concoct to explain the magical appearance of your mother's bauble?"

Alice grinned. "We told Mama we found her brooch on the side of the road on our way back from Ashford."

"And the duchess believed you?"

Alice fought to roll her eyes at such an absurd notion that she would not. "Of course she did. Our mama had no reason not to believe our tale."

"I do not doubt it."

They walked outside and Alice spied her maid walking

toward the inn. "Are you going to be present at the cottages most days, my lord?"

Arndel looked in the direction of the buildings, squinting a little with the sun starting to drop in the western sky. "I shall of course, as I said I would." He stepped closer and Alice had to look up at him. "And you may call me Callum when we're in private."

Callum... Alice decided she liked the name. "Good day, Callum." She grinned and headed toward her carriage, hearing Mary's steps following close behind. Alice could feel the heat of his lordship's attention on her, right up until the point she stepped up into her vehicle. She enjoyed that notion.

CHAPTER 12

*O*ver the next few weeks, Alice hardly had time for anything other than the cottages and preparing for the ball, which was only a few hours away. Her mama had taken her and Victoria up to Town for new gowns for the Season, which, too, was to commence in only a week.

Alice wondered if she'd taken on too much. Everything seemed to be happening at once. Her maid pulled her hair and she gasped.

"I'm sorry, my lady. I cannot seem to get your hair to do as I wish tonight."

Alice passed her a strand of diamonds that would thread through her hair. "It looks perfect as it is, Mary. Don't fuss too much more with it." Only a couple of strands of hair sat against her shoulder, and she smiled, loving the soft but structured coiffure Mary had achieved.

"There, my lady," her maid said, standing back and smiling. "Are you pleased?"

Alice studied her hair a moment and thought it the best her maid had ever done. "You've surpassed yourself. Thank you, Mary." Alice stood and pulled on her silk gloves. "No need to wait up for me tonight, I can put myself to bed."

"Thank you, my lady."

Alice walked from the room and already the sound of laughter floated upstairs.

She headed down the staircase and could see a flurry of people arriving, her mama and brother greeting them in the foyer before a footman showed them toward the ballroom, which looked near full to capacity.

Excited at the thought of dancing, laughing, and drinking champagne until the early hours of the morning, she smiled. It had been so long since she'd attended a ball, well, at least since last Season, but a party was always welcome, especially when held at home, at her beloved Dunsleigh.

Spying her sister, Alice headed toward Victoria. "You look beautiful. Are those Mama's pearls?"

"Yes," Victoria said, touching her necklace. "She let me borrow them for the night."

"You will turn heads." Alice teased, gaining an eyeroll from Victoria. "I think not, but even if I do, I'm not interested. In fact, I may leave early."

"Why?" Alice took a glass of champagne from a passing footman, smiling her thanks.

"My pointer is in labor. I may have puppies even now, and here I am, at a ball where no one holds my attention."

"No one?" Alice looked about the room. Lord Cavendish certainly seemed interested in Victoria, if his study of her was any indication. Poor man, her sister was oblivious to him, as she rattled on about her dogs.

"I am glad that the storms that threatened earlier passed without causing too much strife. It is warm, though, probably too warm for a comfortable ball. We may have to have the staff open some windows to allow in some air."

"Or we could go outside." Alice winked at Victoria, taking

a sip of champagne. "Has Lord Arndel arrived yet? I cannot see him."

"I don't know how you cannot. He's over near the supper room doors and has been staring at you since you arrived. He's awfully handsome this evening, even if he is a criminal."

Alice shushed her. "He's promised never to act in such a way again. You should not speak in such a way, and here, of all places."

Victoria sighed. "I apologize. I'm just not in the mood for a ball. I didn't mean to snap at you."

"Apology accepted. Why don't you go talk to Mama. She seems to have finished greeting everyone, and once you've done that, you can slip away. Nothing will happen here tonight that you've not experienced before."

Her sister's eyes brightened at the notion. "Do you think I could dare?"

Alice shrugged. "Why not? No one will notice." Her sister didn't stop to wish her a good night, but strode toward their mama like a woman on a determined mission. Alice laughed, shaking her head at her younger sibling.

Casually, Alice looked to where Lord Arndel stood. Was he really watching her? He was and the moment she met his eyes Alice realized her sister had been correct. Heat radiated from his look and the breath in her lungs vanished.

Of course, men had looked at her in such a way before, but normally she'd ignored them. She could not ignore Lord Arndel...Callum. He made her yearn for things she shouldn't. Over the past three years, seeing both her sisters marry in love matches had made her more determined than ever to find the same kind of union. To love and be loved in such an unrelenting, intense way would be wondrous. Something told Alice that to be loved in such a way from Callum would be even more so.

His lips lifted in a small smile, and her heart did a little flip. Alice took in his attire for the night, the superfine coat that accentuated his lordship's fine physical form. For the past two weeks, they had been in each other's company quite often but tonight was different. To be near him again where there was no work to do, no choices to be made, or supplies to be ordered, changed things.

And to know that within the next few hours they would dance, enjoy each other's company simply because they could and for no other reason, left her body in turmoil in the most delicious way.

Heat crept across her skin, and she flicked her fan open, waving it idly before her face. She hoped his lordship would disregard the rose hue that burst across her cheekbones. He pushed away from the wall and strolled toward her.

"Lady Alice," he said, finally making her side and bowing.

Alice curtsied, ignoring how the deep tone of his voice made her insides melt like ice on a hot summer's day. She smiled. "Good evening, my lord. I hope you've been enjoying yourself."

"It seems you're most talented, Alice," he said, leaning close to ensure privacy. The breath of his words sent shivers across her skin.

"How so?" Alice asked, noting that she could smell the delicious scent of lemons wafting from his skin. Had his lordship taken a bath prior to attending the ball? Within a moment of thinking of such a thing, the image of Callum in a hip bath, laying back, relaxing with soapsuds about him, left her speechless. She swallowed.

"It seems that you're not only capable of renovating cottages, but you're able to pull a ball together with nary a bit of trouble. You should be very proud. The room looks marvelous."

He smiled and the secure little world she lived in that kept Lord Arndel at a distance shattered about her. Of course, she'd seen him smile before, had even heard a laugh or two, but tonight it was carefree and true, and he looked more handsome and relaxed than she cared to admit.

With less wit than she ever thought herself capable of, she stared at his mouth that continued to talk of the guests and how accommodating everyone was being. His voice was a seductive hum, and his lips looked so soft that she wanted to whisk him outside so she could feel them against hers. The corner of his eyes crinkled and a dimple appeared on his left cheek. She was lost. But worse, was the fact that she was not the only one to notice.

Alice cast a slaying glare to those who dared look at him. "Thank you for the compliment. I am glad the ball meets with your approval, as it is in your honor, after all, to introduce you to the local gentry."

Concern flickered across his face.

"What is it, Callum?"

"I don't feel comfortable for the ball to be in my honor, after what I've done. It's not right."

"Only Victoria and I know of that, and we intend to keep it that way. So for tonight you must play your part. The ball is in your honor and so it will stay. Make peace with it, my lord, for I'm going to introduce you to a great many people, and you'll need to keep your wits about you."

Her words brought forth a grin. "How so?"

Alice gestured to the room and the many eyes that were upon them. "Look around. You, my lord, are the most popular gentleman this side of London. I hope you've brought your dancing shoes, for they'll be in for a lot of use tonight."

"And if I only want to dance with you? What then?"

How wickedly delightful that he was being so honest with her. "I can but dance with you twice, any more than that and we'll be the talk of the county."

His hand clasped hers and he placed it on his arm, holding it there. "You're the only woman I want in my arms."

She bit her lip, pleasure coursing through her. "Come, my lord. You have guests to meet."

He conceded, and over the next half hour, Alice took Lord Arndel about the room and introduced him to an array of people, all of whom lived in Surrey.

The orchestra started up the strains of a minuet, and Alice watched as her mother opened the ball, wishing everyone a lovely evening. Alice turned back to the small group she and Lord Arndel stood with, only to see him bow before Miss Keyworth, Baron Lymington's eldest daughter, and ask her to dance.

For a moment, betrayal coursed through her, before her manners came to the fore and saved her from causing a scandal with her glowering visage, especially when the simpering miss all but fluttered her eyelashes at Callum and gleefully took his arm.

Alice made a quick departure from the group and walked toward her mama, who stood watching the ball beside the musicians.

Alice took her mother's arm and watched the dancers, while really only watching one set, who right at this moment, were laughing and chatting amicably.

Her mother considered her a moment before she said, "Are you well, my dear? You seem a little out of sorts."

Alice shook her head, not liking that her mama was so insightful or that she felt on the brink of tears. How absurd to be disappointed that she was not dancing with the most handsome man in the room. Feeling his arms about her, his laughter and smiles just for her.

The dancers seemed to float together and then apart, and Alice fought not to grind her teeth. Miss Keyworth was too short to be suitable for Lord Arndel, and should this dance ever end, she would be sure to tell him of that fact.

Not that she was considering his lordship for her husband, not now that she was aware of his past as the Surrey Bandit. She was a duke's daughter. She couldn't marry a man with such a shady past. If the secret ever came out, her family would be ruined.

A passing waiter stopped before them, and Alice procured herself another glass of champagne. "I am well, Mama, maybe a little tired, if anything. Do not get overly concerned. Perhaps we should mingle. There are a lot of people here tonight who we haven't seen in some time."

"In a moment, dear," her mama replied. "I'm not sure if you've noticed, but there is a flurry of fine gentlemen here this evening. Many of whom are looking in your direction, not that you have taken the time to notice, so fixated on Lord Arndel."

Alice met her mama's eyes and read the mirth that sparkled within them.

"Of course, there are many gentlemen looking in our direction. Am I not standing next to the most beautiful duchess in all of England?" Alice laughed at the high color that covered her mama's cheeks.

"You tease, but I'm serious." The duchess smiled and nodded toward one man in particular. "That is Sir Liam Sledmere, a baronet. I believe he is the most handsome man here. Don't you agree?"

Alice shrugged.

"He has a small estate here in Surrey, but spends a great deal of time in York. How I would love to visit that part of the country, should I have family there, of course."

Alice chuckled at her mama and her barely veiled hint about whom she should marry and where she should live.

"York is a very great distance from Dunsleigh. I would hardly see you, should I consider such a match."

"I think you should consider any offer that makes your heart not your own." Her mama threw her a knowing look. "And I do believe he will ask you to dance very soon, and I should so love to see you dancing, just as your sister is."

"She is?" Alice looked out onto the floor, having not expected Victoria to still be at the ball, or dancing, for that matter. "Lord Cavendish is very handsome and kind, from all reports. He has three sisters."

"Yes, and all younger than him, with stepsiblings from his father's second marriage." Her mama paused. "Victoria wished to leave only a half hour ago. I'm so glad I wouldn't allow her departure, for we would've missed how lovely she looks dancing and enjoying herself with something other than horseflesh or dogs."

Alice laughed, knowing only too well how much Victoria loved her animals.

"Lord Arndel also seems to be enjoying himself."

Much to her annoyance, Alice looked to where Callum danced with Miss Keyworth. "I introduced them before the dancing commenced. She seems quite taken with his lordship."

"And he as well, although perhaps you ought to tell Lord Arndel that his hand needs to be on her hip and not so far about her waist."

"I will do no such thing." Alice gasped. "I cannot tell his lordship such a thing. Even for me, that's a little forward."

"You are his friend, are you not? The two of you have certainly been in each other's company a great deal over the last few weeks. I don't believe he would see such advice as crass or uncalled for. He's new in Society and we should help those who're capable of making a faux pas without their knowing."

Alice conceded the point, although with any luck she would forget her task by the time she saw Lord Arndel again. "I will see what I can do."

Her mama patted her hand. "Good girl. Now, check your gown, my dear, Sir Liam seems to be heading in our direction."

"York is too far away, Mama. I'm sure I can find a husband by Season's end that is closer to southern England." She didn't want to think about how very close Lord Arndel lived. Although Alice had not wanted to be too close to her family, her thoughts had changed on the subject. Home was beautiful and a safe haven for her whenever she wanted. And Surrey was very pretty, and everyone knew her here.

"Just think, my dear. Having you situated thus would be a blessing for when I travel north to visit Elizabeth in Scotland. We could break our journey with you in Yorkshire. I believe his lordship spends the better half of six months a year at the estate. Beautiful gardens, I'm told."

Alice studied the baronet, watching as he procured her brother before heading more purposefully in their direction. Nerves battered her innards, and she fought not to lose her equilibrium about her forthcoming meeting.

She'd never met Sir Liam before, although there was much gossip about him. His scandalous lifestyle in London had always intrigued her, but to think of herself as his wife, of having to live with a lifestyle that was not what she wished for, made her decision easy.

He checked his cravat as they came to stand before them, and she smiled, liking the fact he was anxious. Maybe his lifestyle had been an exaggeration of the truth. It wouldn't be the first time, she mused, dipping into a small curtsy as he bowed.

"Mama, Alice, may I present Sir Liam Sledmere."

Her brother called over a footman for drinks, and Alice

took the opportunity to study his lordship. He was handsome, to be sure, but not as dark as Lord Arndel, the angel of the underworld. No, Lord Sledmere was golden-haired and blue-eyed.

"Pleasure to meet you, Sir Liam. I understand you reside in Yorkshire?" the duchess asked, giving Alice a pointed glance.

"Yes, madam, at Holbrook Hall." Again he fidgeted with his cravat and Alice wondered if he had a nervous tick.

Her attention stole over his attire. The silver embroidered waistcoat, which suited his complexion very well, made his lordship seem ethereal.

"Sir Liam is Lord Arndel's cousin, although once removed."

A member of Callum's family was here? Alice gathered herself, having not expected such a thing. "You're the first gentleman we've met of his lordship's family. How lovely for you to come and celebrate his entrance into our small society."

"Ah yes, Lord Arndel. We are not close, but as I also have a house here in Surrey, I wished to attend, if only to see you, Lady Alice."

She smiled, although his response was odd, as if he wanted those about him to know Lord Arndel and he were not friends and never would be. "Surely, I should think you'd be happy Kester House is in such capable hands again."

"Again?" Sir Liam asked.

Alice narrowed her eyes, not liking how he was eluding her statement. "The previous earl was also your cousin, I presume. I should think you know very well as to what I suggest as to the running of the estate, or lack thereof."

Sir Liam's eyes narrowed and so, too, did Alice's. "The late viscount ran the estate into the ground and near lost everything before it was inherited and saved by Lord Arndel."

Sir Liam laughed, but even to Alice, it sounded condescending. "It seems you hold Lord Arndel in great regard. How very kind of you." She decided, on the spot, she disliked the man.

Alice shrugged. "I don't shy away from the truth, and what I said is the truth, is it not?" When he didn't answer, she smiled to buffer her assault. What an ass of a man. "Does Lord Arndel know you're here? I should think he would like to see his *cousin*." At the accentuation of his familial relation, Sir Liam looked out toward the dancers, biding time before he spoke.

"I'm sure I shall see him soon enough."

"As a gentleman, I should expect nothing less."

"Alice," her mother chided, glaring at her before smiling at his lordship. Alice stopped listening when the conversation turned to gardens and the hot weather that was well received, but terrible for some of the more delicate plantings.

She looked out onto the dance floor, the strains of the dance slowing toward an end. Although it didn't stop Lord Arndel's dance partner from gazing up at him with a look that bordered on adoration.

Silly little fool. What was she trying to do? Have him propose on their first introduction?

"Would you care to dance, Lady Alice? I believe a cotillion is next."

Alice fought not to roll her eyes. Or perhaps by the little muscle twitch on his temple she didn't succeed. More than likely it was another odd twitch the man had.

At her mother's pointed stare, she took a deep breath and nodded. "Thank you, my lord, I would like that very much." She allowed him to lead her onto the floor.

The dance, as Alice expected, was uncomfortable and

long, so grueling, in fact, that she thought seriously about walking off the dance floor. Sir Liam was a rude, uncouth, boring man—one she didn't need to see, or talk to, ever again. That he hated his cousin Lord Arndel was evident with every barb he could muster against him.

Eventually, she was able to escape, only to see Lord Arndel dancing yet again with the same chit he'd stepped out with earlier. Did he not know the rules within the *ton*? She would have to remind him it was frowned upon to step out too many times with the same young woman or it would be seen as a statement of imminent interest, or betrothal even.

Alice did not find either consideration amusing, and by the time supper arrived, even she'd had enough of the night. The ball was nothing like she'd expected. Her sister had escaped, her mama was deep in conversation with the matrons who patroled the outer fringes of the room, and she was alone.

Alice stood to the side of the ballroom with a glass of champagne, her only company, while not even the bubbles that floated up through the crystal glass were enough to affect her mood. It had soured the moment Lord Arndel walked Miss Chambers, a gentleman's daughter, into supper. Did he not want to spend any time with her at all?

Not once had she caught him looking in her direction to see if she were enjoying the night, nor did he seek her out for a dance. She'd had plenty of gentlemen asking for a dance throughout the night, but the one man she wanted to dance with had denied her the opportunity.

It was not to be borne.

Alice wandered into the supper room, placed a crab cake onto her plate, and went to sit with a group of women friends. Their chatter was amicable enough but filled with talk of the handsome Lord Arndel, which was exactly what Alice wanted to avoid.

She quickly ate and made her escape, walking through the ballroom and exiting through a door beside the gaming room. The hallway was dim, with only a few scarce candles alight, as she made her way toward the terrace.

Outside, she sighed in relief, as this side of the terrace had not been opened for the ball and remained in darkness. The moon was a perfect circle in the night sky, and she studied it a moment, before sighing and walking over to a stone seat nestled within a cluster of ivy.

She caught a flash of movement to her side and Alice stifled a squeak.

"You're free, I see."

The statement, spoken with the deep baritone she'd longed to hear all night, made her stomach clench, along with annoyance at being ignored.

Lord Arndel stepped into the light from farther along the terrace and strolled toward her. Alice remained seated as he came to sit beside her.

"I've been free most of the night, if you'd bothered to look, although by the amount of dancing you've partaken in, I doubt you have."

He grinned, and she ignored the awareness he always brought forth in her, not wanting a reminder as to why all the women in the ballroom were tittering over his lordship.

"I would not have taken you as the jealous type."

Alice gasped. "I am not, sir, and you should apologize for saying such a thing. I'm merely concerned for your reputation. You seem to have forgotten that to step out more than twice with a young lady is frowned upon. Or that your hand, when dancing, needs to be above their hip, not on their ass."

He scoffed, leaning back into the vine. "My reputation is quite sound, I assure you, but as for you, out here in the dark with a gentleman, unmarried...well, I cannot say the same for you. Now who is being scandalous?"

Alice gritted her teeth because his remark was true. Damn it. "I'm safe with you, for we, my lord, are not romantically involved, nor will we ever be." He was scant inches away from her, and Alice was reminded of the last time they'd sat too near each other. Her breathing hitched and she shuffled away.

"My cousin, Sir Liam, is not a gentleman I would suggest as your future spouse."

"That, my lord, is not up to you," she countered, a small part of her delighting in the fact that he sounded as jealous as she was. "And please, pray tell me, who you have in mind for the position, if not him? Until the Season commences, there are not many to choose from here in Surrey."

"He's a pompous ass and I'll not let him have you."

There was vehemence to his statement that sent her heart galloping. "Will you not? And please, do tell me how you're going to stop me if my head is turned in the baronet's direction?"

He looked at her. "Is it?"

Alice shivered from his heated stare and she shook her head, words eluding her. "No, but one day a gentleman will turn it, and then what will you do?" She looked back toward the gardens, her cheeks burning from his continued study of her. "You cannot stop love and I'm determined to find it, whether you like the gentleman or not."

CHAPTER 13

*C*allum was captivated by Lady Alice's lips that shone in the moonlight with a soft pink hue. "It is not up to me who you marry, my lady. I hope, whomever it is, he's as good and kind to you as you deserve." He grinned when, for the first time since seeing her exit the house, a whisper of a smile tilted her lips.

"Do not concern yourself over your cousin, my lord. I came to the conclusion he's an ass, among other things, well before you stated it. In fact, I almost feel sorry for you to be a relative of his."

"My cousin will inherit the title and Kester House should I die, and I suppose being the golden-haired lad whom the family adores, he seems to think he should've inherited this time, instead of me. But"—he shrugged—"the law is what it is, and solely for my daughter's sake, I would not change our situation now, not for anything." His daughter would have a good, secure future, more so than if they'd stayed in the north. Here, in Surrey, with his family's name behind them, she would be elevated in Society where her life would be easy and carefree, as all children's should be.

"And you're going to abide by the law and not slip back into your nefarious past, my lord?"

"I have promised such, have I not? Why you continue to bring up the Surrey Bandit is beyond me, unless you miss him? Or his kiss, to be exact."

He grinned as she threw him a glare, fidgeting with her hands in her lap. Oh yes, she was thinking exactly what he was, of their mouths fused, along with their bodies. Of feeling his blood pump through his veins and reminding him of what it was like to love a woman.

"I do no such thing."

"Really?" He leaned toward her, smelling the soft scent of roses that wafted from her hair. "You don't miss that kiss you shared with an outlaw?" He certainly did. In fact, since that day, he'd thought of little else. With each day they had worked together at the cottages, every time Alice had spoken to him, had been alone with him, he'd become more obsessed with tasting her again, possibly doing more than kiss her, if she'd allow.

Callum stood and paced to the balustrade, needing space.

"The kiss was hardly satisfactory. In fact, the memory has almost been erased from my mind, it was so forgettable."

"That will never do," he said, striding back over to her, having heard enough of her denial. He clasped her hand and hauled her up against him, eliciting a startled gasp from her delectable mouth. Her eyes widened in shock, before challenge lit her blue orbs and it was one battle he was only too happy to best her at. "Forgettable? I must be slipping," he said, taking her lips in a searing kiss.

It was an error of judgment the moment their lips met, for all he wanted was more. So much more than she, the daughter of a duke, would be willing to give him.

Though she'd not allowed him to hang for his crimes, something told him she'd not forgiven, nor would she forget, what he'd done. And as much as he'd love to kiss the chit in his arms for the rest of his life, and to protect and cherish her sweet soul, Callum had an inkling she would never marry him, due to his own misbegotten actions when desperate times had called for desperate measures.

Through the kiss, he punished her for what he'd done, kissing her deep and long, pulling her into a world she knew nothing of, but one he desperately wanted to show her. If only he'd could've walked a different path, their future could be so much more, so different. But it was not to be.

Alice pulled back, staring up at him, her breathing as ragged as his. "I ought to slap you for kissing me so." Her hand came up and clasped the nape of his neck, sending a shiver of need down his spine. Callum gritted his teeth against pushing her up against the vine at her back and showing her what outlaws did with virginal ladies.

"I'm guessing you're not going to?" He grinned as she shook her head.

"No. Not tonight. Maybe tomorrow."

Callum laughed and swiped his lips gently over hers, teasing her with his mouth, making him ache. He wondered if she, too, had a need that pulsated between her legs, making her stomach tumble like a ball down a hill.

"You're teasing me," she said, trying to deepen the kiss and failing when he kept her just out of reach.

"I want so much more than to tease you, Alice." Callum sat on a nearby bench and pulled her onto his lap, positioning her legs to straddle his. "Let me pleasure you, I beg you."

Her breaths came in panting gasps, and he bit back a groan. Damn, he wanted to see her take flight into pleasure, to feel what it could be like between a man and woman— before all the useless fops bowed before her skirts this Season.

"I cannot." She shook her head, but did not move. "I may be forward in some things, but not this. I cannot be ruined."

Callum kissed down her throat, sliding his tongue across the tops of her breasts that with each breath came up to meet him. He slid his hand up her waist and cupped one soft globe of her breast, surprised at the weight of it in his hand. Shutting his eyes he pictured her naked, of him holding her breast and laving her nipple with wanton abandonment. "I'll not ruin you, I promise. I'll merely give you pleasure."

She bit her lip, before nodding her acquiescence. He sighed, although there would be no relief for him. Already, his balls ached, his cock rigid and ready. Callum pushed away as much of her gown from between them and, clasping the cups of her ass, hoisted her hard against him. Her hot core nestled against his prick and he guided her up against him, sliding her excited nubbin against his hardened length.

She bit her lip, watching him with awe and he swallowed, having never seen anything more beautiful than the sight she now made.

"Trust me that what I'm about to do will leave you a maid, but I want more." He ripped open his frontfalls and nestled her against his member. Oh, sweet mercy to have her mons against him, wet and ready, almost broke his resolve to behave.

"Callum, we cannot."

Alice pulled away and he shushed her, shaking his head. "I'll not take your virginity, but let me give you pleasure this way. I want to show you what it can be like between us, if only you'll let me."

She moved of her own accord against his sex and he groaned.

"I trust you," she said, undulating again. "Oh my," she gasped as he increased the glide and pressure of their movement. Alice caught on quickly and was soon moving of her own accord against him. And sweet heaven, the fight to not lose himself before she did was something he didn't think he would conquer.

"This feels so good, too good to be wicked."

Callum groaned, taking her lips as she rose and fell upon his lap. The thought that this wasn't his smartest idea flittered through his mind. To have her in his lap, to show her the arts of pleasure in such a way opened a floodgate of wants and needs he shouldn't have teased her with. They could be caught, her reputation ruined in an instant. The duke would run him through without a second thought and rightfully so.

But the thought of her marrying another pushed the worry aside. If, by having her this one time made her stop and think about accepting another man, this delicious torture, this pain would all be worth it.

She quivered in his arms and he knew she was close. Her strokes became hard as she took what she wanted, pushed herself against a release she'd never experienced before.

"Oh Callum," she sighed against his lips. He guided her hips against him, wishing that he could make love to her, claim her virtue, and make her his forever. He wanted to hear her scream his name, fill her with himself, and watch as her eyes closed in bliss.

Unable to deny himself, he pulled down one side of her bodice and kissed his way toward her nipple. Her hands clasped his hair, her fingers spiking against his skull as he laved the sweet beaded flesh.

She moaned and it was the most exquisite, erotic sound he'd ever heard. "I want you so much, Alice." He suckled hard, pulling her nipple farther into his mouth, and she clasped him tighter against her.

"Yes, like that. Keep doing everything that you're doing."

Nothing would stop him from his current actions. He

kissed her breast with abandon, while kneading the other. The feel of her soft, sweet skin against his lips, of having her in this way even if it left him wanting more, was perfection.

She was close, and so, too, was he. Callum clasped her ass and pushed her hard against his cock with heady abandon.

"Callum…" His name a plea more than anything else gasped from her lips as she shattered in his arms. Small, perfect tremors ran through her, and he ached to come, but not here, not like this.

He gritted his teeth, pushing her to enjoy, to take all that she could in his embrace. For a moment they sat there, both of them breathing hard, and nothing separating their bodies. To control the roaring need that consumed him, Callum breathed deep and promised himself that he would have her one day, not as a tryst at a ball, but as his wife, warm in his bed, for every night of every year they would have together. But first he would finish his dealings with the moneylenders, lay to rest the Surrey Bandit and come to her a man of little wealth, but no hindrance to their happiness, no veiled threats that could injure her or Amelia at any time.

"Was that forgettable?" Callum asked. Unable to deny himself one last kiss, he dipped his head and swept her lips with his.

Alice shook her head, her hands idly running over his cheeks. "That, my lord, I shall never forget."

CHAPTER 14

*A*lice walked back into the ball feeling as if she were floating on clouds. Her body felt heavy, full, sleepy, and yet more awake than it ever had before.

A shiver stole over her as she strolled into the supper room. She took a glass of champagne, downed it quickly, before grabbing another. Her body purred with pleasure still, and the thought of Callum's lips against her breast, the roughness of his unshaven jaw, left her wondering if he'd marked her.

Because he'd certainly marked her in a lot of other ways, ways that deep down in her soul, she wanted to be marked again and again.

Arndel entered the ballroom from the terrace doors, his hair back in place after her hands had messed it up. He pinned her with a hot, intoxicating glance, before moving through the throng and she lost sight of him.

"Lord Arndel seems upset. Did you have a falling out?"

Alice tried to calm her heartbeat that had nothing to do with her mama coming up beside her and startling her. "I don't believe anything I've done has upset his lordship." If anything, she'd left him in a state of uncomfortable need. For if the hard-as-stone bulge against her sex was anything to go by, he'd not found his own pleasure, only given her hers.

And what a marvelous thing she'd found tonight. After shattering in Callum's arms, Alice could see why her sisters had been so keen to marry their husbands, especially if one could find such bliss every night. You would be a simpleton indeed, if you remained a spinster for all of your days, having never experienced such resounding, incandescent sensation.

Her mama pulled her toward a group of old cronies who sat watching the dancing, which had recommenced after supper, the lot of them reminding Alice of a pack of wolves watching the lambs at play.

"No, Mama, Lord Arndel and I are not at odds." Alice looked about the room but could not see him, but she did spy Victoria again, back from checking on her dog and her impending litter of puppies. "I see Victoria is dancing. I did not think she would return to the ball."

"I had a servant go fetch her. You two are my last unmarried daughters, and I'm determined to find you matches this year."

Alice didn't think her sister would find love with her current dance partner. In fact, the grimace on her face that was only thinly veiled by her good breeding, said a lot as to what she thought of her companion.

"Ah, see, Sir Liam is dancing with her now. Doesn't she look happy, my dear? Maybe she will marry the gentleman. He does seem more enamored of her than he was with you."

Alice choked a little on her drink. "Such praise, Mama, I'm sure I'm thankful, in any case. I do not wish to pursue Sir Liam. His character reminds me of Lord Riddledale, and look how mad that man turned out to be."

"No one can be as evil as Riddledale." Her mama studied

her a moment and frowned. "You do look a little flushed, though, my dear. Are you well?"

"I'm perfectly well." Even if her mind refused to cooperate and calm itself after what Callum had done to her not a half hour before. Alice caught sight of him as the throng shifted and swayed about the room. A horde of young women followed his coattails like a raft of ducklings following their mama. He sipped a glass of champagne, laughing and smiling at their jokes, but even she could not fail to notice his attention kept snapping back to her. They may have been standing right beside one another with the effect his gaze had on her senses. Nerves skittered across her skin, and she longed to return to their veiled garden seat to finish what they'd started.

"Your bodice is all askew," her mama said, turning her so her back was to the room, and righting the garment. "And your skin is a little blotchy above your breasts. Have you been eating strawberries again? You know they don't react well with your complexion."

"I only had one. Cook made them look so delicious dusted with sugar, I couldn't go past them. I'm sorry." Thankfully, her mama accepted her fib. Her sister finished her dance and walked away from Sir Liam without a second glance. "I'm going to join Victoria. I will see you later, Mama."

Her mother's parting words to have fun met her ears as she made her way across the room. That she could feel Callum's heated stare also left her steps light and her body singing with new wisdom, and now she had to decide what to do with that insight.

To use it for good or wicked…

*C*allum allowed the chatter of the young ladies, daughters of his neighbors, to wash over him. It was a welcome reprieve to hear the mindless chatter, as it seemed to dissipate his need for Alice Worthingham quite quickly. The little minx currently stood talking with her sister, her sporadic glances his way sending his ardor to rise with each heated glance.

"The Worthingham daughters are beautiful, are they not? You never told me your neighbor the duke had such delectable siblings. I should visit my estate in Surrey more often, if only to bask in their glory."

Arndel leveled his cousin with a lethal stare. "Pity that the ladies looked less than enthused by your presence, Liam. I hope the observation does not deflate your overly inflated ego. We should hate to see you forlorn." Sarcasm laced Callum's words and he turned back to the dancing, hoping his cousin would disappear.

"Do not be fooled by a woman's tricks, both of them loved the attention I bestowed upon their heads." The lout brushed off a piece of nonexistent lint from his suit. "Are you opening the London house this Season? The family expects it."

Arndel could care less what the family expected or what they wished. They had never tended for him or his family, after his mother had married beneath her station. As far as he was concerned, they could hire their own London house and be damned their hope. "I must admit, I'm surprised by such a question. I did not think they paid attention to what I did with either Kester House or the London abode. And, if I remember quite correctly, Grandmother stated I was a blight upon the family name—one she wished she could erase." Should he even wish to open the house he could not. He paused mid-sip of his whisky. He *could* rent it out for the Season, though...

Liam smirked and Callum had the urge to knock him onto his pompous ass. If it were not for where they were, it was exactly where the high-handed miscreant would've ended. "Grandmother wanted me to ask, and so I have. I can see you still harbor bad feelings toward them all."

A simmering anger sparked into a flaming temper and Callum fought not to hit him and be dammed where they were. "*Grandmother* made it perfectly clear, when I came into the title, what they thought of me and my family." Arndel procured another glass of whisky from a passing footman, downing it in one swallow. "Why are you here, Liam? I certainly do not care for your presence, nor do Lady Alice or Lady Victoria, whom you seem so overwhelmed with. Why don't you go back to Yorkshire and work on our family kissing your nether regions some more. You're wasting your time here with me."

Liam quirked his lips, laughing, and Callum gnashed his teeth. "I shall return soon enough. Perhaps with the delectable Lady Alice on my arm. She is a pretty one, if I may be so bold. Victoria is comely, too, but there is a wildness about Lady Alice that I find most pleasing. I believe she would be a bed mate to rival the best courtesans in London."

"Watch your bloody mouth. I won't have you speaking about either woman in such a disrespectful manner." He looked about, thankful no one was listening. The two ladies were the best of women, always looking out for those less fortunate than themselves. God damn it, they had saved his neck from meeting the hangman's noose. They had not had to, but had done so, if only for his daughter.

"Ho. Ho. Ho," Liam said, holding up his hands in surrender. "Why so protective?" The man studied him a moment, before his face cleared with enlightenment. "Ah, so it would seem my older cousin likes one of the Worthingham girls. Oh, how jolly this will make Grandmother. It actually may make her view you more favorably, if you were to marry a woman of such high rank."

"I will do no such thing, and I would appreciate you not speaking about my life, or those around me, to a family I care nothing about." And never would, not after how they had cut his mother off without a penny to her name. A woman without family had not an easy life.

Liam grinned. "Give over and tell me what's going on between you and Lady Alice. I would hate to impinge on your understanding, if there is one."

Arndel fisted his hands at his sides. "I can assure you there is nothing going on, or ever will be, between Lady Alice Worthingham and myself." Not that he didn't wish for there to be. Already, not an hour since he'd held her in his arms, he again wished to hold her, watch her eyes darken with need, whisper his name on her lips. Alice had haunted his dreams for months, and now, after what they'd done tonight, his dreams would be nightmares. With every waking moment, she heated his blood in more ways than he ever thought possible, and that he respected and admired her made the emotion all the more fierce.

"Really," Liam replied, disbelief painting his tone. "From the impassioned looks that are passing between the two of you, something is." His cousin tapped his chin. "I wonder if it has anything to do with when you disappeared at supper, along with the delectable Lady Alice. I hope you've been behaving yourself, my lord. The family would dislike it very much if you fathered another child out of wedlock."

"Amelia is no bastard, and should you state such a fact again, I'll bloody your nose here and now."

Liam shrugged. "Does Lady Alice even know you're a

father, that you were married before? That you killed your wife?"

Callum shook his head, unable to comprehend how vindictive his cousin was. "Maria's death was no one's fault, not mine or hers. How dare you insinuate such a thing to me, and not even in the privacy of my home, but at a ball being hosted in my honor. But then," he said, scoffing, "I know why you're being such an ass here and not at Kester House. You're a coward. A man who prefers to hide behind the skirts of the women present, in the hopes that I will not strike you down for such insolence. Don't be fooled, Cousin. Push me far enough, and I will hit you no matter where I stand."

"As I said, I was merely curious as to what lies you've spread across the county."

Callum took a calming breath, thankful the bastard standing beside him did not know of the Surrey Bandit and his association with the criminal.

"I must admit, I'm looking forward to the Season now. To think I shall be able to court the Worthingham women in London in only a few weeks makes the long journey from Yorkshire worth it."

"I'm sure they'll look upon the opportunity differently."

"They are getting up in age, though, don't you agree? There are certainly smile lines at the edge of both their eyes, but what's that, when such a large dowry comes associated with the chits."

"Neither woman would ever marry you. You're a fool, if you think otherwise." Callum tried to breathe through the simmering anger that roiled inside him. His cousin was baiting him on purpose, had done so for as long as he'd known him.

Due to the fact they had both grown up in the north, Callum had known his relatives who lived in the great house only five miles from home. He'd gone there as a boy once when his mama's sister had married the Baronet Sledmere, and he'd never forgotten the cruelty of the baronet, or the nasty son from the man's first wife, who had looked down on them as beggars in the street. The pain inflicted on his dear mama that day had made Callum realize he'd never seek out the family or fight for their acceptance. And when, as fate would have it, he'd unexpectedly inherited the estate, he'd taken what was theirs and never looked back.

"They would, if I charmed them. There are not many who would not. *You're* the fool, if you think otherwise."

"Why are you here, Sledmere? Cut the veritable dribble and tell me, so I may end this conversation and get the hell away from you." His cousin grinned and Arndel wanted to smash the smile off his face.

"I hear the gentlemen you're acquainted with in London grow impatient."

Callum frowned. "Who grows impatient?" Dread pooled in his gut, and Callum had an inkling that what he was about to hear would not be to his liking. How did his cousin know?

"The debt our late cousin left the estate in is also partly mine." Liam chuckled. "Poor old Robert, he really was a simpleton, always putting his finances on too high a regard than he ought. He offered to pick up some debts of mine from the moneylenders in the East End, had it added to his own. Stupid fool."

"You bastard. I highly doubt you had the decency to pay back your debt before he died. I know I've never received a dime from you in relation to paying what is owed, so tell me, are you going to cough up the blunt, or leave it for me to pay back?"

Sir Liam took a sip of wine, nodding to a passing debutante who blushed furiously at the attention. "Our cousin was a fool and I never intended to pay back the debt. He owed me money and never paid it back. I merely thought it a means to equal the playing field."

"But you're happy to saddle me with your debt, along with his."

"You inherited the estate and what was Robert's is now yours, but I thought I should warn you, since we're family, after all, that the men expect their payment by month's end or they may visit you and your precious daughter in Surrey."

A red haze dropped like a curtain before Callum and he sneered. "I have spoken to the gentleman you so kindly warn me of, and I informed them, as I will inform you, they shall have their blunt, but should they step one foot in my house, they will not be leaving it again, if you comprehend my meaning."

His cousin bowed. "I comprehend you very well."

"Ensure you do." Callum walked away, lest he do something he would regret. He headed for the house's main entrance, calling for his carriage as a footman came out to greet him. He would not stay and listen to another word from Liam, not under any circumstances. On the morrow, he would apologize to Her Grace for leaving early.

Watching as the carriage came to a halt before the doors, he stepped up into the vehicle and sighed in relief as he sank into the leather squabs. Restless fury coursed through him and the need to hit something, or do something strenuous and hard, consumed him.

The thought of the cottages entered his mind and he yelled out to the driver to head toward Ashford. There were a few chores that he could finish by the light of a candle, and it was well past midnight. In any case, morning would soon be here.

Callum leaned back against the seat, taking a deep calming breath, knowing that if he ever met with his cousin again, it would be too soon. The thought that Liam was somewhat responsible for the debt he now carried left him shaking with fury. How dare he come here and demand Callum pay the money as soon as may be, or else. Especially, when none of the financial woes he'd inherited were of his own doing.

It wasn't to be borne, and he would die first before either of the Worthingham girls married anyone remotely similar to his bastard family member. After the reprieve they'd bestowed upon him, it was the least he could do.

CHAPTER 15

*A*lice rose early the following morning, the restless night before made trying to get some sleep a moot point. Her dreams had been filled with the memory of Callum's lips against hers. Of how he had pulled her hard against his flesh, making the ache between her legs unbearable. She wanted more.

So much more.

She cursed and pushed Juno into a faster gallop, needing to rid herself of the longing that bombarded her every thought, her every*thing*. The feelings he evoked in her were not what she wanted. *He* was not what she wanted. All her life she'd prided herself on helping others in need, of being truthful and direct with anyone she met.

To want a man who'd stolen from her and others, and who had broken the trust of his peers, went against everything she believed in. His cutting remarks last season were nothing compared to his escapades as the Surrey Bandit. She could forgive him for being an ass, but a highwayman? A thief? She wasn't so sure.

Damn Arndel and the emotions only he could arouse. It

would take her weeks to get over what he'd introduced in the most scandalous and intoxicating way. That a man and woman, a husband and wife, could love one another in such a way, bring pleasure to the other by doing such things was something she'd never known about. Now that she did, well, she wanted to know what else his lordship could teach her, show her, bring forth in her. If only her conscience would allow it.

She slowed Juno as the outskirts of Ashford came into view, the sleepy village still dormant at this early hour. The birds had only just started to sing when she'd saddled her mount, not wanting to bother the young stable lad who only had Saturday mornings to visit his family.

Alice debated whether to go and check on the cottages, one in particular for which she'd recently received the bedding materials. Her mama had helped her pick what was most suitable for the families going into the homes. It would be one less task to do another day, if she called in now and finished off the rooms.

Being Saturday, no builders would be about, so she pushed her mount forward and cantered into town. Coming up to the first cottages, she was pleased that no one was around to see her attire, her breeches and riding jacket were not exactly deemed appropriate for a duke's daughter, but in her unsettled mood, she'd seen no need to please others.

Riding around the back of the homes, Alice tied up Juno in the narrow alleyway, and pushed through a wooden gate into the courtyard each property came with.

Lifting a small brick beside the back door, she located the key and entered what would be the laundry that sat off the kitchen. Locking the door behind her, she left the key on the built-in kitchen table and headed upstairs, the smell of freshly cut timber, oils, and dust met her senses and she smiled. It was an odor she'd become used to, and it now represented change and progress—two things she loved most in the world.

Making the second-floor landing, she walked into what would be the parents' bedroom and stopped. Her mouth opened and she snapped it shut before her shock was marked.

Lord Arndel stood and turned toward her, his own surprise at seeing her there clearly written across his features.

Alice didn't know what to say, but her eyes certainly had a will of their own. Her attention snapped to his chest, his very shirtless chest, that shone with perspiration in the warm little room.

She'd never seen a man who was not her brother clothed such and the sight of him did odd things to her insides, left her lungs without air, and her lower belly somersaulting with nerves.

"Lady Alice." He seemed to struggle for words. "What are you doing here?"

Alice walked over to the bed and picked up the paper packages stacked on the new straw-filled mattress. "I came to set up the room, as this cottage is almost complete. This room was cleaned last week and I wanted to check that everything had arrived that I needed to finish it off."

He looked at the parcels and back to her. "I came here after the ball to finish off a few small jobs that required my attention. This room is indeed all set."

"You haven't slept?" she asked, wondering if he was as unsettled as she.

"I never tried, for I knew I would not."

She nodded, knowing exactly how he felt. "Are you done with your work? I can leave, if you have more to do."

"No, don't go," he said, holding out his hand to halt her. "I'm finished."

Alice nodded, feeling awkward after what they'd done last evening with each other and now she wasn't sure where that left them, or what was expected of her from this point forward, or if she wanted him to expect anything from her at all. It was all such a muddle.

Needing something to do, she started to untie the strings holding the paper packages together. "Did you want to help me with the linens? Unless you have somewhere else you're supposed to be."

"I can help you," he said, coming to stand beside her, picking up another package and tearing it open. Alice smiled, noting how differently they went about their tasks, she with care, Lord Arndel with none whatsoever.

The linen was dark in color, as her mother had suggested for the working families. White cloth would never do in such households, and Alice studied it, liking the look of the fabric, even though it was nothing like what they had at home.

She walked to the other side of the bed and opened the bottom sheet, watching as Callum grappled to control his side of the bedding. "Tuck it under the straw mattress, the weight of the bed will hold it in place."

He did as she instructed, walking over to the top sheet and copying her earlier action of throwing it over the bed. "I didn't think a duke's daughter would know how to make a bed."

She grinned, throwing him a mischievous smile. "You would be surprised by what I know, my lord."

"Callum, please. No one is here."

Alice didn't need the reminder of how very *alone* they were. The air all but shimmered between them with a magnetism that Alice was fighting with all her might. "Callum, then." She smiled. "Mama thought we should know all about the running of a house, and there was a time when I was younger that I followed the maids about Dunsleigh, bothering them with questions and helping them with their chores. They tolerated me well enough, but I do think they were more than relieved when something else caught my attention."

Arndel laughed, helping her with the woolen blankets that had also been posted up from London. "I can imagine you following about the maids, your golden hair in pigtails, your eyes bright with enthusiasm."

He walked over to her, running a hand through her hair that had fallen down during her hasty ride earlier. "I think, should I have known you when we were children, I would've liked you, Alice Worthingham. Would've wanted to be your friend."

Her heart beat in a rhythm that was beyond control, so much so Alice thought it may jump out of her chest. "And now? Do you like me now?" He moved closer still and her knees grew weak. She licked her lips, eyeing his naked chest that was too close, and yet, not close enough.

"I do."

The breath in her lungs expired. "I like you, too." Her words were but a whisper, and even knowing all that she did of Callum, what she said was true. If anything, she liked him too much.

He stood before her, and why she decided it would be a good idea to reach up and touch his chest, Alice would never know. The hardened planes of his body met her palm and a headiness swept through her, hot and wanting. This moment, right now, was where she belonged and nothing had ever been so right.

Slowly he bent down and kissed her. Without qualm, Alice reached up and wrapped her arms about his neck, pinning herself against him. He reached around her, his strong, muscular arms holding her hard against his body.

Alice let out a little squeak when he lifted her off the floor and walked her backward toward a work table set up against the wall.

She pulled back, gasping as he stepped between her legs, the hardened length she had pleasured herself against only the night before tempting her yet again to sin. And she so wanted to feel what he could do for her, to have him caress her toward the mindless pleasure he'd bestowed last night.

A small frown line marked his brow and she reached up to wipe it away. There was no time for worrying thoughts, no time to think better of their situation. Alice knew very well what she was doing and the risk she took being here with him, and yet, she wouldn't change her decision for anything.

Even her own morals were silent right now.

Here is where she wanted to be, and what she hoped they would continue in this small cottage room was what she wished for beyond anything else. "What's wrong?" she asked, when he sighed, stepping back a little.

Callum ran a hand through his hair, a pained expression crossing his handsome features. "Nothing. Everything." He sighed. "Do you really want to know what I'm thinking?"

"Yes." She nodded, hoping it was equivalent to her thoughts.

He raised his brow, leaning in and placing small kisses against her neck. "I'm thinking that I want to push you up against the wall, slide those very tight breeches that will haunt me for years to come, from your legs, and ruin you here and now."

Alice shivered at his words, her mouth parched from her ragged breathing. His lips left a line of fire across her chest and her fingers curled into his hair, holding him close, loving the sensations he brought forth within her. "And what is it that you'll do, my lord?"

He let out a self-deprecating laugh. "I'm going to set you

on your feet, walk you to the door, and not allow myself to follow you lest you only make it to the kitchen downstairs."

The hunger in his gaze left her speechless and solidified exactly what she wanted. She didn't want to go, nor did she want anyone other than Callum to propel her into womanhood in its most delicious, decadent way.

She clasped his breeches and pulled him back against her, his eyes, dark with need, widened and he shook his head. "You're playing with fire, Alice, and trust me, you don't want to be burned."

Alice leaned forward and kissed his chest, tasting the salty residue of his hard work. "You're wrong, Callum." She untied the little string at the top of his pants that held them together. "I know exactly what I'm doing." Next, she flicked the top button on his frontfalls, watching as understanding dawned on Callum's face. Excitement over what they were about to do made her ache, literally ache, between her legs. "And I've always had a thing for fire, its complexity and heat, its power and wildness." Another button slipped undone and the front flap of his pants fell away. With a boldness she didn't know she possessed, Alice slid her hand in and against his bulging flesh, wrapping her fingers about his length.

She bit her lip, watching him as she stroked his shaft, his breathing ragged. Callum reached out and clasped her face, his eyes fierce with a need that left her breathless.

"Are you certain?" He kissed her quickly, gasping against her lips when she tightened her hold of him, stroking long and sure.

Alice nodded. "I am."

Her words had the effect she hoped, and, throwing all caution aside, Callum did exactly what he'd said he would. He pulled her off the workbench and ripped her breeches from her body, leaving her as bare as the day she was born from the waist down.

With no time for modesty, he lifted her up again on to the table, shucking off his own pants before dragging her against him, rubbing her flesh and leaving her moist and impatient.

"I want you so much," he said, kissing her deep. Alice lost herself in the moment, enjoying the awakening this frenzied need brought forth.

She'd never known a man's penis was so soft, yet hard. It was the most odd, yet brilliant, thing she'd ever beheld. And Callum himself was unexpected. He shivered, pushed himself against her, laved kiss after kiss upon her, touch after delectable touch, so different to how Alice had thought her first time with a man would be.

Having spoken to young wives in town, a lot of them had said the marriage bed, or workbench in this instance, was uncomfortable, over quickly and unsatisfying, unless it resulted in a child.

And yet, the looks she'd seen her sisters bestow on their husbands, and the way Callum was looking at her now, like she was his whole world, that everything started and ended with her, made her wonder if those women were merely unlucky in their choices.

That perhaps there were men in the world who gave and received pleasure equally.

Callum's hand slid down her hip, clasping her bottom before touching her stomach and delving between her legs. She moaned, clasping his nape. The bold embrace against her most private of places relieved a small amount of need that coursed through her, but still, it wasn't enough. She wanted more. Much more.

"You're ready for me." Callum nipped her lip and she moaned as he slid one finger within her. Her body seemed not her own, and wrapping her legs about his hips she pulled him closer, liking the feel of him inside her, pushing against a secret little spot that left her breathless and in need of him. All of him.

"Damn it, I need to go slow with you, but you test my self-control."

Alice liked the sound of his voice, rough and without restraint. That she, Alice Worthingham, had made a gentleman want her, exhilarated her more than anything ever could.

Impatient for more, Alice placed the tip of his member against her and urged him to finish what they'd started. Callum took deep, calming breaths against her neck, the muscles across his shoulders taut and fighting what Alice had recognized as a losing battle.

For today was, when she thought back on their associa-tion, always going to happen. For weeks a simmering attrac-tion, a flirtation, had thrummed between them. Yes, they disagreed, argued even, but always, beneath such repartee, there'd been this. A conflagration of two bodies, two souls that would never be satisfied unless they were together.

"Damn it all to hell. I have to have you."

Alice gasped and stilled as Callum thrust deep and hard into her, taking her virginity within a moment of time. He stopped moving, holding himself against her, kissing the lobe of her ear while whispering sweet apologies over the pain he'd caused.

The sensation of him seated within her was…different, to say the least. Where once she was empty, now she was heavy and full. She realized, with some relief, that she liked him where he was.

"I'm sorry, love," he said.

She shook her head, wiggling a little to accommodate him more. "I'm fine. In fact, I'm more than fine." Her voice sounded breathless, wanton even. Callum swore under his breath before he slowly pulled out and then slid back in again with exquisite care.

"Tell me if you wish me to stop."

Alice pulled him down for a kiss, relishing in the feel of his lips against hers while their bodies were together in other, more delicious places. This act between a man and a woman was truly a marvel, and the more Callum increased his pace, sliding his hands about her bottom and shifting her a little against him, made her body sing and climb to pinnacles she'd not known existed.

She clasped the nape of his neck, holding herself against him as he pushed into her, dragging her into a world he'd only recently shown her to exist. Alice wrapped her legs about his waist, feeling the wood beneath her bottom, and the hard planes of Callum before her. If only they were naked, to have him kiss every part of her body, to tease her as he'd done the night before.

The fleeting thought that this could happen again, if they snuck away and used the cottages late at night, thrilled her beyond anything.

"You're so beautiful," he breathed against her lips, watching her as he led her toward a pinnacle, a relief from this desperate yearning that grew to a conflagration of pleasure. "I can't get enough of you," he gasped.

Alice shivered at his words. She was so close, her whole focus shifted to where they were joined and she fought for release. Needed to shatter in his arms with him inside her.

"Keep going," she begged as he pushed hard and deep, quick strokes that threatened her hold on reality. "Don't stop, Callum."

Callum's strokes became harder and faster and then exquisite torture burst through her body like a ray of light. Alice moaned his name as tremor after tremor racked her core before Callum's own shout of ecstasy sounded against her throat.

They stayed entwined for a little while, until their breathing was level and heart rates calm.

Callum stepped back, a sheepish look to his face that made her laugh. "Are you all right?" he asked. "Truly?"

Alice slid off the workbench and, leaning up against him, wrapped her arms about his neck. His hands came about and clasped the globes of her bottom and even after all they'd done, her body purred with expectation. With a need only he brought forth. "I told you I'm fine. What I would like to know is when we shall do that again."

He grinned, shaking his head. "Minx." He laughed. "Not today, but perhaps in a few days' time. I must travel to London, but I'll be home four days hence."

"London?" Alice stepped out of his hold, wondering what would take him to the city. Was it the unpaid debt he owed that took him there? The thought of him trying to garner more time to pay his cousin's debt, against people who had little care for other's concerns, left dread churning in her stomach. "Why?"

"Estate business, nothing to concern yourself with." He tapped her nose, and bending over grabbed her breeches. As he stood, Callum ran his hand along the inside of her leg. She shivered. "I'll miss you when I'm away, and I'll think of nothing but you and your delectable self."

Alice slapped his arm, taking her breeches from him. "I'll miss you, as well. Don't stay away too long."

"Nothing would keep me away," he said, kissing her deep and long and all thoughts of London and why he was traveling there floated out of her mind when he picked her up and threw her onto the bed, before joining her.

"You may be right," he said, sliding his hand under her shirt and touching her breast. His fingers circled her nipple and Alice bit her lip, her body aching for more of the same. "Waiting four days before I touch you again is too long."

Alice chuckled, but allowed him his way, only too happy to have him exactly where he was.

"I agree," she sighed.

It was many hours later before Alice rode out of Ashford and toward home.

CHAPTER 16

*A*ll was well at Dunsleigh until, two days after Callum's departure, the house was in an uproar. Victoria bounded through her bedroom door as Alice was having her maid put the finishing details to her toilette. Today she'd opted for a few sprigs of blossom in her hair, and overall, she liked the effect the white little blooms had on her light locks.

"Mama is beside herself. Her room, Sister, is beyond redemption, and you must come and calm her immediately."

Alice stood, dismissing her maid and waiting for the girl to leave before speaking. "Why, what's happened?" The despair on her sister's visage raised the hairs on the back of her neck.

"The emerald brooch is missing. Mama swore she left it in the drawer beside her bed for safe-keeping and now it's not there. She's demanding answers from her maid, and the poor woman is half scared to death. If Mama doesn't calm down soon, I'm sure she'll have a fit and collapse."

Alice shushed her sister. "Best that you calm yourself as well, before you, too, suffer the vapors." She walked over to

Victoria, ushering her to the door. "Let us go help Mama find it. I'm sure she's misplaced it, that's all."

Victoria shook her head vehemently, her curls bouncing about on her shoulders. "Mama says she has not. That she especially placed the brooch beside her bed, and that is where it should be."

They left Alice's chamber, walking quickly to the duchess's rooms that her mama had taken over not long after their father had died some years before. They found Josh in the room, going through cupboards and drawers, as well, and a flurry of maids, some on hands and knees, looking for the missing jewel.

"Oh, Alice my dear, it has gone again. I am beside myself." Her mama slumped onto the bed, laying a hand against her brow. Alice sighed, knowing that her dearest mama was wont to overexaggerate.

"I'm sure we'll find it. Now, can you remember when you wore it last?"

"I wore it to the ball, but it pulled on the lace fichu so I came upstairs and placed it in the drawer beside my bed. I swear on all of your lives that is where I put it."

Alice went over to the bedside cabinet and searched through it, noting little letters, no doubt old love notes between her parents, pencils, and some sewing gear, but no brooch. Certainly, the emerald jewel and the case it sat in was missing.

"Have you checked the gown? Perhaps you never removed it and just thought so."

"I did remove it. I may be one of the oldest persons living in this house, but my mind is sharp and clear. I took it off and placed it here," she said, poking the cabinet top.

Alice patted her arm, but turned toward a maid who stood beside the armoire. "Please check the gown, in any case. If we're to determine that the brooch is indeed missing, we need to check everything twice."

The maid did as she was bid but the brooch was not there.

"It's not attached to the fichu either, my lady," a young maid stated, while standing beside a large chest of drawers.

All eyes seemed to be on Alice when it did not turn up. "If the staff could go downstairs and check the ballroom, supper, and card rooms that were used on the night of the ball that would be most appreciated. Let me know immediately, if the jewel is found."

As the door closed and only family remained in the room, Victoria turned a worrying glance her way. "We shall find it, Mama. Do not fret."

Josh walked over to the bed and handed their mother a glass of water. "I'm sure it has not gone far. Do not despair."

"Victoria and I will check our rooms, as you did come and check on us prior to the ball starting. Maybe it fell off and you're confusing this ball with one of the many others we've held."

Her mother pinned her with a withering glare. "I'm not senile. I know what happened to my brooch. Someone has stolen it."

Alice couldn't meet Victoria's hard stare, for the thought had crossed her mind when it had not turned up in the room. Had the jewel been stolen yet again, and if so, by whom? Alice knew who the Surrey Bandit was, and Callum would not have done this, and yet…

"Come Alice, the sooner we start the search, the sooner we alleviate Mama's distress."

Without a word, Alice followed her sister from the room, walking back to her own. Victoria shut the door with a snap, rounding on her. "I knew Arndel wasn't to be trusted. The thieving bastard has stolen the brooch back."

Alice shook her head, not willing or wanting, to believe such words. "No, you're wrong. Callum would not do that." Not after he'd made such passionate love to her and let her fall in love with him, would he break such a trust. He couldn't have done it. He promised the lifestyle he'd led was over.

"Callum? Are you on a first name basis with the gentleman now?" Her sister threw her an assessing look. "You were with him that night for a time, do you think him capable of such an act of deceit?"

"No." Alice could not. "Not at all. In fact, he left early, from what I remember." Had gone to the cottages, where she, too, had ended up...

"Probably because he'd stolen the brooch and didn't want to be caught."

"You're wrong, Victoria. He would not do that."

Would he?

Her sister paced before the mantel and Alice's stomach churned. *I can trust Callum. I can. Can't I?*

"You need to go speak with him, ask him if he knows anything about it. I know it seems wrong, and rude even, but he was the Surrey Bandit, after all. It's not like he's such an honest, polite soul."

Alice sat on the bed, looking out the window and the green rolling hills that lay beyond their land. How would she ever tell her sister what she must? "I cannot do that."

"Why not?" her sister stopped pacing and turned to face her.

"Because," Alice sighed, fortifying herself. "He's gone to London for a few days. *Estate business*, he said."

The condescending laugh her sister bellowed made her cringe. "He's gone to London. Well, how fitting such a trip to the capital is, wouldn't you say?"

Alice ran a hand over her brow, the small ache of a

megrim starting to thump behind her eyes. "He wouldn't do such a thing, not now, at least."

"Not now, what does that mean?" Victoria threw up her hands in despair. "You must admit, the timing is too coincidental for us to be wrong. You've been duped, Sister, by a wolf in sheep's clothing."

"No, I have not. I know him," she said, standing. "He wouldn't do such a thing." But the more Alice said the words, the hollower they sounded. Was her sister right and she wrong? A lone tear slid down her cheek and she swiped it away, beyond mortified that she was crying.

"Are you crying?" Victoria strode over to her and sat. "What have you done, Sister? And don't you dare say *nothing*, for I won't believe it. You never cry, so these tears must be about more than Mama's brooch."

"I cannot believe it of him." The memory of that day, the sweet love that Callum had made to her after their frantic first meeting of souls could not have come from a man who'd deceive her so. "And if such a crime can be laid against his door, then I am ruined."

Victoria gasped. "Oh Alice, please tell me you've not been indiscreet."

"Indiscreet is such an odd word to use." Fast would be a better term.

"The day after the ball, you were gone most of it. Where did you go?" Victoria clasped her shoulders and turned her to meet her sibling's eyes. "What have you done?"

Alice couldn't form the words to tell Victoria what it was that she'd partaken in. More tears streamed down her face and she fumbled for her handkerchief.

"You gave yourself to him, didn't you?"

Alice nodded, shame washing through her, along with despair. "Over the many weeks we've worked together on the cottages, I suppose I fell for his charm and easy manners. I know it was wrong. He'd stolen from us after all, but he promised he was sorry. He swore I could trust him and that he would make it up to us all. That he would never steal again." She shrugged. "I believed him. I thought I was falling in love with him."

"Oh Alice. I think you already are in love with him." Victoria pulled her into a hug, her hand running over her back. "We need to go to London. We received word only this morning that Isolde and Merrick will be arriving in the capital tomorrow for the start of the Season. We could beg Mama to go visit her and use the time to track down Lord Arndel and see what he's about."

Alice dabbed at her cheeks, sitting up. "You're right. We need to find out if he's the devil's spawn who stole the jewel."

"Isolde mentioned they were attending the Cavendish ball that marks the beginning of the Season. We could go along with them. If Lord Arndel is in Town, he'll be there. From what I remember, he's friends with the duke."

"Yes, he is." Although how, Alice didn't know, as they were quite different men. "But I can't believe he'd deceive me in such a way. I'm sure there's a reasonable explanation for all of this."

Victoria's lips thinned into a disbelieving line. "I hope so, but you must prepare yourself for that not to be the case. Now come, let us ask Mama and see what we can do to calm her before we go."

Alice nodded and followed her sister from the room, hoping against hope that all of what happened was coincidence and Callum wasn't guilty as he seemed.

*T*wo days later, Alice stood at the entrance of the Cavendish's large London home, looking over the *ton* who were fortunate enough to be invited before the Season commenced next week. The scent of an array of perfumes and sweat swamped her, and instantly she missed the cooling, sweet air of the country. A year ago, this was a life she'd grown to love, the Season something to look forward to, but no longer. Now, it seemed like a market for debutantes to marry someone they hardly had knowledge of and did not love.

Alice scoured the room for the man she'd been looking for the past day and a half. She'd sent a letter to his townhouse but received no reply, nor had she heard any talk of his lordship that he was even in Town.

So where was he?

She tapped her slippered foot against the polished wood floor. Had he not come to London after all, but had lied about that, too? This morning they had received a letter from their mama stating the jewel was still missing. Alice handed her shawl to a footman and waited to be introduced to the highest-ranking members of London Society.

After their introduction, Alice, with Victoria by her side, waded into the throng of guests. They were greeted with enthusiasm. Two eligible, wealthy duke's daughters were always good sport to have at these types of events. To Alice, it set in stone why she needed a love match, not a match made of social standing and security.

Something she'd thought she had gained with Callum.

They walked down the short flight of stairs into the ball-room itself and Alice turned to Victoria. "We'll look about separately. If you see him, don't say anything, I will speak to his lordship."

Her sister nodded, walking off in the opposite direction.

Alice was stopped here and there by friends, women who wanted an introduction, and the previous year's gentleman admirers. She was polite and jovial as required, but the whole time her mind whirred with thoughts that Arndel wasn't here. That their plan had been a complete waste of time, and they would not find out the truth.

That he had left her. The only consoling thought was that his daughter Amelia was still in Surrey. If his lordship wished to disappear, he would not have left her behind. Alice was certain, above all else, of that fact.

It wasn't until after supper that Alice conceded their plan hadn't worked. She took a deep breath and looked up at the ornate, painted ceiling, anything so as not to allow the tears that threatened to run down her cheeks. Arndel wasn't here.

Gaining control of her emotions, a glimpse of a gentleman, taller than most, caught her attention across the room, and the breath in her lungs seized.

Callum walked toward her, the smile on his face brought forth her own before she remembered why she wanted to see him. Swallowing her unease at how she was to ask his lordship a question that put his honor in jeopardy, she dipped into a small curtsy as he bowed before her. His eyes were warm and welcoming and she fell a little more in love with him despite herself. How was she ever to do this?

"Lord Arndel, we meet again."

---

*C*allum took in the beauty that was Alice Worthingham. He had the overwhelming urge to pull her hard against him and hold her close. How he'd missed her the past few days, and so many things had happened. Things that made his heart ache, but had also relieved him beyond measure. If his meeting with the moneylender went to plan, the debt hanging over his estate and the threat to his family, would be no more. And he could set out to earn the love of the woman before him.

Why he'd never thought to rent out the London property left his mind spinning, and having to sell his horse stock broke his heart. But, in time, he would purchase them back and set out to breed his thoroughbreds as he used to. He hoped they fetched a good price at Tattersalls tomorrow.

"Lady Alice, you look...stunning." He eyed the gold shimmering gown with heavy beading and stitch work across the bodice. That he was aware of what that marvelous bodice held at bay made him impatient to get Alice someplace private so he could kiss her to his heart's content.

She nodded, but didn't venture much in return, and an inkling of concern pierced his conscience. "Is all well with you?"

"Yes," she said, looking fully at him for the first time and keeping her attention fixed. "Can we talk?"

Callum looked about the room and noting everyone was either in their cups, playing cards, or dancing, none of those around them taking any notice of their conversation. He clasped her hand, placing it on his arm, and pulled her out onto the terrace.

The cool night air met his senses and thankfully cooled his ardor a little. He walked her toward the end of the terrace that was less occupied and stopped before the corner of the house. "What is it that you wish to say?"

"Did you receive my note? I sent one to your townhouse yesterday upon our arrival in Town."

"I haven't read my mail from yesterday. I apologize, I would've replied had I known you'd written." The distant tone of her voice gave him pause, and he wondered what had happened in the few days since he'd seen her last. "What's happening, Alice?"

She bit her lip and fear took hold. Something was wrong. Very wrong.

"Why did you leave early from the ball? You never said."

Callum ran a hand through his hair, picking his words wisely. His cousin, the baronet, didn't need to factor in his life, nor did he wish Alice to be burdened with what he now knew of the man. "I argued with my relative over the estate and our deceased cousin. I'll not go into details, but needless to say, I didn't wish to stay and have to listen to him or his septic tongue."

"Oh, I'm sorry, I did not know." For the first time tonight since this conversation had commenced, Alice sounded sincere. His fear eased a little. "There is something that I must ask, and you're not going to appreciate it. In fact, you'll probably think, and rightfully so, that it's unpardonable."

His fear was back. "Go on." Callum spied the other couples returning indoors, leaving them practically alone.

"The day after I met you at the cottages, I awoke to Mama in a panic. The emerald brooch that Papa gave her is missing again—"

Callum held up his hand, not sure he was hearing her words correctly. "And you suspect me of the crime, if this conversation is going where I think it is."

Shame washed over him that Alice would think so lowly of him. Yes, he'd stolen in the past, and from them, but he'd given her his word that he'd never do such a thing again, and that she would doubt that promise hurt more than he thought it could. Especially, after all they'd experienced together.

"I had hoped it was not true, but Victoria thought it too much of a coincidence with you leaving the ball early and then heading for London."

Callum cringed, seeing how that would seem, but it didn't change the fact he'd not stolen the damn jewel again and was innocent of the crime. "I did not steal it." He ground his teeth at having to justify himself, yet it was his own damn fault. If he'd not had to take the life of crime as his way out of financial trouble, none of these questions would be flying at his head now.

Callum reminded himself he'd been left little choice. Blackmail and threats against one's daughter was all that was needed to make a man do as he was bid. A father would do anything to keep his daughter safe.

She studied him for a long while, and he could tell she was unsure of his words. "You don't trust me." It was not a question, just a statement of fact. He shook his head as pain shot through his chest. "Nor, it seems, do you believe me."

"Do you wonder at it? I know who you were, Lord Arndel. I know what you've done."

Looking up the terrace, the last couple walked in the opposite direction to where they stood, and he took the opportunity to pull Alice around the side of the home, the cover of darkness giving them some privacy. "I know what I did was wrong, and I know it is hard for you to trust me, but believe me when I say that I did not take the brooch. That is true."

"Why are you in London? And I don't want to hear it's because of estate business. I want the truth." She crossed her arms and for a moment Callum was distracted by her bosom. Damn it, he needed his wits about him. "Well?" She persisted when he didn't reply. "Answer the question."

"First, I think we're past the point of my lord, my dear. Unless you wish to go back to formalities, which I'm loath to do after I've ruined you most sufficiently."

She shushed him, pulling him farther into the darkness. "Don't say such things out loud."

"Why not, they're true." They stood scant inches from

each other, and Callum was reminded how very delectable, how beautiful his Alice was.

"Why are you here?" The annoyed tone of her voice pulled him from thoughts of kissing her senseless and making her forget her absurd questions.

He wondered if he should tell her the truth, even though to say such a thing would surely make him look even more guilty than before.

"Estate business, like I said." The lie lodged in his throat, and he could see by the narrowing of her eyes that she didn't believe him. Clever girl.

"You're going to meet those men your cousin owed money to, are you not?"

He ground his teeth, hating the fact that the chit had too quick a wit. "It has nothing to do with your mama's missing brooch. I did not steal the jewel again, I promise you on my life."

She stepped away from him, the severing slicing him deep down to his soul. "I don't believe you." She shook her head. "Or I cannot trust you…as to which one I've not made up my mind, but either way, I don't think it's appropriate for you to court me any longer."

Anger threaded through him. Just another person who thought the worst of people based on their past. "Is that what you're calling what we did in that cottage. Courting? I'd call it fucking."

She gasped, hurt registering on her face. A flicker of regret passed through him that he'd injured her, especially when she was the last woman on earth he ever wished to hurt.

"How dare you speak to me in such a way? I'm merely trying to work out what has happened to Mama's brooch. The least you could do is be helpful."

Callum threw his hands up in the air, at a loss. "How can I

help you when you refuse to listen to me? I cannot tell you what you want to hear, for I have not stolen what you seek."

"How are you paying back the men your cousin owed money to?"

"That's none of your business."

She growled, literally growled at him, and he stood there, shocked. "So you admit it, you are going to see the men. And I want to know how you managed to gather the funds you need."

"It doesn't matter how I pulled the blunt together, just let it be known between us that I have, and it was not due to your mother's jewel." Callum walked over to the balustrade and leaned against it, watching Alice as she stayed where she was, her back to him. "Do you believe me?"

Alice turned and eyed him. "After you left the ball the other evening, your cousin was quite vocal in telling me how much you owed, due to your cousin's misbegotten lifestyle. It was quite a sum, and I know I took the last payment that was due. So, tell me, my lord. How will you manage to pay them back?" She crossed her arms, her chin lifting in defiance. "I cannot see how we can go on with such lies, such secrets between us."

Callum scoffed. "You're just like all the rest of the aristocracy. Conspiratorial, viperish Society. I remember why I turned my back on it at the end of last Season. None of you are worth the money stashed in your bank accounts. No matter what I've done in my past, I did not do this crime that you are laying against my door." He ran a hand through his hair. "I've rented out the London home for the Season, and I'm selling my horses, if you must know. After tomorrow afternoon, I'll have two left to pull the carriage and one of those will also have to serve as my own mount. There will be no funds to plant crops or tend to my tenant farmer's homes. Nothing. Are you happy now, my lady? Does hearing how low I've fallen prove to you that I'm the man whom you so obviously loathe?"

She gaped at him, her eyes wide.

Silence reigned between them for a moment and Callum wasn't sure where this conversation would leave them. "To think that I was happy to see you, that I'd missed you." He shook his head. "The lark's on me, I suppose."

———

*A*lice hated the hurt that was written across Callum's face and she wondered, warred within herself, as to how to repair the damage the past had wrought between them. "I don't know what to say."

He shook his head, looking away from her. "If you're pregnant, will you find words then? Will you demand the Surrey Bandit marry you to save your reputation?"

"I'm not pregnant." He looked at her, frowning. "How do you know? It was only a few days ago that we…"

"Because I know, if you understand what I'm saying." Alice wouldn't go into details, and normally she would not venture out to balls under the circumstances, and yet, desperate times called for desperate actions.

"Well, that is perhaps fortunate for you, for I'd hate for you to marry a man you did not trust and could not possibly love."

"Were you going to offer marriage? A gentleman would've asked the moment he took a virgin's maidenhead." Alice made a mental note to shut up before she ruined everything, but his arrogance brought out the little devil on her shoulder.

"I wished to court you." He walked up to her, taking up too much space, and yet, not enough. "But I refuse to marry a chit who jumps to conclusions and does not believe when a man, standing before her, declares himself free of such crimes. I will not go through my life and every time I go to Town, or purchase property, or a trinket and have my wife wonder how I came to own such an item. I want her to trust me, unconditionally. Could you?"

When he said it like that, Alice wanted to reach out and pull him down for a kiss. Make him see through her actions that she *did* wish to trust him, but a small part of her could not. The jewel was still missing, he was in London and, well, he'd been the Surrey Bandit. "I want to believe you, more than anything, but—"

"No more. That 'but' is all the answer I need."

"Callum, please."

He bowed, the muscle at the top of his temple flexing. "Good evening, my lady. I wish you a happy Season," he drawled, sounding bored with their conversation.

An ache formed in her chest and she bit the inside of her lip as her vision of him blurred with the sting of tears.

"Callum, I'm sorry."

"So, too, am I," he said, moving away from her. "I hope you find a gentleman who suits your high standards, who does not bore you to death."

Alice watched him leave and she swiped at a tear that fell down her cheek. Without looking back at her, he entered the ballroom. At the finality of it something inside her snapped, along with the notion that she'd made a catastrophic error of judgment.

Not against Lord Arndel, but toward him, the man he was to his very core, not the title that had been bestowed on his head. For weeks, he'd worked alongside her, more than proven his worth, given her friendship and companionship.

And at the first sign of him needing her trust, she had let him down. She had proven to him that she was like everyone in the Society he'd been foisted onto. If anyone had proved how untrustworthy they were tonight, it was she, for not believing his words.

Alice walked over to the terrace railing, looking out on the darkened gardens beyond. Right here and now she had to make a choice and, once committed, run with it and trust in herself.

Turning about, she headed back to the ballroom and sought out Victoria. She found her standing beside Isolde, their conversation animated with an abundance of laugher. Merrick stood beside Isolde, gazing at his wife with an adoration that left a hollow feeling inside Alice's chest.

She had had that very look given to her not half an hour past, and now she risked never seeing such affection again.

What a fool she'd been. Callum may be a lot of things, may have made mistakes, but he was no longer the thief that had robbed them on the road from Ashford. He was a good man, an honorable, loving father, and of course, he hadn't stolen the brooch. The thought of no funds for crops, how would he support his tenants in the coming months? The money he received from the parcel of land, the renting of his townhouse, and the sale of his horses would only go so far, and not last very long. It was only a matter of time before he faced ruin.

She sighed. None of his troubles could come to pass.

She spied Lord Thetford, her brother's oldest friend, and excusing herself from her family, made her way over to him.

He bowed when she joined him. Alice dipped into a perfect curtsy. "Lady Alice, how very beautiful you look tonight."

She took his arm and guided him along the edge of the ballroom floor. "You should know by now that flattery doesn't work on me, but I do wish to ask a favor."

He groaned and she laughed. "Something tells me I'm not

going to approve of this favor and that should your brother find out, I'm going to have hell to pay."

"Josh won't find out, and if you do as I ask, without raising an eyebrow, I'll put in a sweet word for you in relation to Miss Cynthia Williams whom you've fawned over all night."

"I do not fawn."

She patted his arm and his eyes narrowed. "You do, my dear, but let me tell you, fawning and being sweet to a woman only makes me like you more."

"Alice, what is it that you want?" he asked, a serious tone to his voice.

"Meet me at the doors of Tattersalls tomorrow an hour before the auction. Don't be late."

He groaned. "Alice…"

"And bring money, or however you pay for horses at such places." She went to walk away and he pulled her back.

"Women are not allowed at Tattersalls, or have you forgot?"

Alice grinned. "I've not forgot. Good night, Lord Thetford. I shall see you tomorrow." She didn't laugh at his distraught face, no matter how much she desperately wished to.

CHAPTER 17

"*J* think I hate you." Lord Thetford threw a disgusted look at her as she walked into Tattersalls with him. Dressed as a dandy, Alice itched her nape, as the man's short wig aggravated her scalp.

"Don't be a bore, my lord. No one will recognize me and if anyone asks who I am, tell them I'm your friend from abroad and that I can't speak English."

His lordship looked disgusted at the idea. "I could never know someone who wasn't multilingual."

Alice laughed and at an odd look from a passing gentleman, adjusted her tone to be deeper. "You are such a snob."

They made their way inside, stood in the courtyard, and found a location where they could see the horses when they were showcased to the gathered buyers. Alice spied Sir Liam Sledmere looking about and talking to other gentlemen. He spied Thetford and made his way over.

Alice shifted to the side, not wanting him to recognize her.

"Thetford, good to see you here." Sir Liam slapped Thetford on the shoulder and he winced.

"Sir Liam," Thetford replied, his tone a shade cooler than their guest. Alice watched them and couldn't help but notice that Thetford's dislike of the man was obvious. From the moment she'd met the baronet, she'd been uneasy in his company, and apparently, so were others.

Interesting…

"Purchasing any horses today?" Sir Liam asked, as the first mount was brought out. Alice recognized the horse immediately as Bandit and she cleared her throat, signaling to Thetford to bid on the thoroughbred.

The stallion was run around the perimeter before the auctioneer gave some information on the mount, height, breeding, owner, etc. At the mention of Callum's name, a pang of regret stabbed her belly. She'd been judgmental and allowed her knowledge of his past to cloud her intuition of the man he really was.

Sir Liam scoffed when Thetford yelled out a bid for Bandit. "Do be daft man, look at the horse, it isn't worth a ha'penny."

Alice narrowed her eyes and was thankful that Thetford continued to bid and eventually won the purchase of Bandit. They stayed at the sale for some hours, Alice giving Thetford the signal each time she wished him to purchase a horse. By the end of the day she owned six in total, four mares and two stallions. All beautiful thoroughbreds, and well worth their money.

Sir Liam had slunk away when he realized his continual running down of Arndel's horses had no influence whatsoever.

"Thank you, Thetford, for doing this for me today. I owe you more than a good word in Miss Williams's ear."

Thetford smiled and gestured her toward the gates. "All I ask is that you explain to me one day why I bought all of

Lord Arndel's horses. That will be enough recompense, I assure you."

"I shall," she said, relieved beyond measure that she'd secured Callum's beloved horses. The despair on his face last evening when he'd admitted to having put them up for sale crushed her heart each time she thought of it. He'd looked as desolate as if someone had kicked his puppy right before his eyes. In a way, she supposed, *she* had.

Today had been her first step in showing him she did believe him, and now she wanted to know why Sledmere had taken an interest in his cousin so much that he would purposely talk down the value of horses to a potential buyer.

The man wasn't to be trusted, which brought her to her second point in proving her love: gaining the location of Callum's meeting with the moneylender to see for herself that the debt was paid and they could move on with their lives.

Together.

The following night, Alice, along with her sister Victoria, snuck out of Isolde and Merrick's London townhouse, an easy feat, considering its size, and ran down the street where a hackney cab waited for a fare.

Both of them were dressed as street urchins and were out of place in the heart of Mayfair. The driver yelled at them to be off, before Alice shushed the fellow with a golden coin and jumped up into the cab, sighing in relief when the carriage moved forward.

Victoria adjusted the gun that sat against her hip, yelling out to the driver to take them to an address they had bribed out of Benny, Lord Arndel's stable lad, who had come up to Town with his lordship.

A little guilt pricked her at tricking the boy in such a way, but in order to follow Lord Arndel to where the transaction would take place, then bribe is what they had to do.

"What is the plan when we get there? Do you have any idea what time this transaction is to take place?"

Alice clasped the strap above the door as the carriage rocked about a corner. "No, none. We may have to sit and wait for a time. From what I understand, the cottages that surround this moneylender's premise are washrooms and whorehouses. I'm sure we could persuade someone to allow us to rent a room, which will give us a good view as to where Lord Arndel will be."

"I have a bad feeling about this."

Alice agreed with her sister, although she didn't voice her concerns. The area in which they were traveling was not for the light of heart, which was exactly what they were. It was full of untrustworthy people who were desperate in their need. They would have to be careful and on guard at all time, if they wanted to make it out in one piece.

The carriage rumbled over cobbled roads, and out the window Alice could see the Thames glistening in the darkness, only the shimmering moonlight on the waters to light their way. "All will be well, I promise. We're armed. Nothing will happen to us with such security." Alice hoped, although her words sounded braver than she felt.

"What will you do if his lordship has the brooch and gives it to the moneylender? What then for the viscount?"

Anger hummed through her at the thought and then she dismissed the possibility. No, it would not occur. What Callum had said was the truth. He was innocent of the crime she'd laid at his door and tonight he would prove it to her, if unknowingly. "That will not happen, so it is a moot point."

Her sister sighed. "But if it does, what will you do, Alice?"

She conceded that her sibling would not let this conversation go without an answer. "I will kill him." And she would. Slowly and very, very painfully.

"Alice..."

"I will have to tell the authorities. There will be no other option. But with that, I will ensure that Amelia is taken care of and placed in a gentleman's home, where she will be loved and cared for. I will not allow anything to happen to the girl."

Victoria nodded, satisfied by her answer. "Very well. I concur. This is the right plan, even though I know it must be painful to think of such a thing."

More painful than her sister could ever imagine. To have someone you love locked away would be a devastation she didn't want to think about. "What will be will be. Only time will tell which way fate will play this hand."

They rode in the carriage in silence for a time, both lost in their own thoughts when the carriage rocked to a halt before dilapidated buildings. Alice stepped down and Victoria followed close on her heels.

"Did ye want me to wait for ye?"

Alice turned to the driver. "Yes, if you will, and be on your guard. We may need to leave quickly." The older gentleman's brow rose, and he looked at her with newfound respect, or it could've been wonder. Alice wasn't sure. She handed him another coin and hoped it would be enough to keep him honest and stationary.

The street that Benny had directed them to ran off from a main road of sorts, although with the linen hanging across from one building to another, the piles of rubbish stacked against walls, it certainly didn't look fit for any human habitation.

Taking a deep breath, Alice walked down a narrow alley that no vehicle could travel through and came to a square with houses set out around it, some two story, while others remained only one level high. A water well stood in the center of the square, and the muffled sounds of a child crying somewhere in the vicinity reached them as they continued across the dirt courtyard.

Alice looked about for the reputed whorehouse that was located here, and gaining the opposite end of the square, she spied a group of women lounging in the doorway of a building, their gowns ripped and all but showing those who cared to look, what assets they had for sale.

Dressed as men, Alice boldly walked up to them, but their disguises didn't fool the women for a minute, if their laughter was anything to go by.

"Well, well, well. What 'ave we here? Playing dress ups are ya? Well, lovies, we like all sorts of games 'ere, and if that's what you're into, we're fine with that, if ye have the blunt to compensate us, of course."

Victoria gasped and Alice rolled her eyes at her sister's sensibilities, but then, they had been propositioned by whores, and were dressed as men... "We'd like to rent a room for some hours—one that looks out on this square."

"Oh, aye, you want ye pretty lass friend 'ere and no one else. Aye, we know what you're into now." The whore laughed, and so, too, did her friends.

"She's my sister," Victoria said, outrage lacing her tone.

Her sibling's outburst only made the whores laugh louder. "Our business in the room is ours, and ours alone. I'm more than willing to pay handsomely, if you're able to keep those mouths of yours shut as to seeing us here this evening."

Her words caused instant silence, and a flicker of respect entered the oldest, and seemingly highest ranking whore's eyes who stepped forward.

"This way, then, my lords. We 'ave a room that's perfect for ye and ye private business."

They followed the woman upstairs, and as required they

were given a room that looked out onto the square. Its large window, though grimy and with portions of glass missing from its square panes, was exactly what they needed.

"Thank you." Alice handed the woman a gold coin, along with a shilling, not caring which one she kept for herself, or gave to her madam.

Closing the door behind the woman, Alice locked it and strode over to the window, kneeling beside Victoria, who had already hoisted the window halfway open to see the square better.

"Which building was it supposed to be?"

"The footman I bribed from Lord Arndel's household said he'd delivered a letter to the house in this square with flaking red paint on its door." Alice studied the houses and pointed when she spied the house. "There it is, that's where Callum will go tonight."

"Well, if Lord Arndel does arrive, at least we should see him well enough, as we have a clear sight of that cottage."

"Yes," Alice said, hoping that what she had assumed to be happening actually was. There was, after all, no guarantee that Callum would be here at all. But then, he was supposed to leave for Surrey tomorrow, so it left only tonight to pay off his cousin's debts.

A large, burly man stepped out of the cottage, the red glow of a cigar blinking in the twilight.

"There's a man," Victoria gasped, dropping behind the wall lest she be seen.

"Victoria, he will not see you, he's too interested in the whores talking to him below stairs." Alice studied the man as best she could but didn't recognize him. He wore clothing that looked at odds to the area in which he lived, where there were obviously poor people, struggling families, and whores who walked about. He wore a dark, well-cut suit, and even for his size it fit him well and looked like quality fabric.

His hair was slicked back and looked almost wet with some sort of wax. A small wooden cane dangled from his jacket pocket, and his bulging coat pocket left an uneasy feeling in the pit of her stomach. He was armed.

Victoria brought up her gun to sit against the frame of the window. Alice did the same, forgetting for a moment why they were here.

"He seems to be waiting for someone, so that's a good sign."

Alice nodded, hoping that was the case, and then the sound of a horse trotting on a cobbled road echoed in the night. Her heart sped up when Callum walked into the square, his attire less fashionable than what she was used to seeing him in, he, too wishing to look less conspicuous in this setting.

"Be prepared for anything, Sister, and whatever we do from this moment forward, remember, Lord Arndel is to be kept alive under all circumstances."

Victoria nodded. "I understand perfectly."

---

*T*he older gentleman laughed, crossing his arms against his bulging chest. "I did not think you would come. It's pleasing that you, at least, have more respect for your debts than your cousin did."

Callum fought not to lose his temper with the money-lender. In all truth, he was tired of the man's threats and seedy business dealings. "My cousin's debts, you mean. I, myself, owe you nothing."

The man shrugged, smirking. "I don't care whose debt it is, as long as it's paid in full. Your last trinket is well overdue."

An inkling of unease threaded up his spine and Callum took a look around the square, not seeing any of the man's henchmen but knowing they would be around here some-where. That he had no doubt.

"Do you have the jewel I wanted?"

Callum reached into his coat pocket and pulled out a large wad of cash, instead. The man's eyes gleamed with excitement as he slapped the blunt into the moneylender's outstretched hand. Callum's clasp increased. "I could not get the brooch, but in your hand is an amount equal to its value. This immediately ends our association and my cousin's debt with you. From this day forward, we will have no other contact or need for correspondence. Is that clear?"

The man grinned, snatching the money away and, not bothering to count it, placed it in his own coat pocket. "I suppose the cash will do just as well, but come, Lord Arndel. Let us not be hasty. From what I've been told, your financial woes are many and increasing. I can help you with that, if only you'd let me."

Callum shook his head, in no way tempted by such words. "The payment in your pocket is all you'll ever have from me. Do not ask for more." He started back out the way he came, only too eager to leave for Surrey and Amelia, and if he could prove himself, to Alice.

"Not so fast, Cousin."

Callum stilled, turning and seeing Liam come out from the cottage behind the moneylender. "We have much to discuss," his relative said, gesturing for him to return.

"I think not." Callum continued, and before he had the chance to react, the prick of a knife pressed against his back, halting his steps. Where had that blasted fellow been hiding?

"Turn about, my lord. We are not done here."

Callum did as he was asked, his mind frantic as to what else he could do. He'd not thought to bring anyone with him, not even a servant, dammit, as he'd trusted the man his cousin owed money to, believing the transaction would be simple and over quickly.

Fool!

He should've known better, and now he would be lucky to get out of here alive.

"Why am I not surprised to see you, Liam? You were always a conniving, spoiled little brat who enjoyed trampling those you thought beneath your Hessian boots."

His cousin merely laughed. "And you are a fool who will not see another sunrise."

He frowned, the thought of never seeing his daughter, Amelia, racing through his mind and making the blood in his veins boil to molten liquid. Who would see to her care and raise her as she deserved? Panic threatened to consume him and he swallowed. "Would you care to elaborate, Cousin? I would so like to know what your plan is."

"Oh, there is no plan, other than the one where the authorities will find you floating in the Thames by morn." Liam laughed. "But then no one will care, for who would miss a bastard viscount who should never have inherited the title in the first place?"

"I am the legal and rightful heir to Kester House and the viscountcy, and there are many who, should my death arise, deem it suspicious. Do not be a fool, Cousin, for I have made it no secret the hate that we feel for each other is mutual."

The man merely shrugged. "And yet, I am unmoved by your plight. You will die tonight, and by the hand of my gentleman friend beside me." Liam smiled. "For, of course, I could not do the deed myself, as much as I may wish to. Damn, bloody business it is—too messy for my kind."

The moneylender pushed back his coat jacket and clasped the handle of his flintlock. Callum wondered if he could charge the man, get the gun, and possibly gain the upper hand.

Liam gestured to his henchman. "Get on with it, man. I have other affairs to attend.

"The debt is paid, what's the reason behind killing me. It makes no sense."

"I know you were born poor, but even I thought you had more smarts than that." His cousin snarled. "Who do you suppose inherits should you die?"

You do.

Callum shook his head, wondering if the man before him had anything to do with the former viscount's death, as well. "Did you kill Robert, too? Tell me, dear cousin, did you not look closely enough in Debrett's before you removed him from your path?"

"Robert was a swine, and a stupid one. It wasn't hard to make his death look like an accident. Hell, the man was always falling down stairs or out of carriages. It was no stretch to make his drowning in the Thames a foolhardy mistake."

"You bastard," Callum said, for the first time in his life, feeling sorry for Robert. Yes, the man had been an oaf, had had no idea how to run an estate, or act with any sort of decorum, but to be killed solely due to another man's greed was beyond forgivable. "You will hang for that."

"I will not. It's my word against yours. And if you're dead…"

"And you think that two viscounts, mysteriously dead during the prime of their lives, while you're free and clear to walk away with the viscountcy, will not look suspect?" Callum laughed. "Now who is a simpleton?"

Sledmere stared at him a moment, his eyes without any sort of emotion other than greed and hate. Callum realized the man was cork-brained and without sense whatsoever.

"It is fortunate for me I have friends where friends are needed in these situations," his cousin said and grinned. "Not that you would know of such things, growing up poor, as you did. You have no friends. In fact," he said, looking about. "You came alone. All alone, just as you will die alone. Alone. Alone. Alone."

Fury ran though Callum like a river of revenge. If he was to die tonight, then he would go down fighting.

The cent per canter raised his gun and Liam clapped his hands, smiling "Yes, let's be done with this already. I have a ball to attend, perhaps one where I shall court your delectable Lady Alice and have her on her back before midnight."

"I will kill you for that."

Liam pulled out a small item from his coat pocket and held it up to him. The most prized possession of the Duchess of Penworth glistened before him.

"It was you who stole the emerald brooch?"

"I did. The duchess droned on and on at the ball and told me all about her run-in with the Surrey Bandit, and eventually, she told me of her daughter finding the heirloom some weeks later. Most providentially, I might add. And so, when an opportunity arose, I went upstairs and stole it, since it was on the list of jewels our mutual friend here wished to acquire. It was merely a little bit of fun for myself, as I do love to see people upset."

"You're a sadist." Callum didn't try and hide the revulsion in his tone. Never had he known someone who went out of their way to injure and destroy others.

"But then," his cousin continued, ignoring his words, "I watched you at the Cavendish ball, and I followed you and Lady Alice outside. I must say, your conversation was most lively and very interesting. You really ought to realize there is always someone about who can hear what you're saying. And well, well, well, cousin. You have been a naughty boy."

"I would declare you've been worse. I've never killed anyone."

"La, death comes to those who get in my way. And when Lady Alice asked if you were the one who'd stolen the brooch, and the reasoning why she suspected you, I could not believe my luck. After you're dead, I will place this brooch in your pocket, and when you're found, Lady Alice will know you as the lying thief that you are, and I shall inherit, and all will be well." Liam gestured toward him. "Now finish him off."

Callum lunged at the moneylender, but the blast of a gunshot and the breeze of a bullet that flew past his ear made him dive to the ground instead. He hit the dirt-strewn court-yard hard. His cousin did the same, the man's eyes wide with shock.

Callum looked about the buildings, trying to see where the shot had come from. Above the whorehouse, a plume of smoke floated up into the air, but the person responsible couldn't be seen.

He gained his feet, noting his cousin's henchman was dead, his eyes staring sightless toward the night sky.

Liam crawled toward the moneylender's gun and Callum fumbled for his own, but not quickly enough. *Shit.*

"*T*ouch that gun, Sir Liam, and you'll be as dead as the man beside you." Alice strode up beside Callum, not taking her eyes off his cousin. What a bastard, and how would she ever gain forgiveness from Callum? He would *never* have stolen from her, not after promising not to. What he must think of her being so cruel, so quick to point a guilty finger at him, after all that they'd shared these past weeks.

"You would shoot a baronet? I think not."

"I think you should move so we can find out." Alice glared at the lord, hoping he could feel the hate emanating from her for the trouble he'd wrought. "There are other guns aimed upon your person, and those who shot your friend will shoot you, if you try something stupid. Which, if the conversation I was privy to was anything to go by, you are wont to do."

"You cannot prove a thing. Nothing that was said here can harm me."

"Maybe not," Alice said, shrugging. "But my brother is a duke, who, correct me if I'm wrong, has more influence in Society than you. And a friend of mine, Lord Thetford, told me of your conduct at Tattersalls yesterday, which raised my curiosity over your sudden interest in Lord Arndel." Keeping her own attendance at the auction to herself. "I was confused as to why you would try and talk the value down of horse stock up for sale, your cousin's no less. I had a hunch you would be here tonight, and would you look at that, I was right." Alice could feel Callum's gaze, but she dared not move her attention off Sir Liam. "You, sir, may not hang for your crimes, but I will ensure you never step out of line again, lest I feel like telling my family the truth of everything, and I mean everything," she said, throwing a pointed look at Callum. "I have no doubt my papa's cousin, the lord chief justice of London, will be interested in hearing what I have to say. He's always loved us girls, and has made an effort to remain in our life after Papa died. My word is law to him."

Alice smiled, watching with no small amount of triumph as Sir Liam's color paled to a light gray.

"I wonder if he would be interested in hearing how you whored yourself to Arndel. I doubt he would trust your word, should he know you spread your legs for a highwayman. He is the law, after all."

His words spiked a thread of fear through her, but she

remained steadfast. He could not best her or harm Callum any further. Sir Liam took a step back, and she stilled. "Do I have your word that we shall keep your involvement of Richard's death quiet, if you do not mention Arndel's past?"

The baronet smirked, sliding a little closer to the gun lying on the ground. "I will have to think about it, as I'm unsure as to what I shall do."

"Let him do what he likes, Alice. He cannot prove a thing."

The comforting words from Callum spiked resolve through her and aiming at the man's leg, she fired. Sir Liam went down howling, grabbing at his limb.

"You shot me. Damn it all to hell. How dare you shoot me?"

Alice walked over to the flintlock lying not far from him and kicked it away. She reached into the pocket of the moneylender taking back the money Callum had given him, and the brooch, slipping both into her pocket. Lord Arndel's cousin rolled about as she came to stand over him. "I dare very much, sir. Let this be a warning to you. I shall hunt you down and destroy you, should you seek to ruin me or any of my family. I have more friends in high places, and I do not think you wish to embark on a war you will not win."

An array of curses coursed from Sir Liam's mouth as Victoria came to stand beside her.

Victoria raised her brow, smiling a little. "Does it hurt, Sir Liam? From what I can tell, it's only a flesh wound. Nothing too serious. You are acting quite the baby."

Alice laughed as her sister's words only brought forth more ill manners from the fiend. "Good night, sir, and good luck with wherever your life may take you." Alice clasped Callum's arm, dragging him toward the street. The carriage waited a little up the cobbled road, and Alice sighed in relief, thankful the man had been true to his word and waited for them.

"Is that your horse, Lord Arndel?" Victoria asked, striding toward the brown gelding.

"Yes," he answered, meeting Alice's stare and sending a riot of emotions coursing through her blood. Expectation, relief, fear, and another emotion so great, that she was even too scared to think it aloud.

"I will ride it back to Mayfair, if you'll allow me. I do believe you and Alice have things to discuss."

Alice watched with no small amount of awe as her younger sibling mounted without help and trotted off into the night. She turned and gestured for Callum to join her. "Shall we?" she asked, taking a step toward the carriage.

He followed without a word, only touching her to help her up into the carriage before seating himself across from her. Callum yelled out the direction to the driver, and Alice wondered what was going through his mind. Probably quite a lot, considering the night they'd had.

"Say something," she said, unable to bear the silence a moment longer. Was he angry with her? Did he love her as much as she loved him? Was he repulsed by her actions or his own? All of those thoughts tumbled about in her mind as the wheels tumbled over the road outside.

"I'm struggling to form the words." He ran a hand over his jaw and she waited, trying to remain patient while he debated within himself.

"Are you angry and upset?"

He smiled a little, shaking his head. "Not at all. In fact, I'm wracking my brain to find the words to explain how much I adore you."

Relief swamped her and without thought, Alice threw herself into his arms, welcoming the feel of his tight, strong hold about her body. She pulled back a little, staring up at him.

"You don't know how pleased I am to hear that, for I

adore you, too. I'm so sorry I thought you a thief. I should have trusted your word. I understand you were desperate. Those awful men blackmailed you, and your daughter's safety was paramount. I'm sorry, so sorry that a debt that was not yours was foisted on your back."

He pushed a lock of hair from her face that had come free from her wig, running a hand across her jaw. "I did not give you much reason to trust me. I was the Surrey Bandit, after all."

"You promised me you had stopped, and I should not have doubted you." Alice sat more comfortably on his legs, holding her arms about his neck. "Tell me you forgive me. Please."

Callum nodded. "I forgive you, of course. There is no choice for me."

Unable to deny herself, Alice kissed him, loving the feel of his lips, and the fact he could not seem to get enough of her in return. "Tell me," she asked, regretfully pulling back just as the kissed turned molten. "What will you do now that you've sold all your horses? Will the money I took back from the moneylender help you to gain your financial feet?"

"I cannot afford to purchase the horses back, for even if Liam tried to sully their value, they fetched a worthy price. The money will go toward fixing the estate and planting this year's crops, now that you've taken it back from the money-lender. Horse breeding will have to wait."

The pain that flickered across his visage tore at her heart, but she kept to herself that she had, in fact, bought his horses and so, not all was lost. "I'm so sorry, Callum. But know you've done all you could to remedy a problem that was not yours to begin with. Yes, you were forced into becoming a highwayman, but it was not of your choosing."

"The Surrey Bandit was never who I was, and I shall never forgive Robert or Liam for creating a mess that was left for me to clear up. I was desperate to keep Amelia safe, the moneylenders had shown just how easy it was to get to her, and I could not take their threats lightly. And while there are members of the *ton* who shall never receive back the jewels that I stole, I'm heartily sick at the thought of all that I put them through."

She smiled. "When people are faced with dilemmas that seem beyond their ability, people are wont to act rashly. You have fought against those who bade you wrong, found another way to get what they wanted at no cost to anyone else but yourself, and I admire you all the more for it."

Callum chuckled, and the deep rumbling caused her insides to flutter. "Callum, I have a question for you."

"What is it?" he asked, pulling her closer.

Alice adjusted her seat, shifting to close the space between their bodies even more. Warmth spread through her limbs, and she inwardly purred when Callum's gaze darkened with desire. "Will you marry me, my lord, and make an honest woman of me?" She smiled as his eyes widened in shock. "And if you do, I promise you that Amelia will want for nothing. Not now or in the future when she's presented to Society. Let me love you both."

His eyes glistened and he blinked quickly. "I'm supposed to ask that question and be the man who looks after you. Not the other way around." He paused, concern clouding his gaze. "I don't deserve you."

Alice shushed him. "Like I said, my lord, I didn't have a conventional upbringing, duke's daughter or no. We do things differently in the Worthingham household. And we do deserve each other. Don't ever say otherwise."

"My actions this year are proof enough that you're too good for me. On top of my treatment of you last Season, it only illumines what a cad I've been."

"Will you tell me why you called me a rich, spoiled child?

Not that I think you believe me to be one, but I am curious as to why you were so disapproving of me."

"I have no excuse other than the stresses of being the new Viscount Arndel and the financial problems that came with it. I'm sorry I called you that name. You may be rich, and spoiled, but it has not tarnished the soul inside. You're as pure as an angel and loving toward anyone in need. I love you, Lady Alice Worthingham. More than I thought possible for a man to love a woman."

Alice bit her lip to stem the flow of tears. "You do?" He'd never said those three little words before and hearing them was the most wonderful moment of her life.

"I do," he said, his tone serious.

"Well then, I suppose I better say that I love you, too, and always will."

He grinned and she kissed him. Hard. The embrace went on for some time and Alice had to push him away lest the kiss take them to another scandalous rendezvous like the one in the cottage.

"You still haven't answered my first question." He waggled his brows and she slapped his shoulder. "Callum, answer me."

He pushed off her wig, running his hand through her long locks. "I will marry you and you will marry me and we shall love each other wildly."

"Wildly?" Alice liked the sound of the word, as in all truth, it suited them. "And pray tell me, how soon can this wild marriage take place?"

"As soon as may be, for I would hate for you to be with child."

Alice frowned. "But I'm not. I already told you that." And thankfully, her courses had gone as quickly as they had arrived.

His wicked grin made heat bloom on her cheeks. "We cannot do that here, my lord."

Callum flicked open the top button on her waistcoat. "You shot a lord in the leg...I think you, Lady Alice Worthingham, can do whatever the hell you like."

She ought to feel shame at his statement, but she didn't care enough about Sir Liam and his vile actions to do so. Instead, she delved into the scandalous behavior of her betrothed and enjoyed the ride back to Mayfair, both in the carriage and on his lordship's lap.

*C*allum looked up from his desk as his library door swung open and the two women he loved beyond distraction waltzed into the room, holding hands, with smiles that were wont to melt anyone's heart.

They had been married a month and Callum had to admit, it had been the best month of his life. To find another woman to love and trust him, be his best friend and confidant, was more than he ever could've hoped for. And that Alice knew his faults and loved him still, made his affection for her tenfold.

He adored her.

"Come, Amelia and I have a surprise for you."

He stood, coming about the desk and picking up Amelia, swinging her about as she liked. "What is it?"

Amelia giggled, wagging her finger before his nose. "We cannot tell you, Papa. You have to see it for yourself."

"*Hmm,*" he said, taking Alice's hand and letting her lead him toward the front of the house.

"Now, close your eyes," she said, taking his daughter. The front door opened and the cooling breeze of outside passed across his skin. Taking his arm, she guided him toward the entrance and stopped him at what he assumed to be the threshold.

"Now you can look."

The first thing he spotted was Amelia running down the front steps, before movement brought his attention up to see Bandit, his prized stallion, who stared at him with something akin to boredom. Behind Bandit were all the horses he'd sold at Tattersalls.

Callum wasn't a man who succumbed to emotions, but even his eyes smarted at the sight. "You purchased them all. How? When?" He stepped outside and strode toward Bandit, checking him over as Alice followed close on his heels.

"It was easy. I had my brother's friend, Lord Thetford purchase them for me. I threatened to shoot him should he not buy the horses at Tattersalls. He agreed, of course."

Callum laughed, pulling her into an embrace. "Tell me you did no such thing."

Alice smiled up at him and his heart burst with affection for the woman in his arms. How he loved her. "Of course not." She smiled. "I merely sweetened the deal by telling him I would put in a good word for a lady he's interested in, and he agreed."

He laughed again. "I cannot believe you've done either of those things."

She wrapped her arms about his waist smiling. "I did all those things, because your happiness is mine. We have known Lord Thetford many years, and he's a good man. And now," she said, looking back at Bandit, which Callum did also. "Your horses are home again."

Callum nodded. Home. Two years ago he never would have thought Kester House would be ever termed so, but now, now it was their home—a place to raise Amelia and,

God willing, more children when the time came. A place to make memories and to live their life to the fullest.

His daughter ran up to him, giggling, and he swung her up into his arms, pulling both his favorite ladies into his embrace. "Thank you for my present. It is the best of gifts," he said.

Amelia kissed his cheek. "Happy marriage day, Papa."

He met Alice's gaze, hoping she read all that she'd come to mean to him in his eyes and always would. "Indeed it is, poppet. Indeed it is."

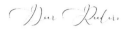

Dear Reader,

I hope you enjoyed, *Only a Viscount Will Do*, book three in my To Marry a Rogue series!

I'm so thrilled you chose my book to read, and if you're able, I would appreciate an honest review of *Only a Viscount Will Do*. As they say, feed an author, leave a review!

If you'd like to learn about book four in my To Marry a Rogue series, *Only a Marquess Will Do*, please read on. I have included chapter one for your reading pleasure.

Alternatively, you can keep in contact with me by visiting my website or following me online. You can contact me at www.tamaragill.com or email me at tamaragillauthor@gmail.com.

Tamara Gill

ONLY A MARQUESS WILL DO

TO MARRY A ROGUE, BOOK 4

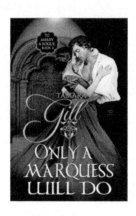

It's a game of instruction and seduction. But who's teaching who?

The London Season is not for Lady Victoria Worthingham. After a disastrous marriage that lasted no more than six weeks, she's sworn off men forever. But that doesn't mean she can't help her brother's best friend find his perfect match. It should be simple...unless she falls in love with him first, of course...

Marquess Albert Kester is everything ladies aren't looking for in a husband—socially awkward and bumbling as a debutante at her first ball. Writing adventures instead of living them seems to be his lot in life. Unless he can convince Victoria to stop seeing him as a project and start seeing him as a man, that is...

She's determined to see him happily settled. All he wants is her. Only one outcome is certain in this game.

Rules will be broken...and if they aren't careful, so will their hearts...

CHAPTER 1

London, 1809

*V*ictoria stood in the modiste on Bond street, the heat on her cheeks as warm as the day outdoors. She glanced about the room, the women of the ton, those who had the power to make or ruin a lady's chances during her Season, stared at her with pity—some with amusement and glee.

Her mother's mouth had not stopped gaping when her sister, Alice, now the Viscountess Arndel, had read the latest on dit in *The Times* that morning. That Victoria's husband, the very man she had married six weeks before, had run off with a maid at the estate.

Victoria stared down at the blue silk gown the modiste had halted pinning the hem for, her face too one of shock, but at least not glee. The modiste would know better than to find pleasure in such news with the daughter of a duke.

"I do not understand," her mama said, taking the newspaper from Alice and reading the article herself.

Victoria felt her cheeks heat with embarrassment. How could Paul do such a thing to her? She had thought they were happy, settled, and ready to start the next chapter of their lives. Only last week she had farewelled him when he went to check on his country estate. That this gossip rag all of London was devouring knew more about the state of her marriage than she did was mortifying. How could she have been so wrong about a person she cared for? She was never wrong.

"Pass me the paper, Mama." Her mother handed it over to her with haste, seemingly only too happy to have the offending article out of her hand. Victoria read the printed black letters, and with each word, her world crumbled about her.

It read: *"Mr. Paul Armstrong, the very one recently married to Lady Victoria Worthingham was seen sequestered at a local inn in Dover, the woman hanging off his every word most certainly not the Duke of Penworth's sister and new wife. That both Mr. Armstrong and his unnamed companion were soused, and too bois-terous for the townsfolk was also mentioned. We can only look on Lady Victoria with pity over her most unhappy union that she so newly stepped into."*

She clamped her jaw shut, an expletive on the tip of her tongue. Paul was a wealthy landholder from Kent. A suitable gentleman for a woman such as herself. Her brother Josh, the Duke of Penworth assured her he was a good match, both financially and regarding the gentleman's reputation. When her brother returned from abroad, she would certainly have words with him regarding his character eval-uations.

Not that their marriage was a love match, unlike her sisters who had found love with their spouses. But Victoria had never been one to think such a thing would happen to her. She was too opinionated, a little rough about the edges,

266

blunt, and loved dogs and horses too much to be a diamond of the first water.

Where her sisters were refined and ladylike, she was, well, a little notched. A laugh caught her attention, and she looked over to find Miss Fanny Christi pointing and giggling over *The Times*. Victoria glared at the social-climbing ninny and thrust the paper aside, the modiste taking it without a word.

"I apologize for wasting your time with this gown, Mrs. DeRose, but it would seem that I'm no longer in the mood for a dress fitting." Victoria held out her arms. "Please help me to remove the gown. I shall return another day to complete the alterations."

"But dear, do you not want to write and demand Mr. Armstrong returns? The article could be incorrect. Why even now he could be on his way back from the country to explain this slanderous piece."

Victoria wiggled out of the gown, leaving her only in her shift as she stepped off the fitting stool in the store and went to change back into her morning dress. "It is not, Mama. Mr. Armstrong has made his choice." *And now he would have to live with it.* "I will not be one of those pitiful wives who allow such insults to stand. While I cannot change the fact that I am married, that does not mean I'll allow him to ruin my life. If it is freedom he wishes so soon after our nuptials, then I too shall live how I like and bedamn Paul to Hades."

Stupid fool to have ruined their future in such a way. Victoria walked into the change room, pulling the small curtain closed to hide her from those in the store who watched them and their reaction to the news like a kettle of vultures over a corpse.

Only then did she allow herself a deep breath, the reaction to the news that she had been hiding from all those prying eyes. She slumped onto the soft, padded chair in the stall. While she knew their marriage would have been a practical and good match, she had liked Paul, even if it were not a love match. He made her laugh and was handsome. She had thought they would muddle along well enough. His estate was large. He had a good stable of horses and was fond of dogs, had stated she could bring her two wolfhounds with her when they married, which she had.

She pulled her morning gown from the hook where it hung. She would not have minded had he wished to break the engagement, but to marry her and then run off? What had he been thinking! The stupid man could have been honest with her. Why did he not tell her the truth, that he loved another and did not wish to marry? That's if he loved the maid at all. For all she knew, perhaps this was the way the man truly was. A gentleman without honor.

Victoria stood and slipped the dress over her head, stepping back out into the store to gain assistance with the buttons on her back. Her mama handed her her bonnet and gloves, and within a few minutes, they were ready to leave.

"I'm so very sorry about your unsuccessful marriage, Lady Victoria," Miss Christi said, the smirk on her face telling Victoria that she was not sorry at all. "And so soon into the union. How you must be suffering."

Victoria looked down her nose at her, feeling the weight and support of both her mother and sister behind her. A duchess and viscountess who would never abide such rudeness for long, and neither would she.

Victoria patted Miss Christi's shoulder, hoping the condescension was thick and clear in her touch. "Do not be sorry for me, Miss Christi. It is not my loss, but my husband's." She smiled, glad to see Miss Christi's face had paled at her words. "I hope we see you at the ball this evening. It's always lovely to see off the Season with a bang."

Miss Christi curtsied to Victoria's mama while mumbling, "Of course. Good day, Your Grace, Lady Arndel."

Victoria turned up her nose and left the store. Their coachman opened the door and helped them inside. Victoria heard her mama tell the driver they were for home, and it wasn't long before the carriage wheels were rumbling over the gravel and cobblestone roads through Mayfair.

No one spoke, all of them too disturbed by what had just transpired, no matter how it may have looked to those who viewed them in the store.

"Well, I hope Mr. Armstrong is pleased with his actions. I shall endeavor never to allow him to step foot in any of our entertainments in the future or those of my children. He is cut off from our family. Dead to us all I swear."

Alice nodded, her lips thinning in displeasure. "You should not allow him to get away with such treatment, Victoria. We ought to pay him back in some way. I could always shoot him. My aim is second to none as you know."

Victoria glanced at her sister, unsure how much help Alice would be since she was in the early stages of pregnancy. "I think Callum may take issue with me having you hie about England searching for a man who does not want to be found and shooting him. Not yet, at least." Victoria stared out onto the street, not really seeing anything other than a city she would be happy to leave. Next week, in fact, she was due to return to Paul's country estate where they were to remain until next Season. That would not be happening now.

What a waste of effort these past months had been. The courtship, the marriage, the expense. Victoria supposed she should feel more upset than she did, but she couldn't bring forth the emotions to do so. That in itself told her that to lose her husband, while humiliating, was not life-ending.

She would clasp the opportunity his foolishness had gifted her and return to Dunsleigh.

"You may do whatever you think is best, Mama. I, for one, will hold my head high at tonight's ball, and next week we shall return home and go on with things as if nothing has happened." Victoria leaned forward, taking her mama's hands. "Do not think that I am so very upset, for I am not. In fact," she said, leaning against the squabs, "I'm certain since he's decided to run off with a maid, society will punish him enough without me adding to his woes. But as for our marriage, it is over and nothing, no persuasion from him in the future will change my mind. As far as I am concerned, I will view myself as a widow from this day forward."

"I think you may be right," Alice said, rubbing her small baby bump. "You are destined for better things, my dearest. Who is attending this evening, Mama? We need to show society that we have rallied around Victoria and will not abide her being slighted."

"Well, as for that," her mama said, rattling off several families, all of whom Victoria knew and classed as friends. They would not offend or slight her in her time of need. They would be home soon. Safe from London and the gossiping ton.

While she did not know what her future held, where she would live, or what name to use, one thing she was at least grateful for... Her dowry was still her own, and no matter where Paul traveled with his lover, he could not swindle her money away. She supposed she could purchase a townhouse in London or a small country estate near Dunsleigh. All ideas would need considerable thought and once they were home, she would be able to set her mind to figuring out her future.

One thing was certain however, her future would not involve her husband. Not ever again.

Hampshire, 1811

*A*lbert Kester, Marquess Melvin wrote the final words in his latest gothic romance novel. His quill scrawled *The End*—a little salute to himself he always signed when he'd completed a manuscript.

He leaned back in his chair, staring out at the inky-black night. Secluded away in Hampshire near Surrey's border, he ought to feel alone, vulnerable perhaps, and yet, he did not.

He loved living in the country. The hunting lodge he now used as his writing oasis was the perfect setting for a man such as himself, a man who did not enjoy crowds or socializing. He'd never been one to have the abilities to speak pretty to females or act as one of the rogues, gambling and carousing about the town without a care.

But he would have to soon. In a week or so, his closest neighbor and influential family were returning to Surrey, and he would have to ride the ten miles between their estates and endure the weekend house party and ball the Duke of Penworth held.

And he would see her again...

Lady Victoria Worthingham, now widow to the late Mr. Paul Armstrong after the fool dabbled with the wrong married lady abroad and received a bullet through his skull for his troubles. The only woman he was certain of in England and perhaps the world to make him question his life. His way of living. So private and alone.

The invitation had arrived today, and he'd sent off an acceptance without delay before he could change his mind and remain at Rosedale.

Albert slipped the manuscript into the leather binder he used and locked the book away in a cabinet before securing the lodge and returning to the main house.

He had not brought his horse this afternoon, knowing he

would be several hours here, but it did not matter. He knew his way back home, even in the night.

At least he could attend the ball at the duke's estate without the nagging guilt he always suffered when he had a book due. With it finished, he could at least attempt to enjoy the ball more.

The lights to the main house flickered through the trees and then rose high before him as he cleared the copse of forest that surrounded his estate. Tomorrow he would send his book off to his publisher and, should they like the next installment of his series, his book would be available within the next twelve months or so.

It may not be the usual occupation that a marquess would do, but he enjoyed writing stories, becoming lost in his characters' worlds. What started as a hobby was now another source of income to his estate, and it pleased him. He could control that world. He could not control the one he lived in.

His mother, who resided on an estate just outside of Bath with her new husband, was forever writing to him, asking when he would return to London for another Season. Find a bride to marry and have an heir. A grandchild she longed for.

He knew his mama had a lot of love to give. His father had been a cruel man, a bullying bastard, and all the love she had for the man withered and died only years into the marriage. Now she was happy. They both were, he supposed, in their small, different ways, but she wanted to share the love she had bottled up for so many years.

Albert, too, would like to love. He would like to court Lady Victoria, but since the scandal of her husband's affair, his running off with a maid followed by several other indiscretions all written about in the London gossip rags, Victoria looked less than interested in entering such a union for a second time.

Who could blame her for such thoughts.

While he liked the idea of marriage, he certainly had no idea what to do with a wife once the union was officiated. A problem he'd been trying to solve with extensive research. He'd purchased a collection of books on the art of lovemaking, sketches of how it was that women and men came together—drawings depicting the act of lovemaking, some of which had taken his breath away.

Albert let himself into the house, his staff well used to the strange times he came and went. He walked into the library and went directly to the latest book he had received from London about the life story of Moll Flanders, having left it on his desk before he'd set off to write this afternoon. An amusing and interesting account, with some bawdy tales that entertained him.

With his books featuring scenes similar to those he found in Daniel Defoe's book, he hoped he at least sounded as true and accurate as this author. His career would be over should the public know the truth. That one of their favorite gothic romance authors who pens tales of intrigue, horror, and passionate encounters was as virginal as a debutante newly arrived in London. A marquess, too, even more humiliating. Lords ought to know how to romance a lady or rake about town.

He was living a lie, at least portraying one. But then, he supposed his books were a work of fiction, and his characters had nothing to prove. But soon, he would need to search for a wife in earnest. Court her, as awkward and clumsy as he was when in verbal conversation with females. The thought made him frown. Next week he would see Lady Victoria, and his ineptitude would be even more noticeable. Her vivaciousness for life, her confidence shamed his introverted self. For years he had wanted the gumption to implement some of the things he'd found in the sketches with her, seduce her into marriage with him.

A dream that was unlikely to come true. He required a wife who at least wished for a husband. Lady Victoria Worthingham, as much as he longed for the position to be filled by her, was the one woman in England sworn off ever marrying again. Everyone knew it, and so did he. Someone else would have to do.

Want to read more? Purchase Only a Marquess Will Do here!

KISS THE WALLFLOWER SERIES
AVAILABLE NOW!

If the roguish Lords of London are not for you and wall-flowers are more your cup of tea, this is the series for you. My Kiss the Wallflower series, are linked through friendship and family in this four-book series. You can grab a copy on Amazon or read free through KindleUnlimited.

LEAGUE OF UNWEDDABLE GENTLEMEN SERIES AVAILABLE NOW!

Fall into my latest series, where the heroines have to fight for what they want, both regarding their life and love. And where the heroes may be unweddable to begin with, that is until they meet the women who'll change their fate. The League of Unweddable Gentlemen series is available now!

LEAGUE OF UNWEDDABLE GENTLEMEN

ALSO BY TAMARA GILL

Wicked Widows Series
TO DREAM OF YOU

League of Unweddable Gentlemen Series
TEMPT ME, YOUR GRACE
HELLION AT HEART
DARE TO BE SCANDALOUS
TO BE WICKED WITH YOU
KISS ME DUKE

Kiss the Wallflower series
A MIDSUMMER KISS
A KISS AT MISTLETOE
A KISS IN SPRING
TO FALL FOR A KISS
KISS THE WALLFLOWER - BOOKS 1-3 BUNDLE

Lords of London Series
TO BEDEVIL A DUKE
TO MADDEN A MARQUESS
TO TEMPT AN EARL
TO VEX A VISCOUNT
TO DARE A DUCHESS
TO MARRY A MARCHIONESS
LORDS OF LONDON - BOOKS 1-3 BUNDLE
LORDS OF LONDON - BOOKS 4-6 BUNDLE

OUTLAWS

ABOUT THE AUTHOR

Tamara is an Australian author who grew up in an old mining town in country South Australia, where her love of history was founded. So much so, she made her darling husband travel to the UK for their honeymoon, where she dragged him from one historical monument and castle to another.

A mother of three, her two little gentlemen in the making, a future lady (she hopes) and a part-time job keep her busy in the real world, but whenever she gets a moment's peace she loves to write romance novels in an array of genres, including regency, medieval and time travel.

www.tamaragill.com
tamaragillauthor@gmail.com